Last November

Last November

—— Short Stories ——

BY Peter Biles

RESOURCE *Publications* · Eugene, Oregon

LAST NOVEMBER
Short Stories

Resource Publications
An Imprint of Wipf and Stock Publishers
199 W. 8th Ave., Suite 3
Eugene, OR 97401

www.wipfandstock.com

PAPERBACK ISBN: 979-8-3852-4362-4
HARDCOVER ISBN: 979-8-3852-4363-1
EBOOK ISBN: 979-8-3852-4364-8

VERSION NUMBER 03/24/25

For my family

Contents

CONTENTS

Notes and Acknowledgments

Several of these stories originally appeared in the online Substack publication *Battle the Bard,* including "Jasper's Here," "Steps," "Heaven," "Stop, Light," "Send Me a Surfboard," "The Blues," and "A Visit to the Gallery That Saturday Morning."

"Margo's World," "The Fisher's Man," and "Alexandra" were all published in *Midsummer Dream House.*

"A Certain Ghost's Long and Final Back to Earth" was published in *The Ana* in July 2024.

"The Observer" was published in *Silly Goose Press* in November of 2024.

Thanks in addition to all who read and support my work, have encouraged me as a writer, and who believe in the need for stories in a society driven by algorithms.

Twenty Bucks

R oy sat next to Adrian in the passenger seat of the Martin's Hospice Care van and told the kid that he'd keep betting twenty bucks that he was going to die the next day until it actually happened. "If I'm dead when you come tomorrow, you owe me twenty bucks, scout!"

Roy kept losing his bets, kept walking out of his room feeling his front pocket because you just never know what those cigarettes might magically reappear, and Adrian kept driving him to the park down the hill with that pack of seed to feed the birds. It was a simple job description. Take anyone from the old folks' home who wanted to ramble around the park for a few minutes, keep an eye on them so they don't fall into the water, and be back before 5 p.m. dinner. Adrian would make more at the gig if Roy paid his debts. They joked about this. "Trying to keep ya humble, son," Roy said. "We both know you'll make the big bucks eventually."

Adrian skateboarded to Martin's like he skateboarded to high school. Every week he had a new crack to dodge on the sidewalk. The board's wheels were loose enough to swerve; he just had to evade the grass. Sure, he'd fallen. Show up sometimes with bleeding hands and wet hair sticking to his temples. Mr. Davies never changed the position of his head when Adrian walked into the lobby. He just moved his eyes away from the computer monitor for about a second, his head falling back in his mid-afternoon loll, lips downturned by the habit of never speaking to anyone unless he had to. He wasn't an unkind man, though. He was just around the near-dead a lot and had started to resemble the tenants.

They'd hired Adrian two months earlier near the beginning of the schoolyear. He'd been doing kick flips in the parking lot and, after about a month of realizing he needed an after-school job if he actually wanted some cash, told Mr. Davies in his interview that he didn't feel weird around the dying. He just needed a job so he could go to college, and he liked to drive around. It's like skateboarding but with glass protection.

"Nah," he had told Mr. Davies, scratching his arm, even though it didn't itch. "It doesn't really bother me. I mean, it's sad they're like that. I guess they could always use somebody."

Alice, one of the caretakers, introduced him to Roy on his first day of work. Adrian went into the little whitewashed room and saw the army uniform hanging in the corner. And then there were the old black shoes setting on the floor by the bed, and a flourish of tulips in a vase on the nightstand that Alice said Roy's granddaughter had sent him earlier that day. Roy himself was sitting upright in the bed with the sheets drawn up to his chest, flipping through a biography of General George Patton. He was licking his index finger and about to turn a page when Alice introduced the gangly senior in high school standing in the doorway and said that he'd be the new van driver for Martin's. "*That's* who ya got to replace old Sid?"

"Mister Roy—be *nice*."

Old Sid was actually young Sid, a college junior who started working shifts at the Applebee's. With his growing assignments for his social work degree, he had decided it was best to hang up the keys and find a worthy successor.

If the group ever grew to three or more, they'd start taking field trips to the zoo, to the movies, but for now, Roy was the only one who wanted to go out, and all he wanted to do was go down to the park. Roxanne sometimes leaned out of her nook in her baby pink dress and say, "Wait up" but then could be heard howling at Wheel of Fortune as Adrian and Roy got ready in the foyer. Mike, another veteran who spent most of his time tapping about the halls in a robe with his cane, stopped and gaped at them before they'd go to the park. Adrian asked him if he wanted to come along. Mike only swallowed his bottom lip and proceeded to ogle at the aquarium. It was like the water reminded him of a memory. But he never came to see the lake at the park. He never went to feed the birds.

That first day, Roy put his Patton down on the bedstand and Alice got his shoes put on while Adrian gripped the edge of his skateboard, wishing he had parked it behind the plant pots by the lobby doors.

Now the twenty bucks joke was recurring. Adrian accurately predicted that it would be about the second or third thing Roy brought up after he got him in the van after "howdy, dipshit" and "got a cig?"

"Twenty bucks seems pretty low, Roy."

"You think I'm worth more than a crisp piece of Andrew Jackson?"

"So long as you keep staying alive, I might as well have a chance at paying my college tuition."

Now it was November, and the best time to be at the park. The trees made a sloping ring around the lake, shedding cloaks of gold and bloody red and purple, with the scattered assembly of strong-seated pines towering like green coronation spikes on a big crown. At this time of the day, the lake was almost undisturbed. And the usual crop of runners and dog walkers slowly orbited its ribbon of newly poured asphalt. Adrian always parked the little minivan by one of the biggest pines in the park and sometimes had to pluck cones from the groove below the windshield afterwards, but Roy said that parking in direct sunlight was bad for the paint. "My daddy told me to take care of my damn truck," Roy said. "So, we better take care of Martin's damn minivan."

It was getting a little colder, days a little shorter, and Roy was the type who was ready to bust out the winter gear in September when it was still seventy-five. He wore a leather jacket that reached his thighs and had a fur-lined hood and felt lining. He never buttoned it, so his flannel shirt could breathe, but it made him look like a fighter pilot who had just gotten out of the cockpit and was ready to reclaim the homeland. It was about the coolest coat Adrian had ever seen.

"All right, give me the birdseed. What have we got here."

They didn't have much company that day. Adrian was just dressed in jeans, T-shirt, and a hoodie worn almost to tissue, and hopped up and down in the grass as Roy hobbled close to the edge of the water and took out a handful of birdseed to spread. A small assembly of geese waddled a way down the walk, cocking their heads at the old man, but they scattered to make way for a woman in leggings and an ocean-blue top. The seed Roy had sprinkled the day before lay in the dead grass, along with the seed from the day before that, and knew that when December hit, they'd basically be sowing seeds for next spring's weevils. "The geese'll come along once we're gone," said Roy.

"Uh huh."

"But I wish I could see a *green* heron. Have you seen one of those, son? Real nice birds. Sleek and purty. And they fly low on the water." He looked up at the lake, maybe to see if he'd jinxed himself and if a heron might rise out of the brown reeds and imitate the movement he just described. "When the water's like *this,* awful still, looks like they're flying over a mirror."

"Uh huh."

Roy emptied his grocery bag of seeds and watched the geese peck at someone's discarded burger in the gravel parking lot. "Sons of bitches don't know what they're missing, do they?"

"No sir."

Adrian checked his phone but didn't have any messages. He lived with his uncle, a late-working nurse who sometimes asked Adrian if he could bring home milk and eggs on his commute home, but that could be quite the balancing act to pull off when all you've got is a skateboard and all of cracked-up fourteenth street to cover.

"You textin' your girlfriend, Adrian?"

"Ha. You know I don't have one of those."

"I bet twenty bucks that you're full of it. You met my granddaughter?"

"Nope, don't think so."

"Yep, my granddaughter, her name's Anita. Adrian and Anita. Two As. A-plus combination. Hehe. I'm going to set you up on a blind date."

Adrian had enough intel to know that this Anita visited Roy on Saturdays and Sundays and took him to the park in her own car. Roy talked about her like she was the state governor who had done no wrong. She was a meteorologist and went on TV, and she got to go up in helicopters to film footage of big prairie storms from a distance. She was thirty-three.

"You know I'm eighteen, right, Roy?"

"What's a lil distance in age?"

"It's fifteen years, that's what."

"Oh. Yeah."

He was just trying to help. Apart from Anita, Adrian couldn't gauge who else came to see the old man. His daughter and son-in-law were the ones to admit him to Martin's, but Alice said that they had just retired out west to Colorado and hadn't lived in Grover for two decades. He had to laugh a little bit at the thought of that, the hint of irony. He had never met his own parents; he was handed off to Uncle Randy soon after he was born when Randy was twenty-eight, too busy with work and volunteerism for marriage, who nonetheless had a streak of parental charity in him.

But Adrian, despite hearing nothing from either Mom or Dad, always imagined that they ran away to Colorado. Maybe Mongolia. Where else could they remain so hidden? They were probably in a green valley west of Denver, living in a shack without electricity and foraging for mushrooms and blackberries. Uncle Randy never heard from them. Every Christmas, which was coming up soon, they got mail from Gramps in Tuscaloosa and a couple of Randy's pals in graduate school from Palo Alto, but no—nothing postmarked out of the deep, ringing forests of the Rocky Mountains or the plaints of Mongolia.

"All right, Roy, you about ready? I'm getting cold."

"Cold? Well hell, take my coat."

"Oh no, that's not what I—"

"Shut up and wear it."

He was leaning back a little precariously for Adrian's tastes, so Adrian helped him take it off. "Seriously, I don't need it—I just thought it was about time to head back."

"I want to see you wear it. C'mon. That's it. You look like a doggone fighter pilot in that getup. Yessir. Beats that hoodie, all right." Roy was breathing hard, leaning against the turf with his cane. His eyes glittered like marbles beneath his brows, irises somewhat melted into the pupils. Adrian kept the coat unbuttoned, blushing beneath his bangs despite the cold. The coat smelled old and like cigarettes and sweat, but it warmed him up in seconds. "Cool coat, Roy."

He wore it even as they drove up the hill back to Martin's. Roy had shifted his mood, and not necessarily for the worse. Sometimes he went quiet. Adrian typically figured he was thinking about the war or his wife or his own death. None of those things were far away from him.

They were quiet for almost the whole five-minute drive back to Martin's. Sometimes Roy wanted to pick up a burger from Shipley's, but he didn't mention anything like that today. He only said two things. He said, "You remind me of my son. His name was Archie, and he was one heck of a kid." And when Adrian couldn't seem to work up a reply at the awning by Martin's, Roy added, "Keep the coat."

For the next couple of weeks, Roy was too weak and sick to make it to the park, and Anita came down from Tulsa more often to visit. Roy's daughter and son-in-law flew out of retirement to see him too. And anyway, they got a cold snap and a bruising of ice and snow that swept through town and left fourteen power lines toppled and pulsing. Adrian couldn't commute to Martin's or school with his skateboard, and he ran out of money fast. He walked the half a mile to the high school wearing a pair of high-top converse shoes, sweatpants, and the cigarette-drenched overcoat that belonged to Roy. He wore the hood and used the drawstrings to tighten it around his face so just his nose peeked through, giving him oxygen. He sat in the back of the classroom in first-hour trigonometry and slipped off the shoes and socks so he could curl his bare feet inside the ends of the sweats, although those too were soaked. Not that many people talked to him at Grover High School, but now they started to pinch noses and veer; he couldn't *not* wear the coat, though—he even tried to layer up with the hoodies like he used to, but no, that wouldn't do. He shed all that cotton stuff and liked the real weight of this coat that had been worn to a mold and yet still seemed to fit him. It was *his*.

December 15th was the first day the roads were good enough to drive on, and the walks to skateboard; though it was still frigid and gray, and Adrian figured the after-hours park program was probably to put on hiatus in exchange for cozier tidings, he decided to go to Martin's. He skateboarded down fourteenth street and went on the road itself since there were no oncoming cars but bit the dust hard at the bottom of a hill and tumbled against the curb. The blood seeped through the sweatpants at his kneecap, but that was nothing. Roy's coat was torn at the shoulder where he'd connected with the concrete. The leather gaped, and the cotton peeked like fluffy guts.

"No, no, no, no." He rocked himself on his butt and grappled with the skateboard, which had snapped in the middle when it couldn't bear the shift in inertia at the hill's low point. Double whammy.

He was too far from home to get a new coat, so decided he would shed the thing at the door in the foyer and see how Roy was doing anyway. He studied the tear. His underlying shirt had gotten scuffed open too, all the way down to the strawberry skin. "Ahhh." His schoolteachers got onto him at least once a week about skating down the hallways and trying to do kick flips in the lobby by the trophy case. It was a miracle he hadn't brought down the 1987 State Champion in Baseball pendant with just an errant flick of his ankle. Now his ten-year-old board, ridden to a grind, pushed to the literal breaking point, fully snapped in two when he picked it up.

He limped his way to Martin's, past the boarded-up flower shop, the Church's Chicken, and the dormant car wash, and set the two pieces of the board neatly on top of each other by the door behind the poinsettia plants.

He saw himself in the glass of the door as he reached for the handle, and paused. Did he always look this despicable? He needed a haircut. Roy was always giving him the suit lecture, too. He wasn't going to get any girl-friends with shoulder length hair and skaw band shirts. He wasn't going to get any with a fifty-year-old coat that smelled like cigarettes either, or at least would have to settle perhaps for a very particular kind of female. He was sure they would catch each other up on all the jokes they had missed over the last month.

He put his coat on the peg in the lobby and did his best to hide the rip in his shirt at his shoulder, but by then, the vaguely familiar woman was already walking down the hallway, holding her hand to her mouth. Thirty-three isn't really old, but for months Adrian thought of it as real, weathered age. So, when he saw Anita with her raven black bangs held to the side with bobby pins, and her pale, pretty face, he didn't really think it was her. The only way he knew it was her was because she was holding her grandfather's military uniform by a coat hanger, and Alice spoke after her, "Call us if you need anything, honey."

He stood off to the side by the aquarium as she came into the lobby, where she draped the uniform on a chair and took a call. "Yeah. I'm here. Mm hmm. Okay . . . thanks Mom. Bye."

Anita's parents, the daughter and son-in-law, walked in just a minute later after he sat down, and disregarded the shadowy figure in the corner of the room and wrapping Anita in their arms and staying there. "It's all right." He listened, bowed head. "It's all right . . . "

He didn't know what to do, where to go. So, he sat down by the aquarium and numbly watched the ocean fish flit and sidle above the bed of pebbles and chunks of artificial shipwreck. He finally owed Roy twenty bucks. He tried not to think about that, but he did, and realized the weird-est part of the joke was that the old man couldn't share it with him. They couldn't spend it on a burger at Shipley's.

He got a text from his uncle asking him if he could pick up hand-warmers and drop them off to him. They were handing out cheap coats to the homeless in the town square and he was running out of handwarmers, and they were going to be out there for a few more hours. Always a few more hours. Adrian stared at the message and put the phone back in his pocket. Roy's family was rejoining by the door, wiping eyes, talking about dinner plans, funeral arrangements. Anita glanced at him and his bloody knee and looked away just as quickly, and then her eyes settled on Roy's ancient coat dangling from the hanger.

"Oh, *there* it is." She plucked it from the wall, frowning at the rip on the shoulder, but then smiled sadly at its undamaged smokiness, its weight.

"Oh wow, good. We wouldn't have wanted to lose *that*."

"You think he would've given it to Archie?"

"Oh yeah. He definitely would have."

They shuffled out the door and of course he didn't go after them and ask for it back. He couldn't lay claim to it. How could he? They didn't know who he was. He got up and started to amble down the hallway but stopped and turned back short of Roy's bedroom, scratching his head. Mr. Davies emerged from his office, smoothing his tie, trying to flatten his downturned formation of lip into something of a smile.

"You couldn't have called me, sir?"

"Happened this afternoon. Sorry, buddy. Very sorry. He was a good guy. Old, though. Very old."

"They all are."

Mr. Davies patted him on the shoulder, his throbbing one, and reached into his pocket with a friendly scowl. "It's that time of year. A little Christmas bonus for you. We'd still like you to drive the van. Could use another janitor, too. We can find something for you to do." He pressed a crisp twenty-dollar bill into Adrian's hand, which Adrian stared at from beneath his drooping bangs. "Go buy yourself a coat, for God's sake. It's too cold to be out in just *that*."

But Adrian had to go spend the money on handwarmers and was left with about eight dollars afterward. The next morning, he layered up in his old hoodies after cutting his own hair in the bathroom mirror.

Professor Carlo

N ot long ago in our town, a man of about forty named Professor Carlo arrived to teach English at the local college and had all the trademark qualities of a sophisticated writer. Whether or not he excelled at writing evaded all of us for a good while. But it became clear after bumping into this Professor Carlo myself that he was something of a restless soul, grinding his jaw or tapping his foot or running his hand through his thinning brown-gray hair. He dropped in on our town from outside of Chicago but beyond that he was essentially a mystery—an alien from the North come to visit our mundane plains of existence.

In the coffee shop where I work, the Blue Bean, Professor Carlo often came in and ordered his Americano with a mumble and stared almost incredulously into the space beyond my shoulder as if pondering life's essence in the chalkboard menu, fingering a slim wallet in his jean pocket. The man only ever paid us in cash, never card. What did he think about in such moments? Whatever grand thought he was going over, he struggled to look at us baristas in the eye, almost like this would bring him back to the real world, which would pain him and remind him he was a human walking around in a physical body.

But I was interested in Professor Carlo from the very beginning. I would try to see what he was reading in the coffee shop corner when I brought him his steaming drink, though he always covered up the title with his hand, indicating that he saw reading as an act of privacy, like a monk poring over texts in a cell. I wondered what it would be like to audit one of his English courses. He simply made me curious. None of us had really met anyone like him before.

In the shop, our manager, Marge, let me set aside a shelf to put books on a few weeks before Professor Carlo's appearance. I don't read much, to be honest, but thought they might add a little something to the space, and who knows? Maybe now Professor Carlo would feel more at home with some literature nearby. Aside from that, none of us saw the man anywhere in town except at the grocery store sometimes. He always seemed to be in the wine section, carefully figuring out which year and brand to buy. I also saw him twice at the park, walking with his hands in his pockets, alone.

A few months went by with Professor Carlo living in our humble little town. The fall semester passed, followed by a frigid two months of harsh winter, and in the spring, right when the ground began to thaw and the buds of the trees blossomed on the sidewalks of Main Street right outside my studio apartment, a flyer made the rounds advertising none other than my favorite band: The Yip Yaps.

The Yip Yaps, a folk band from our state, was set to visit the college auditorium for just twenty bucks a pop. And the college, since it was just a two-year institution with around 900 students, doesn't often nab headliners like The Yip Yaps, so I fully expected a considerable turnout.

I also wondered aloud behind the counter at the shop later that day if Professor Carlo might happen to make an appearance at the concert. He struck me as a Renaissance man who didn't believe in sequestering the ivory tower from the concert hall.

"What's your deal with him?" asked Jess, our baker in residence, as she slid a tray of cinnamon rolls into the display case.

"Yeah, Jamie, seriously. Is he a distant crush or something?" said Mick as he pulled a caramel thread of espresso from the machine.

"No," I said. "I don't know. He's just one of those people you wonder about. That's all."

"He's just a guy," said Jess. "They're a dime a dozen. Or no—a dime a *million*, I'd say."

I shrugged, was met with a couple of deferential chuckles, and we went on with the day without referencing Professor Carlo any further.

However, later that evening when I was starting to wipe down the counters and the espresso machine, Professor Carlo walked in and ambled to the middle of the shop where he hesitated, apparently to study the menu. I assumed he would get a decaf Americano given the hour, but he didn't end up ordering anything.

"What can I get you, sir?" I chimed from behind the baked goods case, which is not very transparent.

"Oh, uh, no, I'm just here to . . ." He halfway held up a small paperback book, like he was giving an awkward wave, and set it on the coffee table by the couches, not far from my infant collection of reader's digest classics.

"You're donating a book?"

"Yes, well, sort of. I, uh, actually *wrote* that one. Thought I'd leave it out here in case someone's interested."

I almost forgot to contain my intrigue and nearly dropped the tiny plate I was drying.

"Oh, fantastic! Yeah, leave it there. That's great."

Professor Carlo nodded, forced his hands into his pockets, visibly reddened in the warm lamplight, and then walked out without another word.

The man of silence had written a whole book. What better way to get to know a fellow of mystery?

I played it cool for a few minutes. Jess and Mick were mopping and doing inventory in the back room, leaving the whole public part of the shop empty and quietly humming with the song "Float On" by Modest Mouse. That's a good song.

I visited the coffee table with the cleaner and rag in hand with the pretense of cleaning and picked up the book. It was a thin volume, maybe 80 pages, and appeared to be a collection of short essays. The title, whitely showing on a simple charcoal cover, read *My Sincere Thanks: Essays on the State of Contemporary Culture.* I only got the chance to flip through it once and glance at the back to read his bio, which stated that he was from Chicago, got a master's in rhetoric and composition, and now worked as a writer in the Midwest. You can't get much opaquer about your vocation than that. "Writer in the Midwest."

Of course, this only served to intensify my intrigue. Or crush. Or unstated spiritual desire. Take your pick. I still can't currently classify my interest in Professor Carlo.

Mick came out of the kitchen laughing with Jess at his heels. I wiped down the coffee table, counted the register, and then went home down a chilly Main Street.

Back at the apartment, I got to thinking about The Yip Yaps concert, and what a shame it is that our town doesn't host more arts and culture events. Sincerely, why is that? We spend all this money going to high school basketball games and Marvel movies, but we can't spare a few dimes for a composition professor's first book of essays? Is this life of ours what we call "culture"?

It's hard to say where my zeal for this issue comes from. I went to the community college and had preliminary plans to be a nurse, but after Grandma got so sick and Mom and Dad split, I found that I was already in something of a rut living here and slinging shots and pining distantly about an interesting, mysterious guy who might inflate the sagging contours of my lifeboat. Maybe it was because Professor Carlo was doing what he set out to do. He knew his purpose from an early age and didn't waste any time getting after his goals.

Why shouldn't we at the Blue Bean head up more cultural events? Why shouldn't we try to bring people together in this town where too many of us abide by the tired old adage of keeping to yourself at all costs?

My idealism carried over into the next morning, and I decided firmly about what needed to be done. We were going to have a proper book launch for the professor's debut collection.

I ran the idea by Marge, who thankfully has a strong Bohemian streak in her, and she applauded the initiative, but with a caveat. She recommended we make it an open mic night where other people could come up to the stage and sing songs, recite poetry, do interpretative dances. That sounded fair enough. The event would be artistically democratic. Marge was always the democrat, after all.

So, I went to the community college directory, found Professor Carlo's online profile, and emailed him to ask if he'd be interested in headlining the event at the Blue Bean this coming Friday—the day before the music concert. Within the hour, I got a kindly worded response saying yes. That was the entire reply. "Yes."

Thirty minutes later he added that he would bring extra copies of the book to sell at the coffee shop for a discounted price, and that he wouldn't take too much time and would stick to reading the opening essay, which was about how cars have reshaped travel and local communities and how furthermore we all ought to engage in a revolution to walk everywhere. Come to think of it, I never saw Professor Carlo step foot into an automobile or interact with a machine of any sort.

"Well done, Jamie," said Mick at the shop. "You got your guy started on a book tour."

"Whatever. We've talked about doing open mics here for a long time now."

"Yeah. Definitely."

Mick and Jess obviously think my sudden advocacy for a renewal of the arts and culture scene is a byproduct of a simple romantic crush, but I genuinely believe that when people hear the words of Professor Carlo, they may just ever-so-slightly alter their perspectives about the world and maybe even change their lives.

Who knows?

It was Monday when I reached out to Professor Carlo, and no one on shift saw him come in until Friday afternoon. Mick and I helped him carry in a box of the books; he was dressed in tan slacks and a tweed brown coat over a dark blue dress shirt, the perfect garb for the professoriate. He spent the hour before the event perusing the opening essay of his book, occasionally mouthing words to himself and gesticulating with his hands in a way that only teachers and maybe HR representatives know how to do.

We had tried to advertise all over town, including the campus, and so we wondered if any students of other professors might show up. Of course, none of us knew of his level of popularity or his reputation at the college, whether he was a bore or a captivator, but his enigma notwithstanding, I was steadfast in the decision to give the man a voice.

"This'll be great," said Marge. She had drawn up a list for performers to sign up on a chalkboard with "Professor Carlo" imprinted at the top. "Way to take initiative! We need to do more events like this."

Professor Carlo ordered his Americano and stood with it by the window next to the door surveying the darkening tunnel of Main Street as he sipped.

More people started to trickle in the closer it got to 6 p.m., including a tall and suave fellow who Professor Carlo seemed to recognize.

"Jim!" the mystery man said. He came in with a guitar case, which he set aside near the makeshift stage, and shook hands with his apparent colleague.

One strange detail about small cafes is that people often forget that baristas can hear conversations from behind the counter, even when their eyes are trained on the steam wand or on the milk designs of a caramel latte. But it's almost impossible not to eavesdrop in this job, particularly when the patrons are boisterous and unapologetic in volume. It soon became obvious that this new dude, who wore skinny jeans, a loose T-shirt, and a gray Carhartt beanie, and had that haze of salt and pepper stubble on his face suggesting a sort of rugged intellectualism, was Professor Carlo's colleague in the English department—a certain Dr. Mann. The whole time they talked, I couldn't help but discern how polite and condescendingly Dr. Mann spoke to his supposed inferior. He congratulated Professor Carlo on the new book, but with an addendum. Dr. Mann vocally remembered when *his* first book came out, how exciting it was, how he got all these pleasing reviews and received the nod from the state book awards, but overall, of course, the reward was simply the work itself. "I know the feeling," he said with a sigh, "that exhilaration of creating a whole world ex nihilo."

"Thanks, Sidney," Professor Carlo kept saying, nodding, sipping. "I hope it'll help someone. Maybe."

"Ah, you can't think about that. You can't be vulnerable to an audience. You have to be satisfied with the work itself, even if it doesn't sell more than seven copies. You wrote a book. You wrote a freakin' book, man!"

I guess there is a whole class of professors out there who try to adopt the vibe of a skater kid who listens to punk rock in a bedroom with a bookshelf of French existentialists on the bookshelf; Dr. Mann seemed like he could be their national representative. He was clearly the cool prof, that much was obvious, and not five minutes after he came in, students started to file in precipitously, mostly women who stepped aside in two and threes, sheepishly putting their hair behind their ears and glancing in Mann's direction.

By the time Professor Carlo shuffled up to the stage, clutching his manuscript, I'd say around thirty students crowded the shop, pressed up against the walls, some braving the chaos to get drinks, a few daring to inscribe their names on the chalkboard of artistic destiny.

Marge got my attention and cricked her head to the stage. That was my cue. I took off my apron, let my hair down, and took my place at the stage before the mic.

The toughest, most volatile part of events like these has to be the technics, along with trying ever-so-courteously to get the people to listen to what you're saying. Neither element exactly fell into place as I tried to welcome the crowd and introduce our opening act—most of the people kept up their excited chatter, and it was impossible to tell if my voice, a low one for a woman's, carried beyond the first batch of oglers.

In whatever case, I said something about supporting local art and the importance of fostering community, and to please welcome the headliner, Professor James Carlo, of a brand-new essay collection, to the stage!

The applause was minimum. Dr. Mann clapped the loudest, and Professor Carlo stepped up, clearing his throat a bit vehemently into the mic and causing a few sensitive souls to screech and the speaker to searingly whine.

I took my place behind the counter again, next to Jess. This gave me a sidelong view of the professor. The overhead lights brought the sweat out on his forehead. It wasn't until he cleared his throat again, muttered, "Thank you, Jamie," that we all realized he was terrified. Utterly terrified. His hands shook, he blinked incessantly, and worst of all, the entire shop had gone quiet, save the occasional blast of the steam wand, the clinking of mugs on tabletops, a couple of uncomfortable coughs, and Professor Carlo's belabored breathing.

He got through one paragraph of the essay about cars and the frenetic pace of our modern life, and then skittered his way through the next two pages at a pace that made it hard to understand the words. I think I was in the middle of handing a regular his evening decaf when the performance went awry, and both of us stopped in the mid-motion coffee transfer to painfully observe. It sounded like he was choking, almost sobbing.

When he finally finished, he tried to inform the audience that the book was available via Amazon and that there were copies in the back, but this too was muffled by another high eardrum buster through the microphone; after that, he walked right out the door and didn't resurface on that street for approximately six weeks.

Dr. Mann performed a few minutes later, and the students and other onlookers were much more enthused by his presence than my cherished opening act. He wasn't a bad musician. His songs were lively, hopeful, tinged with tasteful picking and jazzy eyebrow raises. And it was so obvious to us that his students were mesmerized by this Renaissance man—a handsome PhD who recorded acoustic albums in his spare summers and Christmas breaks.

Meanwhile, as the evening wore on, I leaned against the edge of the sink with a contortion in my gut and an odd disdain for this Dr. Mann and his dedicated minions. Although at the same time, Professor Carlo clearly didn't do himself any favors, and evidently wasn't very adept at public speaking and lacked the popularity of his stellar colleague.

Even so. What did we all miss? Something boring? Or something transformative? If only we'd been able to *understand* him, because now I wasn't not sure anyone would pick up a copy of the book on their way out the door. He had made a complete fool of himself. And I've never felt sorrier for anyone in my entire life.

The event, by standard metrics, succeeded despite the early catastrophe, with quite a few students asking us when we would host another open mic night.

"Oh my gosh, *soon!*" declared Marge with a zestful clap of her hands. "Soon and very soon."

As I mentioned, six whole weeks went by before any of us saw Professor Carlo again. During that time, I wrote and repeatedly revised an email of apology to the poor man but never managed to hit send. I wanted to give him a voice in the community beyond the classroom, not to drag him into the limelight just so his colleague could upscale him with a musical act. But no matter how I finagled the email, it could never quite shed that terrible sense of morally suspect pity and condescension. Sending it admitted that he had goofed, and that it was a mistake to invite him to speak in the first place.

He did eventually return to us, though, on an oddly chilly gray day in early April. He'd slimmed up a bit and had grown out a beard that admittedly made him look more academic, less young. He came up to me and looked me directly in the eyes and said, "Hey, Jamie. Can I just have an Americano in a mug?"

My name being spoken in his low and slightly gritty voice made him sound like a benevolent troll addressing me after a long season of hibernation. I thought about talking about the open mic, but he seemed different today, unseeking for a reflection of the painful past. What was it? Something about the eyes? They were brown. An ordinary and yet luminescent shade of brown.

Professor Carlo took his coffee to the worn blue chair by the window and sat down so the gray light fell right on him, bringing out the hot threads of steam from the top of the mug. He didn't have a book with him. He didn't pull out a laptop or a cell phone. He just supped on the coffee, absorbing its nutrients of heat and happy bitterness, and gave a long exhale that seemed to relieve years of pent-up tension in his shoulders.

"It's really good," he told me five minutes later after another drink. Agreeing about a thing's goodness must have been his way of saying "thank you" to the universe.

Towards the end of my shift, I found myself wiping down the coffee tables and unnecessarily correcting some of the nature paintings on the wall near the blue chair where he was sitting.

"I'm interested in your book," I said suddenly, surprised by my own words falling clumsily from my mouth. "I'd like to understand your essay about cars. Can I hear it again? I didn't really hear it during the open mic night."

He said, "Yes." That was all he said at first. Twenty seconds later, though, he added that I should be prepared to give an account of myself, that I would be called upon to tell him who I was and what I wanted out of life. In short, this Professor Carlo wanted to ask *me* questions. He said, when I sat down to listen, that an audience of one is the best kind to have. We can, after all, only talk to one human being at a time.

A Visit to the Gallery That Saturday Morning

On various Saturday mornings when both the weather and the invitation behoove it, I drive, sully-eyed against the sun, to the local coffee shop to meet my brother George, his wife Estelle, and their daughter Trixie, who is four years old and already a waddling artist in the making.

Today I got out of the Civic for the rendezvous wearing these pants that hang past the knees but leave just enough pure exposed shinbone to invite either polite curiosity or scorn. Usually, it's the latter. To me these capris reflect the essence of the online career. As long as the top half of you is "professional", the bottom half can be in sweatpants or full-on naked. That's called "Zoom appropriate" these days, and for a Zoomer like me, I guess I'll take it with open arms. Unfortunately, that kind of wardrobe often seeps into the world against the world's own wishes. These pants are the defiant garb of the artist—not this, not that. They're not pajamas and not slacks, but a secret third thing. And yes. They are bad news for a guy in search of a girlfriend.

Trixie, with her head of golden ringlets, peered at me through the glass doors as I sidestepped the sign advertising cheerio lattes.

"Uncle Arby!"

This girl, it should be said, absolutely loves me. And I don't really know why, but she does. It's just a fact of nature. I patted her head and tread forward an inch or two, penguin style, after she clutched onto my calves, afraid I'd change my mind and retreat for shame into the Civic.

"Nice pants," called George through his Americano. He sat with an ankle on a leg in the corner of the shop, swishing his marriage ring along his fingers like only millionaires and certain nerds can do.

I like this coffee shop and always have. It comforts me. I like it for its messiness. There isn't a sterile or third-wave bone in its body. It does not try to promote a vague sense of environmentalism. It does not have a creed or a declaration of revolutionary principles on the billboard. It has a coffee. The chairs here are made of *wood*, for Pete's sake. Coffee stains cover the tables, and a stipple art series about the beauty of moon phases hang in various elevations on the wall.

I stood in line behind two college girls, both scrolling phones and ambidextrously talking to each other. The blonde one, dressed in leggings and a Black Sabbath shirt that almost reached her kneecaps, glanced behind her shoulder. We met eyes for a second, and I smiled dumbly, but there you go, it happened, the inevitable. Her eyes soon darted down on my stupid shin shorts. I saw it coming the second she looked at me. And these pants are asking for it.

I'm pretty sure I became the new topic of interest in whatever group chat they were pinging up. Actually, I'm not pretty sure. I'm completely sure. I'd be on an Instagram story in about twelve seconds or less. Who knows the secret to going viral? Maybe I'd be on the weekly fail videos on YouTube. Trixie waved at me from behind the leather chair in the corner. The girls exchanged chuckles, pocketed their phones, and then ordered frappes from a barista who had been clutching the edges of his iPad the whole time they'd been posting my shame to the world.

I returned to George and Estelle with a mug of drip coffee, reddened and suddenly experiencing the world in dyslexic. I had to pause and scrunch my eyes to locate my chair. Trixie crouched at the coffee table, sorting through a row of crayons. A blank piece of paper lay next to the rainbow of color.

"Did that girl take a picture of you?" said Estelle, frowning.

"I think so. Shouldn't have worn these pants."

"What do you mean?" said George, unbinding his ankle and leg and planting his elbows on his knees. "Those pants are awesome.

"Pants or shorts?" said Estelle.

"Maybe both," I suggested.

"Ports," said George, rubbing his scruff. He always has some scruff to rub. It's how you know he's contemplating. "Shants."

"All right." Estelle patted his knee. Then she turned to me. "I will say though, bud—if you want to get the attention of the ladies, you may want to put on a full pair of pants. Just a word of advice." Estelle changed the subject.

"How's the writing going?"

"Oh, it's all right, I guess. Working on an essay series for work on paying attention in the digital age."

"Sounds interesting," said Estelle. Trixie looked up, blue on her button nose, and jittered with delight. "She *loves* you, Arb," said George. "I mean, what did you do?"

"How's work?" I asked in the couple's general direction.

"Slow," said Estelle. "The market is dragging its feet right now. No one is selling."

"Yeah," said George. "He blinked and took off his glasses, cleaning the lenses with his shirt and blinking at the floor. "Work is pretty standard for me. Coding a new part of the website—developing a FAQ section. But you know, I've actually considered going freelance." Estelle sipped her cortado and tapped her foot.

"Just sort of wanting to start my own software company," added George.

"That could be cool."

"Yeah! We'll see. Maybe once the market perks back up I'll make some moves." He winked and flicked Estelle's knee.

Trixie continued to design cathedrals with crayons. I actually couldn't really see what she was creating. She shielded her work with her arm. She was not to be disturbed.

George and Estelle asked a little bit more about work, and I told them it was a good job but definitely could get a bit lonely at times—and all that screentime was a big reason I was writing a new essay on paying attention. See, problem is, I was repeatedly *failing* to pay attention, even to what I was writing, which as a fellow who makes a living in the word-peddling business, is kind of a problem. Someone said Twitter is crack for media addicts. So is e-mail, man. Heck, so is *music*. Infinite sounds, fluxing my thoughts and emotions until nothing's left but a vague smudge of unrefined cognition. I told George and Estelle that my criticisms of the Internet, which I paradoxically depended on for a living, sprang from my own addiction to its glow. I could not judge the group chat college girls. They were fellow inmates.

"I don't know," I said. The cloud of desperation that always follows not so far behind my aching back spat rain, wearied my eyes. "It's like we can't really *see* anything anymore. We only allow ourselves to see through the phones. If it's not recorded online, it pretty much means you didn't have the experience. It means you were never there. Anyway, that's kind of what I'm trying to figure out. In the essay."

"That's interesting, man," said George. The record above him expired and ground with static. He stood up and flipped through the other albums. He put on Joni Mitchell. The barista said, "Whoop!" from behind the espresso machine.

"But yeah. I've been yammering. Things are pretty good. Can't complain. Have you guys talked to Josephine lately?"

Josephine was our older sister who lived and loved and might even die in Scotland. She was getting her doctorate in medievalism. That's about as specific as I can manage. There was so much order in that ancient model of the universe, though. The cosmos, back then at least, had layers upon layers of fine tuning and hierarchy. I bet some of us wished we lived in that world, crass and brutish as life might have been for us peasants.

"We talked about a month ago," said George, glancing at Estelle for validation.

"Yep," said Estelle. "That sounds about right."

"She sends me articles on the medieval cathedral sometimes," I said. The girls, my photographers, left the shop with their drinks and got into a mini cooper by the curb. Their white teeth flashed behind the glass. They were beautiful—truly. The car backed into the lazy territory of Lindon Avenue and sped away with a pointless form of urgency.

"Oh yeah?" said George.

"We don't really talk a whole lot, but for some reason she finds it important that I know how ancient folks thought about architecture." I looked down at Trixie. She'd been observing my pants with a furrowed brow. She mumbled a directive to herself and went back to her business.

"Fifteen minutes and she'll be sprinting around the coffee shop," said Estelle. "I can't quite tell what she's drawing. Can you, George?"

"No. Some monstrous creature, maybe. She'll be an artist!"

"All children are," I said to myself.

Ancy, George folded his hands across his chest and looked out the window. We tend to be pretty cerebral people, by the way. We want to bypass the trivial talk and dive into what *really* matters. That's a form of pressure, though—being forced to relay your insights and vulnerabilities on command. Anything short of the paramount betrays the standards of "real" conversation. But too often, like today, the actual vulnerable thing to say is that we don't have much to say at all, or anyway, don't really know how to say it.

"Do you guys want to go down to the park?" asked Estelle after a few seconds of sipping and Joni's guitar riffs, struggling to stay pure from the undulations of audio. It was an old album. Its fibrous grooves had been carved past their design. Estelle, though, is always our savior in such cases. She pulls us out of our self-consciousness and into the bustling order of the real. Plus, the park was close, and a walk might heal the stalemate in the exchange.

"Trixie, we're going to the park. You ready to go to the park?"

"No!"

"But you can finish that later. C'mon. Don't you want to see the geese?"

"No!"

"Trixie," said George with a note of paternal austerity.

"She can finish, maybe?" I said. I hadn't finished my coffee yet, and clearly, the artist wasn't to be distracted.

"She's usually game for the park in a heartbeat," said Estelle. George eased back into his chair, shrugging off his windbreaker. I started to have insipid thoughts like, *What does Georgie really think of me*? I don't know why I experience myself the way I do around certain people. That inexplicable sense of shame. Why the awkwardness, the forced answers buttressing up defenses? And why does the shame fire its engines around the little child who loves me? She loves me because she can't know me. Not like George and Estelle know me. Not like my fellow fools at the AA meetings know me.

Those who know the details of my life, like George and Estelle, know that I am still hung up on Lucy, who left two years ago, that my Internet addiction is only a branch of very well-established oak, poisoned root to upper tip. It's the addiction that waters down the alcohol—the real doozy, you might say. Internet addicts are allowed to write essays about themselves before they recover. Respectable people can relate and make resolutions. But no one really considers the Internet an *addiction*. It's a forgivable foible. Alcoholics can only report on their stories *after* sobriety. My head hurt.

I had nothing intellectual or vulnerable to say to George. When vulnerability becomes the wall you hide behind, you might just be screwed.

Just as another cohort of young lads and lasses came through the hutch, Trixie coyly clutched her masterpiece to her chest as if puzzling whether to disclose her masterpiece.

"Well, let's see it, then," said George. "Then we can get to the park so these people have a place to sit down."

"It might NOT be all the way done," said Trixie, biting her lip.

"A work in progress," said Estelle. "She's a true artist."

"C'mon Trixie, let's see it!"

"Whale, ok," she said, and the slid the piece of printer paper across the coffee table for me to investigate. Best I could tell, the picture, composed with thick splotches and streaks of red, blue, and orange Crayola, showed me standing in my short pants, holding a chalice of coffee (identified by the rogue brown drops falling to the ground) and smiling into the eyes of observer. My head was a potato and my hands were paws, but otherwise she nailed it. She got the pants just right.

"It's for you," said Trixie, swinging her shoulders with her hands behind her back.

I couldn't say anything. Maybe I smiled, but I don't know. I showed it to George and Estelle. "Aw, honey, that's so sweet."

"You like it, don't you Uncle Arby? Didn't I do a good job with the pants?"

"Trousers," said George, chuckling. "And yes, you did an amazing job."

I'm still puzzling over the reasons why even as I write this, but the piece of art was just about the most beautiful thing I had ever seen. No, there was nothing beautiful about the object of the drawing—at least, not from my perspective. The gal who drew it, though? Who spent some of her existence meticulously poring over my portrait?

"You got the pants spot on," I said.

"Keep it, Uncle Arby. It's *yours*." She ran the backs of her fingers along her cheeks, elbows sticking out, cheeks red with delight.

They invited me over for dinner that night. Of course, I said I'd go. On my drive to my place, which only barely qualifies as a country house, close as it is to the cement plant and its attending conveyor belt, I passed by the windmills. They plowed the atmosphere with their pale blades. Trixie's picture lay on the dash. It was bright in the sun. The glass reflected its image. To look right at the reflection was to be blind to the road and everything else.

The windmills rode on the hills like pinwheels at the foot of an infinite cathedral. Where was the child blowing on them to make them spin so? Whoever she is, she is blowing all the time.

The Celebration on Hudson Street

Someone left the anonymous iPhone on the bar outside the café so it reflected the edges of the Carey Building, Keith's apartment complex, like a mirror collecting action and plotting its own script. It was spotless. Brand new. No fingertips smudged its surface. It had a rubber blue covering, set in the middle of the bar—not even skewed. No one sat near it, since the café was closed now, but a pigeon danced nearby with a cocked head, seeing if it might be some kind of sleek loaf of bread.

Keith's excuse for picking it up was the rain and that the café had just closed. It was seven in the evening, and the last couple of customers were ducking out the door, shoving laptops and books into their bags and looking disapprovingly at the sky. He stopped by the outdoor bar as the first drops began to fall, and a wet smell of spring swept down the street, shaking through the fledgling ornamental orange trees along the sidewalk. It was a Friday night; soon more people would be walking to bars and restaurants in pairs and by themselves, all expecting a long weekend as a due reward for enduring another tediously long week. Maybe the person who had forgotten their phone would be coming out again to look for it. In this day and age, when phones are like sixth fingers, who forgets them except old men and the dead?

But the rain! Keith picked up the phone, scanned it as if he might find a name and address on the back, and slipped it into his pocket.

The bank, a beige building with pillars that made it look Greco-Roman in its austerity, was two blocks behind him, and his apartment shared the building with the café, third floor of the Carey Building with a pretty good view of the botanical gardens and the basketball arena.

Time to unwind.

Inside his apartment, he changed into jeans and a long-sleeved t-shirt and put the mystery phone on the kitchen table next to his personal cell, work cell, and ring of keys. His plan for the weekend? No clue. Loneliness and alcohol. Another round of Batman films, another round of wishing Anna was there. But she wasn't. And he was more comfortable that way.

The rain now streamed down the long windows in his bedroom and cast liquid gray shadows along the wall. He always felt tired beyond repair at this point in the day, especially on Fridays, but then would kick back into gear around ten p.m., as if his circadian rhythm was out to ruin his life. And it was more than just a tired feeling. A full day of going over loan repayments, checking excel sheets, and scrolling through mortgage plans with customers on the line, asking questions they could have accessed in the initial information emails, drained him; his leisure time was co-opted by this after-work emptiness where he didn't want to do anything except lean back, put on a jazz album, and stare into the ceiling wishing it was the grate of a woodburning stove like the one he used to have in his room as a boy.

He had a good job. A promising job. He was three years out of college and made six figures. Good enough for him—not much more required at this point. His family lived two hours north, close enough for a weekend trip. But days like these made him realize that no one had taught him what to *do*. What's a man supposed to *do* after hours? Might someone invite him to a party? A non-work related function? An ice cream social? A game of pick-up basketball? Something?

The mystery phone pinged on the kitchen table.

The ping was crisp as a hammer on a boxing bell. He got up and approached, a little warily. What else was he supposed to do? Tapping the phone, it lit up with a backdrop of an ocean tide crawling up a beach and there were two messages from an unnamed contact.

Before he could put it back down, though, the lock screen flipped up; he was in the phone, unrestrained. No passcode. Nothing.

He opened the messages.

He planned on saying that he'd found the phone at the café on Automobile Avenue and would return it in the morning on his way to work. He was no thief. He was no digital voyeur. He was Keith, and he was going to drink a beer from the fridge after he sent the text. It was going to feel cold in his mouth and when it settled in his stomach. Then the bottle would warm up, half-empty in the light of the window, and he would do pushups against mortality and fatigue on the edge of the rug he should probably vacuum. Then he would cook asparagus on a steel pan. Two boiled eggs on the side. A slab of steak to boot. He'd have the course on his lap, cradling the beer, and sift through the infinite catalogue of his Roku on the tube. That's what he was going to do.

The two messages, though, were the first in a conversation thread. The first read, *Walk to the corner of Hudson and Terrace.* The next said, *Pls let me know when you're there.*

There weren't any more threads in the inbox. The phone had no email set up, no social media apps, and no phone call records. All it had was a clear AT&T signal and the time, which was 7:39 P.M.

He wrote back, *Who is this?* but backtracked and realized he was going to go to the corner of Hudson and Terrace. That was what he was going to do. Forget the asparagus.

Maybe he'd stumbled into a drug deal or a secret affair. But he was going. Forget the Roku. He didn't care what he'd find.

The rain thickened, pared down to a drizzle, and then gave way to a humid swelter as he walked out of the building in jeans and T-shirt. He still had more than two hours of sunlight.

He turned on Hudson, passing the concrete box of a law school and its tidy, green lawns. A homeless man sat on a bench by the stairsteps with his arms crossed and his head bowing up and down, like he was about to fall asleep. Beyond that was a barbecue house with a tin roof where waiters wiped the rain off outdoor tables and chairs, fanning out cloth awnings as a group of college students milled outside the door. He checked his own phone, with the other in his pocket. He had no notifications except for an update on his incoming meal delivery.

He was familiar with this part of the city and liked going to the coffee shop on the corner, where, by all appearances, he was heading now. He hadn't put two and two together initially, but a block away and there it was: Element Coffee, with its tall glass walls, outdoor patio with the usual hound licking its paw at the feet of a forty-year-old urbanite sipping espresso and dabbling at a poached egg.

He crossed Hudson and ambled up to the coffee shop doors, peering as inconspicuously as possible at the array of customers within. A young woman emerged with an iced drink and massive bug-eyed sunglasses perched atop her ponytailed head; she and the small boy who bounded after her holding a burrito disregarded the incoming customer. Another ping: *Oh, and order a hot chocolate at the counter.* He laughed to himself.

When he ordered the hot chocolate, a little sheepishly, the barista frowned at him and checked her watch. Then, with an eyebrow raised, she took his bill and asked if he'd like whipped cream, and he, unperturbed by her surprise (even though he thought it wasn't *that* weird, getting a hot chocolate, was it?) said no thanks, he'd not like whipped cream.

He sat in a tall chair by the window two seats down from a couple absorbed in conversation, toying with wine classes. Her hand propped her head and he sat with his fingers laced at his stomach, elbow on the window bar with his eyes trained outside into unknown heights as he spoke, as she listened. Keith watched them with hints of envy for a few seconds, then appraised the rest of the shop. Classical music, perhaps Bach, trilled through the speakers, though the chatter of exchanges drowned out all but the triumphant swells of the song. Clean shaven fifty-year-olds and their divorces in hand, scrolling through new business ventures. Single college girls, iPhones in one hand with latte and sadness in the other, sitting in the comfy chairs in the corner next to the slim bookshelf holding philosophy, self-help, and traces of really good literature.

There beanie crowned thirty-year-olds who never worked out, rubbing their own trim cut beards in admiration as they spoke across small tables, grinning at their mirrored counterpart, decrying conformity and right-wingers. An old woman, seemingly out of place as she milled near the pickup counter, clutched a purse at her hip and stared at the ceiling above the espresso machine. Keith breathed in. That wondrous pungency of chocolate, sharp coffee grounds, and wine sifted over to him, joined ranks with the music, clamor, and variety of human beings, and he realized that *this*, something like *this*, was what he was missing out on.

"Hot chocolate for Keith!"

They really had to shout it out, huh? He walked up to the counter, earning a maternal smile from the old woman, and took the paper cup to find not only his name scribbled under the rim in Sharpie, but the following addendum: *One block south, beneath the happy lights . . .*

He glanced at the barista, who *winked* at him, doggone it, and then vanished behind a film of steam from her machine. He was beyond questions now.

"On a scavenger hunt?" the old woman laughed.

"Something like that," he said.

"Hope you find what you're looking for!"

"Thanks, I hope so too." And with the sense that every strand of society represented in the café was now scrutinizing his next move, Keith slipped out the side door and almost ran the final block southwards. He actually passed one of his colleagues on the way. Bill. Yes, it was Bill, walking his terrier, who scoured the walk with its restless tuft of a snout. They didn't look at each other. It didn't make sense to "see" people outside the bank.

He was led to an empty courtyard with, indeed, celebratory lights crisscrossed through the air and attached to two centennial buildings he'd always admired in the past. One building was rustic brick red and the other a pastel yellow, and together, with the dark sky above him, made him think of a wedding party, one that was supposed to last for a long time. He checked the phone. Nothing. And there was no one in the empty courtyard.

The phone pinged after five minutes of his anxious standing, concerned that he was about to get sniped from the rooftops by some dark avenger he'd forgotten about. He didn't think he'd made any real enemies in his life. Wouldn't that be exciting? He read the text as follows: *Oh my gosh. I'm so sorry. There's been some mistake made . . . this was supposed to be a surprise birthday for my husband, and I see someone else got a hold of the phone. If you'd be so kind as to leave the phone here and I'll pick it up later.*

He paled and his hands went clammy, and without a proper thought henceforth, he spun on his heels and ran back onto Hudson street while a dark-haired woman leaned her head out of the window of the brick building and watched him flee.

Keith ran, cursing himself, until he reached the foyer of his apartment, where he retreated into the elevator and finally allowed himself to catch his breath. Here he was alone, sweating and sick to his stomach, with the phone still greedily clasped in his hand.

"Oh, Jesus," he half prayed. "I'm so so *stupid. Stupid, stupid idiot!*" The fact that he hadn't left the phone assured him that he was now portrayed in the worst possible light in the texter's eyes. She'd seen him milling the courtyard, staring at the phone, and he'd run off with the dang thing in hand without leaving it behind. Who was he to her now? The joke of the party, the creep who now had her number.

He undressed and sat in the shower, pressing his hand against the wall, then lay on his back in bed, staring at the ceiling with the silence weighing on his chest as a substitute for bedcovers. It wasn't that the coordinator of the whole event had caught him and had to cancel the party on his account.

It was that, for some reason against all reason, he thought that somehow the party was for *him*. That a stranger had left a blank Apple device outside of a coffee shop hoping that he would find it and follow it to another coffee shop, order a hot chocolate, and be led all the way to the happy lights. The religious remnant of his childhood even suggested that God was texting him.

He buried his head into the covers and fell asleep crying.

It was the last kind of wake-up alarm he expected. The phone gave an old timey, 1950s ring. It was waiting for a Humphrey Bogart to answer dismissively with a cigarette and bourbon balanced in hand, a desperate woman on the other end. Keith sat up. It was almost dark out, now, about forty minutes since he fell asleep. Crawling through the darkness, he secured the mystery phone, no longer so mysterious, and answered it.

"Hello?"

"Hi . . . um." It was a woman's voice, high and sonorous. "Are you the guy who came to Hudson on mistake?" She had a little bit of a lisp, especially when she said "mistake." She sounded like she a fifteen-year-old girl, but she was in fact twenty-nine.

"Yeah," he said, rubbing his face, no longer caring about hiding his humiliation. "I'm really sorry about that. I'll return the phone immediately. I don't know what happened . . . just got sort of caught up in the adventure, I guess. I found the phone and was going to try and return it when I started getting your messages."

"It's totally fine. Don't worry about it. Actually, the reason I called is because we wanted to invite you back. Back to Hudson Street where you just were. If you want to."

He frowned. He heard voices and laughter on the other side of the line. "Well," he said. "I don't think . . . you don't know me, do you?"

"Not at all. Do you know *me*?"

"No."

"Didn't think so. No, we just wanted to call and say more the merrier. It was a funny mishap and we want you to come by. I got that extra phone by winning some dumb raffle at work. Thought it would be funny to see what I could do with it. It wouldn't be right if you didn't come. We're sorry about what happened."

"Well," he repeated, more to himself than to her. "Thanks. I'll try to drop by in a few minutes."

"Great!" Click.

He anticipated another hoax on the walk over to the celebration on Hudson Street. He walked past Element and ambled by the place he'd encountered his colleague and the terrier. He saw the glow of lights a block away, getting closer, spelling mockery, enhancing doom. But he couldn't stop walking to the light. He couldn't stop approaching the great joke, again cursed with the slightest hope that the party might still somehow in part be designed for him.

Standing between the two buildings, blinking under the light, he saw a crowd of about twenty people mingling by long tables full of wines, grapes, coffee, and other hors d'oeuvre.

A tall Black man came up to him with an outstretched hand, smiling. Keith took the hand in apprehension, trying to smile back. "The guest is here!" he said. Then he said in a soft voice, "You can leave anytime. But I'm glad you came, man. My name's Keith. That's my wife, Candice. Today's my birthday."

"Happy birthday," said Keith.

"Thanks. Can I get you anything? Anything at all? We got coffee. Wine. Tea. C'mon, you want to meet Candice? The great orchestrator?"

Keith wrung his hands, wiped them dry on his pant legs, and smiled. "Sure, I'd like that," he said.

"All right, great. Here she is." He put his arm around Keith's shoulder, adding, "Oh, and you can keep the phone. She got it through a drawing, totally random. Or you can just give us your actual number so we can hang out. Whatever you want to do, man."

Keith led Keith deeper into the celebration on Hudson Street, and the strangest thing wasn't that he was one of the celebrants. It was that no one seemed surprised that he was there.

Jasper's Here

A mayfly slipped into the dark bedroom in the middle of the afternoon. Blackout shades were drawn, and old star stickers glittered upon the ceiling with the little phosphorescence they maintained; the bug made unimpressive dashes at the cloaked window and sidled up a ruffle of one the curtains. It was too forgetful to retrace its trajectory and go to the kitchen downstairs, where soft bananas and an array of food-crusted dishes might better satisfy its existence.

The girl in the bed raised herself upon the intrusion, exploring the room before her through a veil of disheveled bangs. She reached to her nightstand, securing a half-smoked cigarette, and relit it with a hand still weak from sleep. Her name was Stormy, and she was nineteen years old and badly in need of rehabilitation.

It was strange that a fly should wake her up. She and her father lived on a busy street that was not immune from brazen trucks and the crackle of arrogant Dodge chargers. She had trained herself over a lifetime to treat the engine of the neighborhood as inconsequential white noise, but the buzz of a fly unearthed her from her sleep and held her where she sat now, baffled in a haze of fatigue and dimness. She covered her chest with her covers, inhaling the cigarette and wondering what time it was, and reached to the windowsill near the right side of her bed to draw back the blackout curtains. The sun was halfway through its afternoon descent and nestled ripely between the neighborhood houses, all of which slumped with weak architecture, hosting inhabitants as reclusive and mysterious as herself. "Shit," she said, wishing it was nighttime, and sank back into the pillows with the cigarette sticking straight up out of her mouth.

The fly must've noticed the stirring of the hibernator. It flitted to the surface of a dresser littered with coins, hair clips, empty vials of polish, and faded polaroid pictures. The fly explored its real estate but was disappointed by the prospects and retreated to the other window by the girl's bed.

Stormy watched it perch on the edge of the sill and rub its silky paws together with mischievous intent. Her father coughed in his bedroom, and even louder than a truck, a girl screamed bloody murder on the sidewalk.

"What now," she whispered to herself, hoisting herself back up ad peering to investigate. Her brother, Jasper, who she had not seen in two years to the week, was wriggling away from the vengeful grasp of a girl in a tank top and too much eye shadow. The girl screamed, "You're not *leaving* me!" Among other expletives, she made it clear that his betrayal would invite many future visitations, but Jasper slipped through the open door before she could wrangle him back into custody.

Stormy rolled out of bed all the way, laying her feet on the hard wood floors and flicking the newly dead cigarette somewhere into the covers. She couldn't quite wrap her head around her big brother being back inside the house—the old hero who was driven out into the blinding sun so long ago. Well. Not *that* long ago.

Now Jasper was at the bottom of the stairs, gasping for breath, and launched nimbly up the stairwell as if he was scared Dad would reach out and grab him by the scruff of his neck.

He crept into Stormy's room and went straight to the beanbag in the corner, accidentally knocking the TV stand so a couple of his old Star Wars bobbleheads fell off. Stormy blinked at him, leaning back a little bit upon his entry. He sat down with his knees raised up, elbows resting on the caps.

He probably wondered where his bed was. They used to share the room, after all. Dad had moved it out mere hours after Jasper ran off, presumably never to return, and used it to "patch" a hole in the fence in the backyard to deter the neighborhood cats from coming in. They still got in, of course. Creatures always got into their backyard or tiny garage or their house some way or another.

"Well, Stormy, how the hell are you?" Jasper said, still staring at the floor.

Stormy almost wondered if she was still dreaming, and the man's apparition had come to visit her to punish her dislocation from reality. She looked at the fly, still dormant on the windowsill, and blinked.

"I'm all right," she said. "How are you? I haven't seen you in so long."

"I'm just great!" Jasper said. He clapped his hands together, grinning at the ground. Then he leaned back on the beanie bag and put his hands behind his head.

Stormy stood up, straightening out her T-shirt so it went below her knees. She had to steady herself using a bookshelf with not very many books in it, and itched her foot while quizzically appraising the specimen before her. He had a buzz cut, which was different. He had a lot of tattoos on his arms. That wasn't different. He smelled like cigarette smoke and sweat and a third thing she didn't want to know about. She wobbled again, and then leaned over to her nightstand to turn on the lamp.

"I guess you're wondering where I've been all these months."

"Years," Stormy corrected. "You've been gone years."

"You don't sound like you missed me."

"I missed you. I'm just very, very tired right now."

"You're tired and you're something else, too. What've you been up to, sis? You were always such a sweet soul back in the day. Don't do what *I* did."

She laughed, shrugged, and sat down on the edge of the bed with her small hands joined on her lap.

"Why are you back?" she asked.

"Just to say hello." He sat up with a grunt. He scratched the back of his head and let his shoulders relax. "Is Dad home?"

"Yes. Sleeping before his night shift."

"So he's still working there."

Stormy shrugged.

"You don't know?"

"He never said he's *not* still working there."

Jasper nodded. "He ever mention me?"

"No." She sighed, then added, "I mean—I hardly see him. He sleeps all day and is gone all night. You know. It's the same stuff. But where have you been?"

"In Cantor, if you can believe it."

"Why would you move to Cantor?"

"It's a long story."

"Let me guess. That's where your girlfriend is from."

"She's not my girlfriend. Wait, you saw her?"

She nodded. "She doesn't quite look like your type, if you ask me."

"Oh yeah?" Jasper leaned forward, eyes narrowed. "Who's my type?"

"Some girl who's nice. And actually cares about what you care about. You know, someone *normal*."

He gestured to himself. "You don't think I'm normal."

"That's not what I said." She hankered for another cigarette and unearthed the one she'd tossed in the covers.

"You think I attract the worst kind of women."

She shrugged, lighting her medicine again. "I just think you have a type, and that's not it."

"What do you care?"

"You're my brother."

"Ah."

Jasper stood and clapped the ball of his fist against his palm, then complained about how dark it was in the room and asked if he could roll up one of the shades.

"No! Leave them down, please. It's my room—it's the least you can do."

"I thought it was *our* room, but whatever." He didn't pull down the shades, but sort of melted into them, dressed as he was in a dark hoodie and jeans.

"You're not going to be able to stay here," she said.

"You said you never talk to Dad. He would probably never realize I was even here. And you know, I could slip out in the daytime and try to, you know, find a job or something." He turned around, trying to attain some of the lamplight. She peered up at him. She cursed herself when she realized. Yep, she did really miss him.

"He's going to find out."

"Why does he hate me?"

She hated that all she could do was shrug, but all she did was shrug, and give an innocent frown. Then she said, "He doesn't hate you."

"Yes, he does."

"You have to say that."

"Are we really going to talk about this?"

"What else is there to talk about?"

"You haven't told me anything about your life for the last two years." Her cigarette expired, and getting another one would mean a trip to the kitchen downstairs, where she had left the pack next to the stack of unpaid water and electric bills.

"I didn't have a life, Stormy," said Jasper. "Isn't it obvious that I have no other place to go? I mean, don't you *want* me back?"

"There's not much life here, either," she said, leg jittering. He noticed an empty pill bottle of prescribed opiates on the floor and picked it up, studying the label. "Jasper, don't . . . "

"You have a prescription?" he said. "You're kidding. What for?"

"Hmm, I don't know . . . how about debilitating *pain*? Ever think of *that*?"

"I'm sorry. I didn't know. You're in pain? What kind of pain? Huh?"

"I don't want to talk about it." She rubbed her knees and scanned the room briefly for her phone. It was buried somewhere in the covers, and too knotted up in the sheets for her retrieval. "Let's talk about you," she said. "What do you feel like?"

"What do I *feel* like?"

"Yeah. It's been two years. You've probably been feeling a lot of things. I, however, haven't really managed to feel anything since . . . " She cocked her head and drummed her fingers on her chin. "Oh, yeah . . . two years ago. Around, coincidentally, of course, when ya left."

Jasper returned to the beanbag and shucked his shoes off, rubbing his feet and wincing. "What do I feel like," he mumbled. "Do you know how *old* we sound right now? We never used to talk like this."

"Yeah we did," she whispered. "We really did used to talk like this."

"Fine." Then he paused in silence for a little while, the one ray of light escaping the shades and throwing itself like a sword over his close-cropped head. Stormy saw the scar on the scalp from the time she threw a frying pan at him when they were kids.

"I feel like a waterfall. Or no, that's not it. I feel like I'm floating in a pool at the top of a waterfall but never falling over it. Always kind of circling around and around in this pool, on my back looking up at the sun, but never falling over."

"You need a soothsayer to interpret," said Stormy.

"Yeah, maybe. Anyway, I'm just floating next to the edge of this giant waterfall, and every time I circle back around I think, 'this is it. Now I'm going to fall over.' But I never do."

"What's at the bottom of the waterfall?" Stormy asked.

"Great question. I always thought it sort of represented when my life was going to really start. You know? That finally I'd go over the edge, leave it all behind, and start something." He shook his head. "Nothing ever starts. No matter how long time goes by."

"That's an interesting way to feel," Stormy affirmed, stroking her chin, imagining she had a philosopher's beard. "From my perspective, you went over the waterfall a really long time ago. And I was like, whoa, hey there, Jasper, you've gone off the deep end a little bit, and I don't see you anymore, and we used to kinda be pals."

"You're mad at me."

"What? Mad? No way, man! Like I said, I haven't *felt*—" She raised her hands and gestured quotation marks when she said "felt," and went on, "—angry, sad, hopeful, disgusted, excited, in quite a long time. You're off the hook."

Jasper twiddled with the cross necklace below his neck, studying the silence and the room, and they heard a door downstairs close and the chatter of a talk show host emanate from the source.

"Crap," Jasper whispered, jolting upright. "He's up. It's only four in the afternoon. What's he doing up?"

"Probably getting a snack and a beer. You'll be fine."

The shuffling steps halted. The video stopped. Dad's voice arrived groggily, only half there, going, "Stormy, why the hell is the *front door* open?"

"Your little scuffle outside must have roused him after all," whispered Stormy. Jasper, meanwhile, had crouched between her bed and the wall, right beneath the window, breathing hard and quiet. Stormy slipped into the stairwell and flicked on the light so Dad, a remarkably skinny man of forty, peered up at her in the phosphorescence. He was just in his boxers and all his tattoos of anchors and buxom women stood out against his pale body.

"The door?" said Stormy. "I don't know. I've just been up here sleeping."

"The door was wide open." He mumbled something else, then closed the door and clicked the lock. Looking at the door, he ran the chain into its sliding groove, and turned back around. "The door was locked. I know I locked it. Your brother here? He's the only one I can think of who got another key."

"No," said Stormy. She put her hand against the wall. "Why would he be here?"

"Because the door's open, and we always lock the *door*." He started up the stairs.

"Dad, c'mon—he's not here. Why would he *be* here? He hasn't come around in two years. Don't you gotta get some sleep?"

"Smells bad up here," he said, brushing past her and into the bedroom. "And God, dark as hell. What are you doing, hibernating in here?"

Stormy followed him, arms wrapped around her stomach. Her father rubbed his eyes and kicked through the dirty clothes on the floor. He picked up the beanbag and tossed it so it upset more bobbleheads, then flung the door open to the closet and rooted through her private wardrobe as if he had every right to do it. "I'm sorry, baby," he sighed, after coming up empty. "Sometimes I miss the kid, you know? He's a total failure, and I'd bust him up bad if he were right now, but man, wouldn't it be kinda nice to be a whole *family* again." She smelled whiskey on his breath when he passed her again, and once he was gone, she fled to the restroom and vomited.

"You sick, honey?"

"I'm fine."

"All right. I'm goin' back to bed. Got that late shift again."

Stormy lay next to the toilet for a few minutes, hand resting somewhat inside the bowl. There were no windows in this bathroom. Only a band of grayness bled under the bathroom door. But she felt a little bit better. The withdrawals were excruciating, yes, and there was only so much that cigarettes and sleep and valium can do for you, but she felt a bit better. She got up and rinsed her face, then, still dripping, went back to her bedroom. She had to squint, pull her hands over her eyes. The window above her bed was open, curtains ripped apart, with a hot August wind teasing the bedsheets. She recovered from her disorientation, then scrambled over her bed to peer into the waxing afternoon. She didn't see him. There was a child playing in a sprinkler across the street, leaping and laughing and falling joyfully into the sweet tang of freshly mowed grass.

Jasper was a fast runner. He always outran her to get to the front seat of the minivan, when Mom was still around. He probably dashed around the corner the second she'd gone into the bathroom. It was about a twelve-foot distance from the window to the walk. It would have hurt at least a little bit. It was bad there wasn't a pool of water at the bottom.

She brushed the hair from her eyes and settled her chin on her folded arms, letting the sun shine on her face. The cars whined and the birds chattered and the wind whooshed in the trees—all this, right outside her window?

Of course, by that time, the residential fly had buzzed to freedom, and would try to avoid dark rooms for the rest of the twenty-four hours it had left to live.

"He'll come back," Stormy whispered to herself. "I'm pretty sure of that." And she fell asleep in the sunlight that flowed into the room behind her.

On Cold Days

On this cold day, I see you walk in with a backpack and a swallow in your throat. You order the same drink—a medium drip, and coyly transport the cargo to the corner table beneath the morose portrait of Poe. Fitting. On this cold day, *unbefitting* for April, I see you open the laptop and bunch your brows and begin to scroll through work related items. And you sip the coffee without taking your eye off the screen. We are both regulars at this coffee shop, in this miniature temple of anxiety; we share the same daily patterns, the same lot of white-collar work in the twenty-first century, but I've never spoken to you, nor you to me. I imagine speaking to you, of course—like now. I imagine asking you what you're doing in the corner beneath the sad Mr. Poe, behind that screen which casts its sheen on your own pale, wondrous face, eyes flitting with doom. You can't bear to be home alone—that much is obvious. I can't either. I wake up in the gray tangled sheets and sit at the edge of my bed wondering how every day can be so identical. Except today is one cold day, a Spring anomaly sent to tell us that some events remain unexpected. I don't even look at you—not really. I have my own corner, my own Slack channel, my own headphones making nice sounds in my ears all day. Here for the free refills. But we see each other. Peripheral sight makes up for a lot. You take another big gulp of the coffee and there it is—the first hand through your hair. Scratching your wrist as your leg begins to shake. You look like you're about to cry as I answer Steve's email about proper invoicing format. I take a sip of my own cup of drip.

On cold days I like to work by the fireplace and take laps around the house for breaks without wearing a coat. My father calls from Arizona at noon, which I take with a raw hand and listen as he asks where my brother is, and I have to tell him, on cold days like these, that I have no clue where he is.

"Oh. Oh. Where do you *think* he went, Rod?"

"I think he went to Miami."

"Miami?"

"Yeah."

"Do you think we can . . . *find* him down there?"

I go to the woodpile and split a log thick as a thigh bone and bring a bundle back to exhume in the woodburning stove. On cold days that's what I do—and alone.

But today is cold and you are wearing a sweater with green and burgundy stripes. You are kneading your forehead with one set of fingers and drumming the table by your laptop with the other. You don't have any awareness of the other dozen or so customers in the room. Frankly, neither do I.

When Dad went to the home in Arizona and Jamie vanished into the ether without even a note to show for it, I got another job that let me work remotely. You know how that is, maybe. People in the office smile at you and ask you how the family is. In your cubicle of faux productivity, there is no hiding from the well-intentioned colleague. Who are these people, anyway? How are they bound to us? By human resources in the back department? They carry their white cups of coffee to their chests with the spare hand in their cargo pockets, smiling through beards, woman suits, and . . . do I miss Jamie and my father? Do I know why Jamie spent his days running his hand through his hair like you are doing now only to flee to another corner of the universe once all his options ran out? He was drinking too much and showing up to work too little. And he kept telling me what I ought to be doing, because that's what big brothers do, right? They never relinquish their authority as quiet sages who know more than you. "You should date that one girl . . . what's her name?"

"Jean?"

"Yeah, man. Jean."

Jean has not lived in our vicinity for three years.

You are halfway through your coffee now and biting your lip as you type a message. The barista calls out two hot matcha teas. A man and woman go to retrieve them. They look like they're in college, not all that younger than us. How on earth are they speaking with each other? And what's this— they're smiling across their little table? That was supposed to be statistically impossible. No one in this generation is supposed to be human enough for that. But it begs the question. Why aren't *we* connected? Why haven't we talked? We've marched into this shop to work for three months now. Have you ever wondered about this?

Maybe you do. You get up with your coffee and slip outside into the cold day and make a phone call with your chin nuzzled in your scarf. You bounce the toe of your boot softly on the concrete walk. You made the call yourself, though. Personal or work-related?

You hang up and hug yourself on this cold day until a Ford F-150 rolls up and a man with a crewcut, dark denim jeans, and compassion on his face wraps you in his arms. Is he your father? He looks old enough. I don't hear much of what you say, except, "I can't do this anymore. I can't do this anymore."

It's right after you get into the truck with him that noon hits and my own father calls from Arizona. He is breathing raspingly. I hear him lean forward. "I don't know where Jamie is, Dad."

The truck leaves and I know that when you return, you will go back to work, and I will go back to work, and we may never say a word to each other as long as we live.

"No, no, no," Dad says. "Where are *you*, son?"

The Voyage of the T-shirt

The whole third-grade class brought their sailboats to Lake Smitty at Sallisaw Park, where goose refuse made hopscotch champions of the oldest of walkers and an old bridge, only recently mended from last summer's baptismal flood, stretched over an overflow as the connector of two forlorn dimensions newly reconciled. Only, Jenni didn't bring a sailboat. She brought something, in her eyes, much better.

The third graders flooded out of the school bus in twos and threes like liberated prisoners of war. Each one held a small foam sailboat in tow, painted various pastels, that they each had made without any intervention from parents, teachers, dumb uncles, or big brothers who knew what was what. They took an oath before God and their fellow classmates that they would each serve as the sole proprietors of their creations.

Jenni, who was the last student to get off the bus, blinked lovingly at the sun once it shone on her face. She cradled not a sailboat but a twenty-year-old red T-shirt in her arms, like it was baby Moses ready to be set down on the Nile. She had found the frock that morning from her own dresser, but the shirt didn't belong to her. It belonged to her big brother, Bobby, ten years her senior and two years deceased. The shirt used to have a Coca-Cola bottle on the front, but now there was just the lid, sloshing with specks of soda pop that could have been mistaken for holes. Her brother used to wear the Coke shirt every single day in the summertime. When the dogs got out of the pens in the middle of the night, he'd flee into the darkness with nothing but the red T-shirt on, hanging well past his knees. No one could remember where he ever got it. Maybe it was some last-minute Wal-Mart gift in a dirty Santa giveaway. Whatever the case, the shirt became an extension of the kid. To see the shirt was to see Bobby. It was his knight's visor and his worn-out crown. He used to shove Jenni into the shirt at night like it was a sleeping bag and haul her around the house as she yipped in delightful protest. He swung her up in the shirt and let her sail to the couch, where she wriggled out, bottom first, and clamored for more. It was a real stretched-out shirt. Sometimes Bobby would lay it on the grass in the back pasture and say, "Magic carpet, sis. Get on and let me take you to Tokyo."

Or, better yet, it was the Titanic, befitted with a wiser captain, and could jump across the ponds on windy March afternoons after school. For a girl who could never manage to separate the shirt from the man, she knew now that she carried her brother in her arms, and he was laying there quietly ready for the voyage.

Jenni's main companion in the class was an asthmatic named Christopher, but he was absent that day with a purported illness of the laryngitis.

And Bobby, who knew what was what when it came to making toy boats and just about everything else in the world, and would have positively been there if the circumstances allowed it, was dead from a drowning accident. Two years he'd been that way, haunting her with his old shirt in the old dresser. It had been swum in plenty of times, even died in, dirtied and roiled in oil fields, and clung to by a certain little sister who was not so keen on his departure.

Now, the young'uns swarmed the banks of the lake, observing with open-mouthed wonder the many diadems of glory specific to Lake Smitty—like the mud-grafted oyster shells, plastic water bottles full of bilge, and lumps of goose droppings in quantities that might humiliate American's biggest poultry farm.

Jenni, though, stood back from the happy mob and pet the cuff of the T-shirt, as if it was an ancient tabby cat still on the mend from its arthritis shots. Mikey and Tony, resident tormentors of Sallisaw Elementary School, hustled up to Jenni with their sailboats suspended above their heads in mid-voyage and making car noises. "Where's *your* sailboat, hey Jenni?" demanded Mikey.

"Yeah," said Tony. "Where's *your* sailboat?"

"I *have* my sailboat," said Jenni, tossing her tiny noise in the air so her bowl-cut black hair wrangled around her cheeks in joint retort.

"Is it in that shirt ya got there?" said Mikey.

"No! This *is* my sailboat, morons. I've been working on it for months now. Day and night."

"That is NOT a sailboat," Tony said, bending down to peer up at the shirt from below as if this might disclose a secret rudder and boom. He straightened again, fruitless.

"Of course, it's a sailboat. It's going to sail majestically across the whole lake. You'll see. It's a perfect day to sail."

"Majestically," Mikey mumbled to himself. He was maybe uncertain about the meaning of the word but seemed to like the way it sounded, and proceeded to investigate his paltry vessel of slipshod craftmanship as if to see if it merited a similar adverb. Then he glanced back at the T-shirt and repeated, "*Majestically,* eh?"

"Okay, kids! It's almost time to set sail. Ricky, don't splash him please— Maya Lou, *please* don't stick that up your nose! And hey, Jenni, where's *your* sailboat?"

Mikey and Tony hooted and fled at the sound of their teacher's impending footsteps.

Jenni glanced at the folded red T-shirt, briefly chewing her lower lip before replying. She was less confident than in the face of her former antagonists but stated with no less resolve that *this* was her sailboat, that she had tested its maritime efficacy in the pond in their back pasture, and that if Teacher would keep her *pants* on, she *might* just witness the most stunning voyage of her life.

"Oh Jenni," said Mrs. Hannigan, holding her forehead with her skinny, thirty-year-old wrist upon her hip., "Oh Jenni. You had, what, three *weeks* to make your boat? And you had *all* the materials you needed to build it: the block, fabric, scissors, glue, paintbrush!" The list escalated in volume, promising to end in etcetera.

"I made the other sailboat, Mrs. Hannigan, honest I did, but when I *compared* 'em in the cow pond, the T-shirt was just majestic. You know? You'll see what I mean. Give it a try and you'll see!"

"Jenni," Mrs. Hannigan sighed, looking more the damsel in distress than ever with the back of her hand now softly curled against her forehead and her tennis-shoed foot postured in the 45-degree angle needed to demonstrate her teacherly plight.

"Mrs. *Hannigan,*" Jenni replied, with even-keel gravity that made her teacher blink and observe the little girl in front of her as if to make sure this was indeed a *child* and not an old widow who by virtue of loss and experience has the right to veto certain responsibilities. "Please let me sail with Bobby."

Mrs. Hannigan lowered her thin arms, clad in a cardigan to fend off that day's forecasted wind, which now rustled treetops and woke the water, and stared at the folded T-shirt and by some sixth sense perceived something deep and untouchable, and nodded.

Jenni smiled and skipped to the lake alongside her classmates.

"Okay!" cried Mrs. Hannigan, hands now up in mime configuration, facing her little tribe.

"You're letting her sail a shirt?"

"Shush, Ricky. What did we learn in class about the *wind*? Anyone?"

Zoey Shellenberger flung her hand up and jumped so she partially sank into the fertilizer of a shoreline, and her sacrifice went duly rewarded.

"Yes, Zoey?"

"Wind is when the temperatures, kind of, you know, get mixed up, and then there's all that business with the jet stream, this massive river of air that flows and flows and never stops for nobody, ever."

"That's very well put. Thank you, Zoey. And can anyone tell me why a boat *floats*?"

This time Ricky offered a sheepish finger which formerly he was using to scratch his left ear in meditative rhythm, and after his selection, squeaked, "Boo-yancy!"

"Buoyancy," Mrs. Hannigan said, nodding. "Indeed. Anything you can tell us about buoyancy, Ricky?"

"Well, the wood of the boat isn't as dense as the water or whatever, so it floats."

"Very good! And do you all remember the photos we looked at from the Dead Sea in the Middle-east with people floating on the water and not even trying to? Do you remember that?"

The class gave a semi-confident chorus of yeses. Jenni, meanwhile, furrowed her brows in concentration as she observed a toddler balance on the bridge hand in hand with his mother. Or probably grandmother. The woman had her back to the class but enjoyed a head of mostly gray hair, and beneath the bridge the lake's excess water dribbled over and down a stone wall, across a lichen spattered runoff, and into the woods where the kids weren't allowed to play.

"Today we're going to see what we've learned in action," Mrs. Hannigan continued. "So, in the order of your assigned numbers, you're each going to put your boat in the water. Riley, you're up. And *remember*, Mr. Stone from the shop is coming out with his big boat in a few minutes to pick up all the sailboats, so none of them will get lost. Okay?" She scanned the blinking, restless faces for signs of disillusionment, but was met with jittery feet and soft exclamations of glee. "All right then, line up, line up! We haven't got all day," she cried, clapping her hands as the kids scrambled into formation. Jenni's last name, some might say unfortunately, was "Zamboni," which afforded her the number 22 and a certified last place in line. She stood in her place on a flat stone farther up the bank, as the wind picked up and ruffled the unclipped mass of her heavy black hair, which everyone who saw it in such lighting and disarray could agree had a primal, unhinged beauty to it.

Turns out, though, that launching a fleet of miniature sailboats takes a miracle of fine-tuning. The wind rolled down the hill in wafts at 25 m.p.h., enough to bowl the boats over upon their feeble departures and send them quickly to the overflow beneath the bridge, where they were sure to plummet as if over the world's edge. However, a slight amendment to the wind's direction altered the cohort's trajectory and had them bobbing lopsided in a patch of algae a few yards away from the contestants.

"It's okay!" Mrs. Hannigan said. "The water's a little rough, but it's okay! Let's keep setting sail."

One by one, the kids sent their ships into the dark good night, but never unto gentle results, crouching by the water and biting their lips in hope and terror that *their* ship might have the engineering aptitude to survive the turmoil of Lake Smitty. Sadly, all hopes were dashed. Some of the sailboats even flipped upside down, belly up.

Mrs. Hannigan tried to quell the disappointment by telling everybody that they had all *learned* something today, and that next time they would test out buoyancy at the local university's swimming pool.

But really the only thing left to do now was ridicule the final voyager, who stepped up to the edge of the water with the ancient red T-shirt now unfolded and fluttering wordless and brandless in the up-and-coming wind.

"That's *definitely* not going to sail," sniffed the miffed Zoey Shellenberger.

"Nope!" said Mikey, freshly prejudiced.

"You call that a *sailboat*, Jenni Zam*boni*?"

Jenni, under the watchful and now silent eye of Mrs. Hannigan, knelt down and laid the shirt on the water in perfect flatness, taking two sticks in either hand and urging it under the armpits towards its offing. At first, the T-shirt drifted slightly sideways, as if insecure in its coordinates. But with another draft of wind, it seemed to almost catch a deep, hidden, and abiding current. The wind fiddled its way into the shirt's chest cavity, bloating it like a pair of lungs and shooting it across Lake Smitty. It disregarded the shipwrecked and parsed the choppy waves with a dry deck and a full mast. She wasn't sure why she felt like she needed to know her brother's old T-shirt could sail. She just figured that it would. Her mom and dad had tried to get her to build the actual sailboat last week, and she actually did at the last minute in the garage late at night, but come this morning she reached for the alternate vessel.

The skeptics now ogled, and Mrs. Hannigan clapped her hands again and saying, "Okay, kids, you see, do you see? It's floating *and* it's moving with the wind at the same time. It's *sailing*!"

Mr. Stone from the school rattled up the gravel drive and parked next to the bus with a metal canoe sticking from the back of his far-too-long truck bed. He sighed and flicked away a cigarette before getting out.

And still the T-shirt sailed, now halfway across the lake and attracting the confused attention of some nearby geese. The toddler and the grandmother, now safely across the narrow bridge, watched it from the opposite shoreline, cusping their hands to their brows. The shirt had no apparent intention of slowing or sinking.

"Hey, where's Jenni going?" said Tony.

Mrs. Hannigan turned along with the rest of the on-looking class to see Jenni clomping across the bridge. By the time she got to the shirt, the thing bobbed blood red and human shaped on the other side of the lake.

Stone's Throw

The Jackson family, residents of Brownwood, Texas, drove in a long Volkswagen into the parking lot in Pacifica, Oregon next to a blue double-story building that acted as a sentinel and snack shack with the beach and far-reaching ocean behind it. Mr. Jackson smoked a cigar in the driver's seat. Mrs. Jackson, flummoxed by the smoke, wanting to exchange it for the smell of sea salt coming through the open window, asked him to put the wretched thing out. "This air is *divine,* honey—cain't foul it up!"

"Is this it?" said Constance, the eighteen-year-old middle-seater and eldest of the four.

"Looks like it!" said her father through the impediment.

"Woah!" This came from Al. He flung his hands over the middle seat and inhaled. "Smell the mariner's whiskey!"

"Shut up," said Sarah, Al's twelve-year-old dissident, two years his senior. "You've seen pictures."

"It's not the same!"

"He's right, Sarah," said Mr. Jackson. "This ain't nothing compared to what you'll see in a dumb Nat'l Geographic. Right, honey?"

Mrs. Jackson glowered at him. She plucked the cigar out of his mouth and plunged it into a cup holder. "You have to *smell* it, too, not just *see* it."

Mr. Jackson pulled into an open spot in a parking lot that, at ten in the morning, was almost full. Surfers walked shirtless and broad-chested through the cars. Some were like them, though, organized in families and provided with a luncheon box, quilts for the sand, and a big umbrella that could shelter them from foreign elements.

49

"You're awful quiet, Stone," said Mrs. Jackson once the ignition was off and everyone fought for the exit.

"I'm all right," said the back-seater. This Jackson sibling was watching a surfer not much older than he was walking with a board under one arm and a blonde-haired girl tucked warmly under his other. Like the other Jacksons, he never saw the ocean before. Not even at Galveston. They did, however, own a swimming pool in the backyard that he liked to dive in on the hottest of days. He would exhale underwater and let himself sink to the bottom of the pool, and lay there in the ephemeral quiet, pressed lightly against the concrete. He didn't suppose you could quite do that in the ocean, but he was game to try if push came to shove and he exhausted all other options of adventure.

They all got out of the car and stood behind the Volkswagen. This was their very first vacation of this magnitude and so they had overpacked, like real Americans. They had never zipped past the state line during the summer, but Mr. Jackson's unexpected promotion and Mrs. Jackson's subscription to a travel magazine broadened their horizons. "Oregon," she sighed when she swept the kitchen. "The Pacific coast . . . Highway 5 . . . can't you see it, honey? We ought to go. Before Constance is off to A & M."

That sounded all right to Mr. Jackson. His promotion, which was to manage three hundred sofa and office chair factory workers, came with five extra vacation days, and a trip to the exotic west was the very thing he needed to make conversation to his new underlings in the break room. "Oregon's *beautiful* in the month of July, boys," he'd chat at 8 a.m. as other admins started to file in. "I mean, really, you ought to just snatch your pension now and beat it. Took the whole posse out there and we lived it up. Hoo-whee, yessir, fresh, Pacific air, big ol' rocks taller than the Brownwood courthouse . . . heck, taller than the *Dallas* courthouse . . . you really ought to have seen it."

Mrs. Jackson heralded the efforts to get everything they needed for the day—picnic boxes, wool blankets, and yes, the yellow beach umbrella, an embarrassment and a hassle to establish. Stone stood behind the others. Al caterwauled for a sandcastle. Constance glanced at the incoming surfers and Sarah kept telling Al to shut up.

Mr. Jackson came up next to Stone and slapped him on the back. "Well, what do you think?"

"It is quite cool," said Stone. "It's excellent that we've finally arrived after hours of acute anticipation."

"Yep. Not as hot as Texas, that's for sure."

"Yeah."

"Ah, it feels *great* to finally be here!"

The family reached the edge of the parking lot, where a film of beach sand obscured the lines of paint, and waving prairie grass poked up on to separate knolls between which ran a narrow trail leading them to their long-envied destination.

Mrs. Jackson put it on herself at the beginning of this crazy voyage west to wrangle Al without encouraging Sarah's insults against her little brother, and to let Stone wander from time to time apart from her tutelage. Stone liked to wander off lately without explaining where he was going. He never really *knew* where he was going. Some Saturday mornings before anyone was yet up in the Brownwood house, he slipped out the backdoor, compressed himself beneath the ragged wooden fence in the backyard, and walked no farther than a stone's throw into the back pasture where the electric lines made mile-long perches for refugee birds and where, if you timed it right, the sun rose between the two hedges of oak trees.

Now the hedges were sand knolls and the great beyond the Pacific Ocean undulating in rolls of blue out past a pair of rocks pocked with seagulls. Stone stopped on the path, arrested for breath, toes planted in the sand—so cool, so unlike the tangle of bramble and weeds in the back pasture in Brownwood. His family ambled on until resigning themselves to a spot by a log glistening with years of being sat on. Here, Mr. Jackson planted the umbrella into the sand like an American soldier claiming victory in Europe (which he had, twenty-three years before), Constance shrugged off her cardigan, Sarah sat pouty-mouthed in the shade, Al took off towards the foam-lipped waves, and Mrs. Jackson rummaged in their picnic baskets for lunch. It was around eleven o'clock in the morning, warming fast, with another bout of surfers filing down the trail. A couple of them brushed past Stone in his revery, nudging him off the path.

"'Scuse me, dude," said a kid his age wearing a straw hat, smoking a cigarette, and holding a redheaded lass's hand, who walked behind him. He caught eyes with the girl for one divine second. Her eyes, emerald green in the sun, flashed at him from a pool of freckles and then glanced away again. He watched them evolve from an excited amble to a full-fledged sprint to the water, as if life's essence was tucked in droves within the tide.

"Stone, there's no agenda here," said Mrs. Jackson as the boy approached with hands in his overall pockets. "My only rule'—" she kicked

Mr. Jackson, who was whistling to himself and working on igniting another cigar—"is that you don't go so far off that we can't see you. It's a flat beach, so you'd need to go pretty doggone far for that to be the case." She straightened up and settled her hands on her plump hips, and scanned the beach with her hand over her brow. "But that does *not* apply to Al. He can't be wandering. He'd get lost. Isn't that right, Daddy?"

"Huh? Ah, yeah. Let's rendezvous here at one p.m. for some lunch," said Mr. Jackson. "In the meantime, swim, loaf, surf, do whatever you want. It's vacation!"

"Al!" screamed Mrs. Jackson. "You're *not* running off by yourself?"

Stone looked after the girl and her friend in the straw hat. They joshed around in the shallows, laughing in their sunglasses. A few others who must've been part of their group came up to them, exchanged some words, and then they all started off down the beach with all their surfboards, gear, and batches of firewood.

Stone watched them as they walked, then trotted, then ran all the way to a bend in the coast where a crag jutted out into the water, where they veered in unison like a herd of wild animals and disappeared.

"I'll be back around one, then," he said, and started to wander off just as Al dragged himself back to the homebase.

"Where's Stoney goin'"? he demanded.

"Nowhere. He's old enough to wander a little bit. But you! You sir, are stayin' right here until we get our bearings together a lil bit, hear?"

"Aw, Mom! But, Mom!"

Stone visited the water first. He stood a few feet out from the tumbling waves and waited for the tide to swarm his ankles, tickling his Achilles when it rushed back out to sea. After five minutes, though, he turned on his wet heel and walked towards that jutting crag. He put his hands behind his back and looked at his feet while he walked. The gulls swooped twenty feet above his head, squalling in their disordered symmetry, and retreated to the heap of stone in the shallows.

Who were those kids? And who was that girl with the green eyes? She had a name, surely. Oregonians must have names just like Texans. Do they speak in ordinary English? Are their movements godlike? Around the corner, out of sight from his parents, he would know. There was no other way *to* know.

As it happens with beaches, the crag was farther than it looked. And he felt lonely and vulnerable earlier than he expected to. The crowd of voices behind him quickly dissipated with the distance and crashing waves, and his only company consisted of the gulls and blue-bellied swallows that fired and rebounded from little nests and sutures in the crag in front of him. But he didn't look back. He was fifteen years old now, teetering, as noted in his history books on Native American culture, on the brink of manhood, in need of initiation. He guessed this place was as good as any to fly through the gauntlet and emerge on the other side as a victor. Those kids! Being as they were from this faraway land of impossible beauty, maybe they had the answer. Maybe they *were* the answer.

He registered the moment he'd disappeared by instinct, almost; he reached a black boulder and planted his shoe upon it and looked back one last time at the moving specks of human beings behind him, and then hopped up and over the stone and towards a stretch of beach where last night's tide had deposited a motionless sheet of water, still as a mirror. He shucked off his shoes and walked on the water, pretending he was Peter in the Bible story. The water was warm.

He got the impulse to run and so did, letting his legs and arms fly-wheel until he skidded, heart pounding at the onset of a small boulder field where the tide seized the spaces in between the rocks. He jumped on the first one in sight, testing his balance. He tasted the salt from the air as well as his own sweat, reveling in the solitude, but then froze. The voices of a boy and girl floated up just twenty feet away.

Sure enough, it was the red headed lass and her surfer man. They sat with their backs against one of the stones, wearing nothing but sunshine and sexual liberation. The tide flowed beneath them. The boy had put his straw hat over his penis and the girl hugged her chest.

Stone crouched behind his boulder, heart pounding, and scanned back over his route for an escape. He would have crawled to safety right then and there if he hadn't started hearing the conversation. He was on his hands and knees, stooped low, eyes like egg whites. The girl said, "This might be it, you know."

The boy said, "Nonsense. What are you talkin' about? We'll always be right here."

"But we won't."

"Sure we will. No reason why things need to change."

"High school's over. College is up. Or whatever's next. It's the law of the universe."

"Law? Listen to the movement. No law but love, baby. C'mon."

"Not now, not now . . . I told Melissa we'd follow them in ten minutes. Don't you want to go to the bonfire?"

"Melissa! Why does she always want to have everyone there all the time? Groups aren't so great, you know."

"It's almost like she's sentimental."

"Can't relate."

"I'm the one trying to have a mature conversation about moving on."

"Nope. You're trying to be a party pooper and I'm trying to make love. Like usual."

"Stop it. We're barely out of sight. Someone could walk right in us. Spoil the whole thing."

"I don't care if they see us like this. What, are you thinking of that kid we bumped into on the trail? Looked like he was on another planet. Haha! Did you see his eyes when he was staring at the ocean like that?"

"I saw their license plate. Family's from Texas. They drove a long way to get here. Try to be nice."

"Texas. Oh boy, what's in Texas? I can't figure what it's like down there."

"I was trying to talk about something important and you keep sidetracking."

"I don't want to talk about the fall. About the future, babe."

"Oh really. Great. We'll just let it slide, then. I'll go to the University of Oregon and you'll . . . what? What're you going to do? Make money by making love, baby? Don't start."

"You're going to learn a crock full of nothing at that place," said the boy. Stone situated himself on his rear. "And we've talked a million times about how America is a corrupt capitalistic beast that must be quietly but firmly resisted. Boys my age are dying in 'Nam. Did you know that?"

"They've got a few months on you."

"Military industrial complex. Lies from the White House on how things are going over there. Draft dodgers in Canada. Right-wing fundies vying for power. Nah, I'll kindly opt out of what those fools call 'society.' Give me the Zen of the mountain range. I'll be your precious Buddha. Sitting naked on rocks by the sea."

"You're one carnal Buddha, buddy. Isn't a Buddha supposed to renounce all earthly desires?"

"You're sounding too much like Christianity. My Buddha can both renounce and indulge. He's a two-sided coin—a real yin and yang. Takes severe concentration to achieve this kind of inner balance."

"You're full of crap. Back to the point. Are we going to stick it out after I leave or what?"

"You know how I feel about promises."

"You're afraid of them?"

"You know what—if you're so excited about the group, how 'bout we jaunt on over? It isn't far."

The boy vaulted to his feet without bothering to don his underpants and shot off over the rocks. He scrambled for balance and scraped his knees once or twice. The girl shouted for him to stop. Stone slipped into the open from behind his rock. He was determined, now, to make a run for it.

"Whoa, there's somebody here! Hey!" He froze. The girl was talking at him yes, that was no misfire. He waited a good twenty seconds to ensure she was no longer in the nude, and when he shifted his head, was disappointed and relieved to find her back in overalls with her freckly arms crossed. She was squinting at him, but the boyfriend was long gone behind the crag and didn't turn back.

"Were you spying on me?"

He stood up, crusted with wet sand, and faced her. She was even prettier on second notice.

"You're that Texan kid, aren't you?"

Stone nodded. He backed up, slowly, fists clenched.

"I think you owe me a little bit of an explanation." Arms crossed again, hair like fire in the wind. Stone cleared his throat, smelled the heavy salt in the air, and replied,

"I was just walking along the beach. I've never been on a beach before and I wanted to see what that group was up to. I hear so much about how people like you are in touch with the essence of the universe and whatnot. Free people. I came up on you on accident and then I hid. I hid during your conversation because I was afraid. I was technically mortified, I'd say, unleavened unto an unconscionably small decimal into the earth. I was deteriorating with humiliation." He paused, adding, "I've never seen naked humans before."

"Geez, you're a wordy Willy, aren't you?"

"I try to choose my words carefully and with an eye towards the truth they convey," he said. "It's hard for me to do otherwise and has gotten me expelled on three separate occasions from the high school for it. For instance, you're undoubtedly the prettiest girl I've ever seen, and since I'm in the midst of puberty I was having thoughts. Lustful thoughts. Thoughts I'm so ashamed of I could die. Thoughts and feelings that I'd like to ask my own father about but don't know how to phrase the words. He will not ask me and I will not ask him. But I blurt and I regret and my family has no idea what to do with me." A ream of tide rushed in and swallowed his volume. She asked him to repeat himself. He did—the whole paragraph, and she frowned and stepped toward him until she was within spitting distance, and said, "What's your name?"

"Stone Mason Jackson. Feel free to poke fun at the punny configuration of my name. My father wanted to be a comedian when he was growing up and has made a pastime out of wordplay ever since the comedy acts backfired and he became a secretly disturbed veteran and the overseer or a furniture company." Stone wiped his hands free of sand and asked, "What's your name? And is your boyfriend a jealous type? Does he plan to put on his clothes when he joins the rest of your cohort?"

The girl got a cigarette from her breast pocket and lit it against the wind. "My name's Liz. And no, he doesn't plan on it, but at this point none of them have clothes on. They're nuts. We're all nutso up here in Oregon. Didn't anybody tell you that?"

"I know there are radically strong focal points of the sexual revolution in certain parts of the United States and that rural Texas isn't necessarily on the list of hot spots, but I didn't imagine this beach in Oregon to be partially nudist, either."

"How old are you?"

"I'll be fifteen and three quarters in seventeen days. How old are you?"

"Eighteen. I'm an old, washed-out high school student. Now I feel weird."

"Why would you feel weird? Is it because you're a legal adult and I stumbled in on you when you were having a quasi-sexual episode with your boyfriend?"

"That has something to do with it." Liz swept her hair out of her eyes and glanced at the crag.

"I was very interested in coming to Oregon," said Stone. "I had never been out of the state of Texas, and I've only been out of my native Brownwood a handful of times, mainly to see my Aunt Rosa who is very lonely and who my father loves and feels sorry for, although he won't say that, and many mornings lately I've been crawling beneath the fence and visiting the back pasture. I'm not sure why I do this. Maybe to imagine that I'm someplace else. Someplace expansive." He pointed to the ocean. "It's the great nothing and the great everything. You know?

"Here's the thing, Stone."

"Yes?"

"I don't seem like it, but I'm incredibly embarrassed. That you overheard us. Saw us. It's actually something that my voice isn't shaking right now. And you want to know something else?"

"Sure."

"I was embarrassed to be seen like that the whole time I was talking to Jim. I feel like you might understand because you're from Texas and you don't seem like to type to shed your loincloths on the beach."

"I like to keep my clothes on in front of people."

"That's good, probably. But you know, if I tell that to Jim he'll call me a crazy prude. He'll call me a housewife and a Victorian. I'll be a traitor to the cause, that's what *I'll* be."

"That doesn't sound fair."

"It's not. The point is that here's something I've learned. I don't even know why I'm telling you this but maybe it's because this is what I was about to tell Jim before he ran away. Texas . . . " She held her hands up as a balance of justice and weighed the left downward. "Oregon." Right hand downward, the Texan hand up. "Free love, happy, liberated, naked love . . . rural, conservative, little town Texas." Up and down with the balances. Stone gaped at her and the girl sighed.

"Oregon . . . California . . . Zimbabwe . . . Lichtenstein . . . Bolivia . . . ummm . . . .Oklahoma . . . "

"You're weighing the balances of these particular geographical locations to indicate that no one place is inherently better than the other and that my tendency to slip beneath the fence to go to the back pasture shows a desperate though understandable adolescent mode of escapism," said Stone.

"Couldn't have put it better myself."

Before Stone could extrapolate, someone shouted Liz's name. She turned around, shading her eyes like she was confused about why in the world someone might be calling her name when she was in this remote locale with this strange youngster, then said, "Have fun today, Stone. It's not such a bad thing, you know. To have some fun."

He was tempted to follow her when she turned on her heel and left him. He started to murmur a goodbye, but nothing came out, and it was like he was stuck there by an invisible hand, convincing him that his following footsteps might forever determine his destiny. The girl's old mannish wisdom had stumped him.

After a minute's deliberation, he hobbled the rocks, reached the sand, and waded into the ocean. The waves were getting bigger. A blue-black storm curled up on the horizon, poised to strike like Leviathan. Stone cast a couple more glances towards the crag but gave up his original plan, choosing a thigh deep slice of water to fall into instead. He depressed his lungs, felt himself sink, and waited in the chill. Unlike the ponds and pools of Texas, summer salt water in Oregon does not warm. And what was he waiting for? He didn't know. The girl's face shimmered in his head. No matter how far you sink, you can't escape your own head, and for many kids trying to become men, that's a real agony.

He felt his body wriggle with the waves, get pushed forward by the rush of water and then sucked back. He tumbled, had to plug his nose, then surfaced with the foam strangling at him like fingers. Then he was under again, handled by gravity and power, and realized that this was no peaceful warm pool in Texas. This was the Pacific Ocean, not a parent. This was the sea, brusque and impersonal, not his backyard. He tumbled again and got spat on land akin to Jonah, and when he looked up, saw his paunch bellied father standing above him smoking a cigar and with arms concernedly outstretched.

"What are you doing, son?" he said, kneeling in the sand. He dirtied his slacks. He smelled of aftershave and cigar smoke, a combination that vaulted Stone back to their living room in Brownwood. There was his father, sitting with a paper and said cigar in his leather recliner next to the fireplace they used but twice a year, socks loppy and eye quizzical, searching for obscure facts in the margins.

"I was swimming," said Stone. He spit some water out and shivered. "I don't know why I was swimming but I was."

"I've seen swimming and that seemed more like limp-fish planking, sonny," said Mr. Jackson. "I got a little worried when I didn't see you and so I came looking for ya."

"Mom didn't come looking first?"

"Nope. Took a little walk myself after you went out of sight, against protocol." Mr. Jackson took off his cardigan and settled around the boy's shoulders, then sat next to him despite the incoming tide and asked Stone if he was doing all right.

"I am not *fully* all right," said Stone, gripping the cardigan and closing his eyes. "I saw a crowd of young adults flock to that crag yonder and I decided to pursue them because I thought they might include me in their group. You know probably better than anyone, Dad, that back at Brownwood, Texas from which we hail that I don't have said *group* to be a part of. I hate sports. I'm very bad at sports. I'm too arrogant for chess club."

"Too *good* at chess club," corrected Mr. Jackson. "Ain't easy being the object of envy."

"I don't have an ingroup that I can successfully claim to be a part of except our very own family unit, which up until recently I felt I'd never leave but now sense that I must as all boys must at some point become men, seeing how every traditional culture save ours has rites of initiation for young men such as I."

"Well, that's true, I guess." Mr. Jackson sniffed, then added, "So you want to be a man, huh, son?"

Stone shrugged. He didn't know what he wanted to be. Seen and spoken to by beautiful redheads? Maybe. Given high fives by cool surfer dudes in straw hats? Or to be left alone in a solitary meadow behind the house, where once a gray fox perked its head above the grass and bounded away towards the electric lines?

"I'm sorry if it's been a tough time for ya, son," said Mr. Jackson. "Heck, I don't hardly know what to say. My daddy didn't talk to me much, and the best I can do is clap ya on the back and crack jokes. Ain't very fatherly."

"Tough time," said Stone, nodding. "Unsure of anything. Unsure of what's good. TV says war is a necessity. And that young people are finding freedom on college campuses and in high school and that your generation is out of style. Out of the moral zeitgeist."

"How many books do you read every week?"

"Approximately seven, Pops."

"Seven. I don't know where ya get your brains from. Your mama, clearly." Mr. Jackson coughed up some smoke and watched the birds circling them overhead. The storm billowed but was blowing north, away from them, with the midday sun reemerging a band of stratus and gleaming on the swells.

"Honestly, I feel like I've got nothing to teach you," said Mr. Jackson. "Every time I try to, you're three miles ahead of me. Remember when I wanted to show you how to change the oil in the car? You already knew how, doggone it. For some crazy reason you'd already read the manual on

Volkswagen repairs. Beats all, Stone. That don't mean I ain't proud. I am. You're going to go places. Make fools of your teachers when you go off to Princeton or Harvard or some other school up in the Northeast. I fought in Germany and came back to work at a furniture factory. Exciting life, huh? Point is, I want to be there for ya, but you're way beyond your old pop, and that's a fact."

"I don't think it's a fact," said Stone. "It's a fact that all I been hankerin' for is a conversation with someone. It's hard to believe it's that simple. Just a back and forth, like people do. I tried to talk to a girl today, Dad. I think I scared her to Pluto."

"A conversation." His father laughed to himself. "I guess I had to go all the way to the Pacific Northwest to have one of those with my son. Huh!"

"Must be a pretty good place after all," said Stone. "Can you tell me about girls and all that?"

"And all that?"

"Yeah."

"Well."

"Can you tell me why Truman chose to drop the atomic bomb? Did Oppenheimer object to it?"

"Uh, well . . . "

"And is there the slightest possibility that the moon landing was fabricated to goof with the Soviets?"

"Now *that* is a load of baloney."

"What about Vietnam? Why are kids two and one quarter years older than me going over there to get shot?"

"That's a long story."

"Can you tell me about the theory of relativity?"

"No, but I bet you could tell it to *me*."

"I don't know everything, Dad."

"Anything else you wanna know?"

"Just one other thing. Do you love me? Do you think I'm all right? Am I going to hell in a handbasket?"

Mr. Jackson's cigar fell from his mouth and the tip of it singed his wet kneecap. The storm had buffed itself out and moved on to the Puget Sound. The middle-aged veteran's wrinkles popped with sweat and an old sadness. The mysteries around the corner of the crag nudged Stone's weak ribs.

"You're a wunderkind. A wonder upon wonders. A champion and a king. Sure, Stone, I . . . I love ya. Got the best son in the world."

Sink into that ocean, mister.

Stone and his father pulled out of the hug only by the call for lunch, with the corner around the crag gone unexplored. But Stone still threw his glance toward the great everything and the great nothing as they walked away from the water and kept talking about girls and love and Soviets and all that—just one more glance was all. He tasted salt, and mystery.

Thirty Grand's Worth, Honey

"Clary? Where ya going?"

"Going out. Don't worry."

He buttoned up his pale denim shirt and matted his trucker hat on his head.

"Second night in a row?"

"There's just somethin' I gotta do baby girl and I don't need more questions 'cuz it's complicated."

He stood up after shoveling his pants on and glanced back at her when he was in the doorway. She was twenty years old now but still looked sixteen, which was when they'd gotten married. She sat up with the covers held up against her chest and pawed for a cigarette on the nightstand, moodily lighting up and staring at him through the fog. "You keep lyin' to me and then I won't trust you."

"You can trust me."

"Tell me where yer goin.'"

"Tomorrow."

She blew smoke and he turned out the lamp, so she was a hunched curvature against the light of the window, which was only illuminated because of the brash streetlight in front of the meth house next door.

He had recently won ten thousand dollars gambling at the brand-new casino on the edge of town, stashed the money underneath the very mattress Joanna now lay on without knowing it, and was back for round two. That's where he had to go now. Again.

He won the money on one of those slot machines. He'd played one once when he visited Reno, Nevada. Or, he wasn't really visiting—just driving through with Joanna when they were with the temp agency. The ring of the machine and lever tug gave him the sense that he was actually working for the rewards, and now he was on the road going fifty in a thirty just to get there before the night rush.

He wished he could have slipped out without Joanna's notice, but then again, she would have woken up at two in the morning, because she *always* woke up at two in the morning, only to find him gone with the kerosene lamp dangling on the front porch in an eerie swing with no wind. And then she'd interrogate him during breakfast in the doorway of the kitchen while he laced up his boots. So, turning on the light and waking her up was better. It was better for her to see him leave and then to show up at five with ten thousand *more* dollars, and then he'd grab around under the mattress with his grin and pull out all the secrets from the night before. Then they'd have this laugh about it and maybe retire. He didn't know. He hadn't figured it out yet. But he thought he was about to make her the happiest woman in the world, and really that's all he wanted. He just liked drawing it out and imagining what her face would look like when he got the stash up to one hundred grand. Could it be possible? One hundred grand?

Wolf's Eye Casino brimmed with locals and commuters alike when he got there. No surprise—it opened the week before and Holdwater County was out in spades to gather up the goods.

He grabbed a beer from the bar first, tipped his hat at a girl who dandled her hips at him on her way past him, and then had to wait in line to get back to the slot machine he'd used the night before. He didn't realize it, but he was exhausted and wide-eyed at the same time. What from the night before and trucking for Braums all day today. And he had to get out to western Texas tomorrow by 10 a.m. the next morning. Or this morning, technically.

He finally got to the slot, pulled the levers after betting all of two hundred dollars that he'd brought along, and when he left an hour later, he had a haul of another ten thousand. He couldn't believe the luck. He really thought, at first, that something magic was in the water. But he didn't push the goat past its pasture. He recalled the stories of fortune won and quickly lost; he was dog tired by the time he got back to the apartment and fell back into bed next to Joanna. He was, however, careful to tuck the money under the mattress, listening to her deep breathing while he did it. She was asleep. Somehow, she was still asleep.

The next three nights in a row, he lucked out and won big, convinced after raking in thirty thousand by Friday that God really had given him the big break he'd begged for, and he even courted notions of spending it responsibly. *Investment.* That was the word. Invest your money in stocks. Open a bank account. Put it anywhere other than your mattress, man.

He'd have actually taken it to the bank, too, if on Saturday morning, he hadn't woken up, scrummaged under the yellow foam of the mattress, and found nothing but clean copper wire and banged-up section of bedspring.

"Well." He knew he'd find it clumped in its three rolls of bills on the shag carpet beneath bed. All he saw, though, was an old baseball glove and an opened bottle of pills.

Joanna still slept, her forearm draped over her eyes with her bare leg hanging over the edge of the bed, shingled with a couple slats of light coming through the window. For just a second, Clary loved the way her raven-black hair made a storm cloud on the pillow. She deserved a lot more, right? Thirty grands' worth more?

Clary scrambled to his feet and swept his hand as subtly as he could all the way around the mattress. He went back to the original spot and stuck his head into the crevice, thinking that maybe it got jammed between the lip of the sheet and the underbelly of the mattress. No such luck. The money, the whole week's worth, was gone.

He slunk into the kitchen and turned on a dime by the door to retrace his journey from the night before. He hadn't been drunk. Tipsy enough to do a little more than tip his hat to the bartender after her shift, but not out of his mind. He had walked in with his latest bundle, and . . . set it on the counter? No, the counters were clean, and the dishes were set in the dry rack by the sink. He had walked to the bathroom to pee and brush his teeth and . . . dropped the cash on top of the toilet? He slipped into the bathroom and investigated, finding a pair of his boxers next to the shower mat but no cash.

He tramped outside and scoured his pickup truck. It was just seven in the morning and the whole block still slept; the crisp November sun made his leather seats brashly glow, almost like they pointing out the stupidity of his investigation. All the truck had to show for was the collection of empty beer bottles on the floor on the passenger seat side.

"Son of a gun . . . "

He had gotten back at one a.m. with the money in his pocket, rolled up. He had taken the money out and tucked it under the bed. He planned on showing it all to Joanna this morning and taking her to the bank to put it in a nice big account that would make money from the interest. And he planned on quitting the trucking business forever so he could love her like he should, be with her as she tried to start up her knitting business (she sold sweaters and caps) and figure out that trip to Washington state they always talked about.

"What in the every-living hell . . . "

First, he'd thought it fell through the bedspring. Now he suspected foul intent. He went back inside. Joanna combed her hair on the edge of bed, yawning and facing the corner full-body length mirror.

"Very funny, Jo."

"Huh? Mornin' to you too."

"All right. I'll come clear about where I been. Seems like you already figured it out."

"Figured what out?"

"Hardy har har, let's not get cute, baby, I know you stashed it some-where and I'm sorry I didn't tell you where I hid it." She looked puzzled at that, pausing in mid-brush and looking at him with an exhausted contor-tion of her brows that piqued Clary's fury a little too fast for comfort.

"C'mon now," he said. "I ain't kidding. Where'd you put it?"

He ducked under the bed again, grunting like a hog, and then sat on his heels.

"You know how much I got for us," he said.

"Baby, I don't know whatcher talkin' about."

"Oh c'mon, Jo. C'mon, Jo, it was thirty grand worth right under the mattress. That's what I was out doin'. I had the best run of luck in my whole life and I ain't even a gamblin' man, you know that. I was desperate. You know. Tryin' to get us out of our ditch we're in. And I kept goin' and I kept winnin'—"

"You been gamblin.'" She said it like she was giving herself a flashcard to memorize. "Honey, you idiot, you been gamblin'? What's my daddy gon' think?"

"What? That's what you're worried 'bout?" He stood up again and hoisted the mattress up so she almost fell to the floor.

"Clar, can you not?"

"I put it RIGHT here." He pointed at the spot. She peeked over the edge of the mattress. "This whole week I've been comin' back in with the money and landin' it right here. Now it was here last night at 2 a.m., so either I'm absolutely off my mother effin rocker, you hid it somewhere else, or we got a dude comin' in here like a ghost in the middle of the night."

She didn't say anything. She was bothered, sure, and he could tell it in her eyes, which he knew well enough to realize that she wasn't lying to him. "Oh shit, Jo."

He swept through the kitchen again. His heart pawed at his throat. Sweat beads popped along his thinning hairline. He snatched his trucker cap and went back outside. A couple of trucks swished by, rumbling with country music and diesel. He upended the seats in the back of the truck. He crawled underneath and rolled all the way to the other side. Joanna stood on the tiny front porch of the trailer by now, shielding her eyes against the sun and cooing his name.

"Somebody stole it. Ain't no other explanation."

He got up and scanned the neighbor's house, a square sallow thing with the concrete foundation exposed above the ground. There was a small hole, half-boarded up, leading underneath the house. A gray cat slipped through with a kitten in her mouth, darting her head back and forth in search of predators, and ran through the yard to get to a little patch of weeds by the fence.

Did he see any scuffle at the base of the foundation? Was there anything that might tell him someone crawled under there to hide his money? *His* money? He jogged over to the opening and bent down to look into the black.

"Clary, please don't."

"Honey cheeks, this is all out war. Understand? Somebody done stole our whole life savings. That's what it 'mounts to. Do you understand that? Please tell me you understand that."

"Maybe you ne'er brought it home." She was stepping out into the lawn now in her robe. Clary handled one of the unkempt boards, glancing to his side to make sure no one was coming out of the house, and yanked. "Clary!"

"Get back inside. Just gonna have a lil look-see."

"Clary, good Lord, don't crawl under their house. They're weird people in there. They'll kill you. I swear I seen one of 'em in there pop a pistol out on the porch when somebody ambled too close the other day. *Please.*"

"Exactly. They'd be the ones to steal it, the buggers. And hush up! They'll hear!"

He slipped inside. The sweet musk of insulation, mold, and air conditioner hit him hard, and he couldn't see a thing. He sat up and banged his head on a beam. But he blinked a few times, rubbing his head, and started to make out the jungle of cords, animal bones, and boxes of what he assumed contained bags of drugs.

"Clary!" Joanna hissed. "Someone's *moving around in there.*"

"Get back inside! Now!"

He scooted across the dirt. He got a hold of one of the boxes. Taking out his pocket knife, he cut through the tape on the top and opened the box to find stacks of perfect thousand-dollar bills. They were just stacked there, held together in the ten thousands by rubber bands. He stared. He picked up a bundle and weighed it in his hand. It was the cleanest dirty money he ever saw. These people were real stupid to store it here, but sheesh. They must have had some kind of operation. Major, in fact, to have a lab of that caliber in a dumpy house and neighborhood like this one. They had to have stolen his own thirty thousand. The rich never stop with the millions. They get wind of a poor man's fortune and they'll swoop to steal it. Right? That's what he told himself, sitting there on the cold floor of dirt under this drug dealer's house flipping through thousands of dollars. And he couldn't hope to find his own thirty grand under here. It was probably somewhere else, probably upstairs under their own mattress.

Right?

He scooped out the thirty thousand, no more, no less. There. Now we're even. And then he crawled his way back through the door, seeing Joanna perched back on their wood porch smoking a cigarette, her leg jiggling in anxiety.

"Found it," he said. "Now hurry, hurry, hurry. Get inside, *now!*"

They went inside and sat down at the kitchen table. Joanna's hands shook, but she still smoked, inhaling and blowing streams through her nose. "God, Clary, what in the *hell* are you doin'?"

"I was right! They stole my thirty grand." He held up the money. She gawked at it, like she didn't believe it was real. She held up her fingers to touch it but then wilted away. It was as if she didn't think she was worthy of touching something so wonderful.

"Are you sure?"

"Sure I'm sure. It was layin' right there just like I had it bundled. They musta just thrown it down there this mornin' or last night when they took it."

"I cain't believe it . . . yer tellin' me that someone come into our house and grabbed that money from under our mattress. Right under our noses."

"Yep. And when they try it again I'll be ready this time. I'll be sittin' up waiting."

"Oh Gawd lawdy, Clar!"

She put her head in her heads, crumping up the cigarette and burning the base of her thumb. "Ow!"

"Easy. Easy. It'll pan out."

"Should we get outta here? We can stay with Daddy for a few days."

"God no. What'll he think of me gamblin'?"

He grinned at her.

"Ain't funny, scout."

"You believe me, though, don't you? This is gonna be a big thing for us. I mean, just think. We could buy a house. I mean a real house. On the edge of town where they're buildin' all that new stuff."

"Stuff like the casino. You know I hate them casinos."

"Not no more you shouldn't. That casino dug us out of the ditch. 'Member we talked about the ditch?"

"Yeah . . . "

"All right. Now I got to go to work but just tuck this under the mattress and I'll be back at eight this mornin'. Okay?"

She took out the cigarette and kneaded her forehead with her spare hand.

"I don't know about it," she said.

"Know about what?"

But she just shook her head some more, hiding her face, and he walked out after kissing the top of her head.

He had to drive a shipment to Amarillo that day and by the time he was docked at the warehouse and signing off with the manager in the steaming hot parking lot, watching a range of sparrows dip and flit above the aluminum, he said, "Damn."

"What's the matter?" said the manager, clicking the end of his pen.

"Oh. Well. Can't be helped right now. Nothin' to do with the meat, anyhow."

"Gotcha. Well, hope it clears up. You know sometimes things just work themselves out. It ain't my business, but sometimes things really do sort of work themselves out."

"Thanks."

The drive back to the Holdwater headquarters was a straight line although it felt like he had to grip the steering wheel with both hands just to avoid the ditch. It was like the wind and the whole world with it was trying to topple him. Part of him wished it would. He didn't know what lay back at Holdwater. It should have been called Hell and Highwater at this point.

He sped up to eighty, then down to fifty-five when he saw a whirl of cop lights a mile down. He stopped only once to pee and pick up a pack of Zyn, and when he got back home, the house was dark as it should have been, and Joanna had gone to her night shift at Walgreens. The drug house was dark, too.

"Oh, man."

He took the money from under the mattress when he got inside and put it on the bed. He rubbed his neck and chin, shaking his head, wanting to kick in the wall, kick himself for somehow losing his original stash.

"I can't do it. It's dirty money. And I can't steal money, even if it's dirty."

He scooped it up and crept outside on the porch. The crickets were out. The crescent moon was just a grin at the rim of the oak trees on the edge of the trailer park. There were only two streetlamps on the block. Neighborhood kids had busted one, so the glass lay in shards at its base. The other one stood by the drug house but was on its last stash of wattage. It gave just the barest orange glow on a patch of sidewalk, dim enough to let the first stars blink down on him in their beauty. He looked at the stars, then looked back at the money. Man, it just wasn't worth it.

He crawled across the grass dividing his property from theirs, slid into the enclosure, and army-crawled the rest of the way to the cardboard box, still cut open just the way he'd left it that morning. He arranged the money back into its original place and army-crawled his way back. He stuck his head out, so his eyes pointed upward, and the back of his head brushed the grass. Oh, shoot. The big man of the house was leaning out the window right above him and pointed a pistol at his face. The nuttiest thing was that from here, he had a great view of the stars. And another wheel of sparrows made a final dive into the world of men.

Joanna hugged herself on the edge of the bed the next morning, covered again in morning sunlight. She knit her brows at the empty bed. The cops had come and gone, asked her all the questions, and the druggies must've been halfway to Kansas City at that point, or the border, or God knows where. She dropped her face into her hands and fell to the floor, then from the floor she shoved up the mattress. The three bundles of ten thousand dollars, which had gotten stuck in the elastic lip of the sheets, hiding like old receipts, toppled to the floor.

She picked them up, knowing full well this was casino money, not dirty money. This was cleanest money she ever saw.

What on earth, though, was she supposed to do with it?

The Owl of Hackney Woods

L izzy just wanted to know where the pigs went every year.
In the morning before school, she ran over to the stalls when the hoarfrost still tinged the lawn and said hello to the little fellows as they oinked and rooted in their beds of hay. She named them, watched them grow, touched their blinking snouts, but after a few months, they were gone—poof! No explanation.

"Daddy, where did Rocky, Boingo, and Toodles go?"

It was November, nearing Thanksgiving, and Christmas after that, when Lizzy and her family could expect a sudden rise in the household population due to cousins, aunts, and an ancient grandfather who liked to sit in a recliner in the gray sunshine and smile at everything. She had no siblings, and her closest neighbors lived four miles west.

"Those some of your friends at school?"

"Nope, I'm talking about the pigs."

Daddy glanced at her Mama as he wiped his chin. Mama stirred gravy and told Lizzy to try a biscuit without slapping a load of strawberry jam on it. Then her father peered out the window into the lavender morning, patting the frock of his overalls and clicking his tongue.

"Pigs are world travelers," he said. "They're nomads. You know? They can't stand to stay in one place for very long or else they'll start feeling cramped up. So, we generally strike a deal and I send 'em off through Hackney Woods over yonder so they can choose their destination."

Lizzy's mother raised an eyebrow and Lizzy stopped chewing, and also looked out the kitchen window toward the tall band of trees her father had indicated. She was allowed to explore over there—it wasn't off limits. They weren't all that dense and thinned out into more gentle hills and farmers' plots in the great beyond.

"And in the summer they travel sometimes by way of the corn maze."

"Huh?"

"The corn maze hooks up with an international airport—it's just so hidden in the maze that only pigs, smart as they are, can find it."

"Why haven't we been able to see the planes?"

She stabbed a section off a continental biscuit and ate it, gravy dripping, hungry for answers. She could only hope Boingo brought an extra scarf. He tended to be pretty absentminded.

"Oh, well. That's simple. Owl."

"Huh?"

"The planes turn into owls when they take off."

"They fly in owls?"

"Yeah. Sometimes swallows and cow birds, but you know you got a flying pig taking off to Amsterdam when an owl takes flight over the cornfield."

Lizzy's mother poured her more juice and checked her watch. The school bus bustled a half mile down the gravel road, kicking up dust, bouncing over bumps and into potholes with no apparent concern for the passengers.

"So Rocky and the rest probably got the heck out of dodge, honey." His cell phone vibrated in its little hip holster. Lizzy tried to turn her attention back to what remained of her biscuit, scrambled egg, and ham chunk, but she could only think of Rocky, Boingo, and Toodles in route to Naples or Tokyo, somehow tucked in the tummy of a little barred owl that didn't mind the baggage. Where were the billboards? *Fly Owl Wing—Air Service with a Stomach That Can Take It!*

She thought about it at the back of the school bus where she gripped her books to keep them from falling and where Remmy the class clown rolled under seats collecting gum that he would use to glue teachers' mug to their desks.

She wondered if old Rocky would like the fjords of Norway. They talked about the fjords of Norway that day in Mrs. Hanson's World Geography class. Would the owl drop them off on a great big cliff and just leave them to reflect on the valleys and snowy peaks and the blue veins of river water? Toodles would want to bring a sweater since he was the pinkest of the troop. Boingo would need some looking after with his tendency to wander off to the corner of the stall for better real estate. But they'd be all right. They were smart pigs and always were since they were white piglets suckling at Mama Candy's teats six months earlier.

At recess, Lizzy swung alongside her best friend, the flame-haired Rosemary, and announced that the pigs were currently flying via owl to somewhere foreign and probably mountainous.

"Huh?"

"Yep. They're probably way out over the Atlantic Ocean right now." Another piece of World Geography applied in so little time!

"Owl?" huffed Rosemary. They weren't swinging in concert and so had to transmit comments when they swooshed past each other.

"That's what . . . my DAD . . . .said!"

"My dad has . . . pigs too! But, we . . . eat them!"

"Huh?"

"Eat!"

"You treat them? How do you treat them?"

But the siren blared before they could converse any longer and the teachers stormed the playground like FBI agentry and the hundred or so 2nd graders funneled under the awning by the storm shelter.

"We have chickens that we just keep for eggs, too!" whispered Rosemary as she filed in line behind Lizzy. It wasn't until they got to the helm of classroom that Lizzy made the disturbing semantic connection between "eat" and "treat" but she wasn't close enough to Rosemary to check if she heard right. *Now lemme get this straight. You treat the pigs and you eat the chickens, right? Okay great. Just making sure.*

In Phonics they learned about contractions and conjunctions. Mrs. Hanson wrote a list of contractions on the whiteboard, so her blonde mop of hair swayed, whilst Lizzy doodled owls in the margins of her homework, flying over a cathedral in Rome, pooping pigs in France and New Guinea.

Would they ever come back? That was sort of the unanswered question. Would their sojourn to the Holy Land bring them home renewed and cultivated?

What else did she learn that day? Basic division. The strait of Gibraltar. Erie Canal. Thomas Jefferson. Next year you're gonna have to deal with decimals, so stop your wailing, Paul Mason. A snack for the best score on the spelling test. That would be Edith Lev, thank you very much. End of the day story hour: blue whale meets school of krill, befriends them, then eats them and carries them to a krill society that the entombed would never have found if not for Mr. Whale. The moral of the story? Mrs. Hanson asked the children, some ogling, some dawdling their hands and pulling ears.

"Would the whale carry pigs?" Lizzy asked.

"Pigs?"

"My dad says our pigs travel by owl every year. Looks like the whales are in the same business but with the krill."

It was that Allen Powers who guffawed, and Rosemary who put her hand to her mouth, and Lizzy who one day would wonder how she could ever be so alone in her suspensions of belief.

"Your dad kills those pigs!" said Allen.

"Allen, hush!" Mrs. Hanson snapped. Lizzy froze and reddened and tried to come up with a rebuttal with the dozen pairs of eyes leering at her, but ended up bowing her head and staring at a run in her white stockings that hadn't been there that morning.

"Let's get back to the lesson. Now—the moral of the story is that sometimes when it seems like something bad has happened, really some-thing *good* has happened. So we can't always assume that the whale wants to eat the krill." Mrs. Hanson didn't seem too convinced of her own inter-pretation of the text, or maybe had to second guess the cohesion of her argument. She hesitated with the book in her lap, cross legged and thirty years old. She tossed her hair behind her shoulders and clapped her hands at the kids and—

The bell cut her off and the students fled for the open door as she pre-scribed homework from the floor: contractions, spelling test Friday, how many vowels are there, the difference between a monsoon and a typhoon, multiplication tables, Tenochtitlan. Land run reenactment Thursday at recess.

Lizzy, slower than the others and with a pulsing heart, dizzy head, went outside and waited by the flagpoles with her hands stuck disconso-lately in her coat pockets. It had grown colder over the course of the day. The cars that passed all gave visible puffs of exhaust out of their mufflers. The principal, a squat man who wore a cowboy hat everywhere he went, ducked into a Ram 3500 and almost vanished behind the steering wheel.

Rosemary joined her and they stood quietly under the American and Oklahoman flags until the bus started up and they got on and sat across the aisle from each other in the back. Remmy the class clown had decided to ingest the gum he found that morning and so was now greenly folded in half a couple seats up, groaning, asking for the end.

"Hey Rosemary."

"Huh?"

"Do you ever wonder where the people go?"

"Whatcha mean where do the people go?"

"I mean . . . when they die. I don't think *we'll* ever die, of course. But what do you think?"

"They go to heaven."

"Oh yeah, heaven. What do you think it's like up there?"

"They are lots of lollypop fields and unicorns."

"Do you think pigs go to heaven?"

"You're still worrying about your pigs?"

"I'm just curious is all. If people get to go to heaven, how come not pigs?"

"I don't know. There are unicorns in heaven, so I guess there could be pigs, too." Rosemary sighed and slouched in her seat so her collar collected her chin. "Tuesday!" she mourned. "It's only Tuesday."

It took thirty minutes to get to Lizzy's house from the school. Rosemary got off two stops before hers, and so she was left alone among the remnant watching the gray November skies collect themselves like a dark banner and suggest an early panhandle snow.

She got off at the gate and hobbled over the cattle guard with her books and knowledge of the day clutched to her chest, still with the great mystery unsolved. Where *do* they all go?

She decided to detour the house and set her books down by the rusty post by the cattle guard and tramp through the cow padded field to Hackney Woods—named that way because her father once had a brother whose middle name was Hackney, and who had never showed up during the annual Thanksgiving and Christmas population surges.

Good Lord, the cold. It nipped at her face and ate through her corduroy.

She reached the woods as the first flake of snow fell down, stepping over decaying ribs of fallen trees and the creek, which was almost dry. In no time she was in the middle of the copse with a view of the plains extolled through an opening established by the deer trail, but there was nothing living that she could see. Snow fell and landed on the brown bellies of dead leaves, melting on the bridge of her nose, her open neck.

She didn't know exactly what she was looking for or why she had come. There was no Boingo or Rocky or Toodles. There was no Uncle Hackney or whales bearing krill. There was only the unexpected barred owl, shuffling its head and blinking down a brief curve of beak with black-lantern eyes, saddled on its knob of oak, a piece of forest furniture, awaiting passengers.

Lizzy gasped a little when she first saw it, afraid it might start talking to her, or bear her off in its talons. But it only observed her for a second, then swiveled its head on its flexible axis, and closed its eyes as the snow thickened and sleet made a hushing sound against the leaves.

It was only when Lizzy left the trees and started running for home and warmth to tell her father that it was true, that he was right and everyone else was wrong, that the owl flew above the trees into the gentle oblivion of snow.

Notes to Petron

Note to Petron: Today we will be meeting inside Club Petron and talking about stories.

Note to Petron: Tell Joetron he is running low on independence dots on the great wall of independence. So just tell him to be a bit careful about that. He's a good sergeant and Petron would be sorry to lose him.

Intel report: Club Catron is has broken ground on the other side of the creek, which is an act of treason since Petron won that territory fair and square in the Two Fork dispute of the Bloody Spring of '07. Catron is building his club out of rebellion against Club Petron.

To do today: Gather army and march against Club Catron.

Casualty report: None so far. Catron still building his dumb fort so attack could not fairly be executed according to fair statutes of law.

Joe acting like a fole at the dinner table. He thinks we need to make Club Petron bigger than the box that Mom's China cabinet came in. Fole!! He does not know the ways of camouflage and secrecy.

Intel report: Our spies tell me that Club Catron is nearing completion. Intelligence sources report that he is laying planks across the big oak across the creek. He has the foolishness to think this will protect his sorry butt from attack. Joetron and I beg to differ.

Note to Petron: Get more snacks in here for battle strategy sessions. Get Joetron new clip for his airsoft gun. His keeps jamming.

Intel report: Our spies tell Petron that Catron is nearing completion of his dastardly fortress, and that we will be able to attack said establishment in two days' time. More direct communications came from Catron himself from across the dinner table tonight. Petron and Catron's mutual benefactor, unfortunately a peacemaker, had to scoot the respective chairs of Petron and Catron apart so shins were not overly bruised.

Note to Joetron: Another insubordinate comment from you, eh? When Petron built this kingdom as an eight-year-old man two years ago (feels like a lifetime, now) he had a vision, you know. A vision of what these woods could become if he could only be lord of its perimeters. Now you say you have homework, despite it being June. Now you say it's because you are studying for something they call the "a see tee." Then you say you have a date. What even *is* that? Now you say you have a life beyond Club Petron. Will the excuses never end?

The wall of independence won't look kindly on this.

Intel report: Intel tells Petron that Catron now broods in his lair across Two-Fork creek. That he had that the gall to invite Petron over for an opening luncheon. It's been further reported by Petron's best spies that an attack on Club Catron would mean a lot of casualties, and that going nuclear might be the only alternative. Catron has stored many pinecones and tennis balls in his lair and is building an armory of airsoft guns to boot.

Note to Petron: Petron will have to gather our entire intelligence committee to figure out how to defeat Catron. He thinks he can stay safe as an island. True, he does have the advantage of Two-Fork creek, that torrent of water that comes up as a primordial fount from the inner keeps of the earth. But he has underestimated the cunning of Petron's powers.

General report: Morale not good among the men. Joetron's absence and Catron's defiance has left a hole in Petron's stalwart heart. Several allegiant crows have watched Petron leave his abode and walk the bike trails he, Joetron, and Catron raked last summer for the purposes of inter-forest travel and commerce via bicycle. One crow followed Petron as far as the barbed wire fence by the tunnel beneath the conveyor belt. Petron wanted to see the swallows in their nests and to make echoes in the tunnel. This tunnel is very close to Club Catron. You might even say he ventured into enemy territory.

Note to Petron: Pull yourself together! July underway and we haven't even figured out a way to make turrets in the cedar trees! A leader must have aplomb. He must be alert at all times!! And he must cram in everything before stupid school starts in t-minus one month!!!

Intel report: Catron still spending a lot of time in his admittedly cool fort. He has been fishing with a bamboo pole off a branch and catching perch, little catfish, and even crawdads. Last night he roasted the feast in the backyard of the familial estate (which is of course divided by our terrible feud) and even offered Petron a piece of underbelly, which the fearless warrior and tyrant reluctantly took and ended up enjoying, although it could've been crispier and Catron could have possibly been trying to kill Petron via food poisoning.

Note to Petron: Tell Joetron that is two meetings away from an indefinite suspension, and that he doesn't want to know what happens when he tests the patience of his capacious overlord.

General report: Joetron was seen this afternoon standing by himself in front of the kitchen window looking out into the background with his head leaning against the wall. He reportedly didn't respond when Momtron said his name and Petron is fairly confident he saw a tear form at the lids of Joetron's eye.

Point of interest: Petron was walking down the bike trail on Monday around 8 p.m. wearing his coonskin cap and carrying his pistol for protection when a gray fox darted from behind an oak tree and stopped with its paw raised to look at the resident tyrant with its little green eyes. It sniffed and then bounded into the brush. Perhaps such critters can later be recruited for intelligence purposes.

Note to Petron: Don't wait to talk to Joetron about his teetering allegiance to the cause. Don't let fear hold you back from what you know you must do.

Intel report: Catron hosted two companions (thus, enemies of freedom and prosperity) at Club Catron and again, probably by the promptings of Momtron, invited General Petron to partake in their tomfoolery. Whether

Petron surveyed the festivities from a distance remains a case for the Pentagon to work out. Whether he wanted to join them as they swam in Two-Fork Creek really is anybody's guess.

General report: Joetron was absent from the premises the entire day studying at the college library and was only seen slipping into his bedroom last night at around 10 p.m., holding a fat book under his arm and appearing generally slumped, fatigued. If this continues, it will be uncertain whether he can be fit for the office he currently holds.

Note to Petron: Remember to send a due warning to Catron about the impending attack that will leave his traitorous roost in ashes. Timing on this announcement is sort of ambiguous.

Intel report: The crows of Petron report little activity at Club Catron over the last two days. Catron has, however, been seen throwing his fishing line into the lake off the dock and spending more time with his two (dastardly) compatriots. A naïve military mind might take his hiatus as a simple diversion of fun and games, but to the trained eye of General Petron, it means plotting. Conspiracy. A plan to reduce Club Petron and its wondrous corridors to rubble. Petron is under no delusion. He is still at war with Catron.

General report: Joetron took his a see tee test in a classroom at the local college, after which Momtron and Dadtron took him to get pizza and pop at Teddy's. Petron and Catron were begrudgingly forced to suspend their vow never to eat at the same table together and joined the party. Petron thinks that, with the test over and done, Joetron can now turn away from such nonsense and get back to priority number one: orchestrating the downfall of Club Catron.

Note to Petron: Remember to ask Dadtron if he will help rebuild the roof on Club Petron, given the recent rains and the moldy smell that's starting to form on the insides.

General report: A dark day for Club Petron. When Momtron and Dadtron took a look at the interior of the glorious castle, they were disturbed by the belts and blobs of black mold covering all but a section of its walls. Petron tried to contend that the mold would repel enemies, including jaguars, but by nightfall, Momtron and Dadtron, in horrific tyrannical fashion which history tells us always ends in civilizational destruction, disassembled Club Petron with axes and hammers and are now burning the "health code violation" in the firepit. Needless to say, this amounts to the worst humiliation and defeat in the history of the Petron franchise. The censorship! The Big Brother madness! The Communists! Surely Catron is gloating. Joetron stands by the fire with his arms crossed. Petron is mourning on his knees, hands outstretched to the heavens, decrying his fate. Momtron and Dadtron, though they are demigods in this realm, have dealt cruelly with their mortal underlings. Joetron's failure to weep and wail will be dealt with. For now, all is gloom, all is death, all is for naught!

Intel report: Despite Club Petron's newly nomadic condition, Petron's kingdom has not faltered. The homebase may have been destroyed by the parents, but Club Petron was always about more than brick and mortar. It's about dominion! Control! A kingdom far and clear! Petron reports that Catron spent a couple of hours raking leaves around his fort and is now working on developing a trail through the Eastern Woodlings. Fole! Does he think he can connect his estate to Mom and Dadtron's estate with a shortcut through such hostile territory? He will be met with missiles and projectiles and mobiles!

General report: Joetron's attention still diverted away from the cause. He was seen eating cereal early this morning with the early morning sun making red-gold blobs on the table, with the cat rubbing its head against his ankles. He tells Petron that he has a lot on his mind—stuff that's hard to explain to a military man of valor. Petron is in process of writing an amendment to the Constitution that allows a premiere sergeant an extended leave of absence for emergency-related reasons.

Intel report: Catron erected a camping tent and slept at Club Catron last night, perhaps fearing that Petron's midnight spies would raid his estate and reclaim the territory. He's a clever one. Of course, Catron has put out a statement contending that his night stay was due to his boyish desire to camp in the woods, but every villain has his lies!

General report: Last night Momtron and Dadtron visited Petron in his cavern and said they were "deeply sorry" about ripping down the heart and soul of his precious kingdom, but that the old crate he'd been using wasn't meant to be lived in—it was meant to hold a China cabinet. Dadtron offered funds to help rebuild Club Petron into something even more glorious and dominant than it was before—a real outpost of strategy, warring, and s'mores. Petron agreed after negotiating prices and is now colluding with advisors on real estate. There's the fertile land of rich soil and tall trees that lines Two Fork Creek, but to rebuild the holy temple so close to Club Catron would mean inviting direct conflict. There's the old spot where the crate used to sit, right next to the boulder, but on second thought it's too close to the mega-house. The new headquarters needs to be secluded. Hidden. Inviolable.

Breaking news: In a remarkable twist of events, General Catron has offered his own fortress as the cite to rebuild Club Petron. In a statement to the press earlier today, he said that he would be willing to "merge" the two kingdoms and even submit his estate under the name "Club Petron," with all the rights, privileges, and assets pertaining heretofore witherforth. General Petron had to ask his nemesis if he was crazy, but Catron said no—he'd simply had a change of heart and had hopes for peace and a stable democracy for both the East Woodling and the Lower Scrape. Petron, of course, noted to intelligence sources that should Catron ever backtrack on his promise and try to oust him, it would be a fight to the death to keep that coveted real estate. Rumors are swirling that Momton and Dadtron urged Catron into the deal, calling it "mutually beneficial" and "a wise diplomatic move in these dark and stormy days."

General report: As of Saturday, the Petron and Catron merger is underway and Dadtron has hauled in the lumber to start construction of what some critics are expecting to be the greatest treehouse ever built. Catron and Petron worked on the architectural integrity of the fortress for approximately twelve straight hours, taking only lemonade and sandwiches at lunch, and decided, once the floors and walls were up, to sleep the night up there under the branches and stars. Petron reports that it feels odd sleeping next to one who has so scarred his ambitions and dreams. But he also reports that he slept well that night. Better than he has in a long time.

Note to Petron: Tell Joetron thank you for bringing breakfast to Petron and Catron this morning, and thank you for putting up the roof on the new fortress. Now this shining beacon of glory and dominion will beam forth for centuries to come, 'til rot and mortality take it!

Petron has agreed to start over with Joetron's independence points and offer a treaty of forgiveness. Joetron has smiled and accepted.

Further note: Note that it's been what feels like decades since Petron, Catron, and Joetron sat down to munch on salami and pop tarts together in the East Woodling. Joetron even shared some of his coffee with Petron, who took this as a sign of initiation into manhood. Cheers! But always be watching for treachery, Petron. Let not this turn of events or this happy reconciliation blind you to the woes and foes of the forest. Let not the school that starts on Monday dissuade you from the righteous path . . . all glory to Club Petron and Friends!

Lines

"It's only peanut butter."

Right. Only peanut butter. It wasn't gasoline or tar or honey. Just innocent peanut butter designed for innocent pranks in the darkn.

Cameron brought the jar, pilfered from the kitchen, under Joseph's nose. It smelled sweet. Like an hour-old pumpkin pie. The room, meantime, was black like a tarpit, ready to catch fire and eat worlds. The lad couldn't see his hand, or the peanut butter jar, or Cameron's wicked grin. The exit sign had glowed red at the back of the room the night before, but had died, or the Pastor Todd had turned it off, so now they were just ten nine-year-old boys laying on their backs in an abyss of a tin room at Crater's Creek Baptist Camp.

"Don't talk so loud," said Joseph.

"We gotta follow through. This is *war.*" Joseph didn't know why whispering sounded louder than speaking when it's that sort of quiet, the "shooshing" of the dusty air conditioner unit notwithstanding. All he knew was that ever since Pastor Todd's opening speech over dinner three nights before, condemning reprehensibility among today's youth and warning that all and any pranks would be tried in "Court Todd" without partiality or mercy, he'd been struck with mortification while Cameron felt only more compelled to conspire.

Pastor Todd's belly rose and fell in the darkness. But they weren't after *him.* They were after Markie, the elite, the favorite, the athlete, the ascetic, the godly one. The one Pastor Todd loved.

"Right on his forehead," Cameron said. "He won't even feel it."

"I tell ya I can't *see* anything." The darkness. Pastor Todd's sermon at the tabernacle that night echoed in his head. How there is a physical darkness like the kind you encounter on a starless trail in Colorado, akimbo with the monsters of the mountain, and how such is the metaphor for the wandering soul. Hadn't Pastor Todd, that week's honorary speaker and the owner of a commentary for every single book in the Bible, preached how there is also the darkness that comes not from the lack of light but from blindness? And how *that* is the final horror?

Joseph and Cameron sat hunched on their knees seven feet away from Markie's bottom bunk. Usually, Joseph's eyes could adapt. Every time his father tucked him into bed back in the day, when he was much younger, he'd turn off the lamp and then sit in the old threadbare chair in the corner of the room, waiting for him to fall asleep. At first it would be all black. Not a light except the green dot from the smoke detector. But he watched, and waited, and the generosity of the moon and the kitchen lights and the remarkable perception of the human eye all combined in his bedroom and generated figures. Lines. The edge of the bed and the rumpled sheets. The square window and the heads of oak trees against the light pollution four miles away. The rocking horse and basketball goal sticking out of the closet door. The head of his father, somehow visible against the wall behind him, and the occasional glint of his glasses. Even when his father left the room after he'd fallen asleep, that shape remained like an imprint of quantum ink the whole night long.

Now, even after twenty minutes, Joseph saw nothing—no silhouette of the bunkbeds, no band of light bleeding under the door, not even his own shaking hand when he put in front of his face.

"Let's go back to bed," he whispered. He grabbed Cameron's arm and tugged. "We'll get in trouble and we can't even see him!"

"I've measured the distance, nimrod!" he hissed. "Three bunks down, bottom bed, head against the wall. We debriefed during our protocol session, soldier. No turning back!" The protocol session was so compelling to Joseph when they machinated in a purely lit dorm room. But now— what did Markie do to have deserved this desecration? He gave Cameron a profound noogie at the dinner table the night before. He'd demolished both Cameron and Joseph in ping pong. And he won the Bible Bee contest that very afternoon, racing his way to Revelation 17 with the agility of a medieval scholastic. He was among the brethren, sure, but he was due for a salvo in the war for dominance. According to Cameron. According, by concession, to the more pacificist minded Joseph. Now on the brink of battle, in a blackness so deep that no widened iris could absorb, he realized his allegiance to the cause was lukewarm at best. He started scooting backwards through strewn underpants and Axe cologne bottles and empty chip bags until bumping against what he presumed was his bunk.

"What're you doing?"

"Going back to bed. Go ahead if you want to."

Pastor Todd stirred, muttered "nyup nyup" to the ceiling, and refocused on snoring.

"Don't tell me your scared of the dark."

"I'm not afraid of the dark. I just don't want to do it. Isn't that reason enough?"

Joseph found the edge of his sheet and teased it with his finger— anything to grant him some familiarity. Cameron muttered, "Scaredy cat. Scaredy cat."

Joseph felt his way to his pillow. He sought he disordered edges of his blanket, realized that his sheet had rubbed off the mattress, and that he had to roll to the far side of the bed to blindly reconfigure the mess. He was making too much noise. Cameron hissed at him. Pastor Todd whispered a mid-dream report. Johnny Travis raised himself in bed, hesitated, and then laid back down with a sigh. Finally, Joseph settled beneath his blanket and lay looking into the void above him while his expatriate companion remained stranded on mission.

"You're *afraid*," Cameron whispered. Joseph didn't reply. He wished the edge of the bunkbed would form in his vision. He wished someone would stumble their way to the bathroom. He would, but he didn't want to get up again. He wanted to fall asleep and wake up with gray light coming under the door. He wanted to wake up and see his father sitting in the old threadbare chair.

"Aw nuts, forget it." Joseph heard scooting and little gasps of exertion. "Ain't no fun doing it by yourself." The bunk trembled as Cameron grappled its rungs and clambered aboard. He tossed, turned. He was quiet. Then he let out a long sigh and whispered. "You're afraid of the dark."

"No I'm not. I just want to go to sleep."

"All right, *fine*. Just go to sleep."

Joseph swallowed. Beads of sweat formed at the edge of his hair and slipped over his temples. "Cameron?"

"What?"

"I feel like I'm blind. Like Pastor Todd was saying tonight."

"What?"

"I said I think I might be *blind*."

"Are you kidding me?"

Joseph didn't reply. The air conditioner gurgled and went quiet.

"Why would you be blind?"

"Cause I did something wrong. I don't know. Maybe I did something wrong to upset God and now I'm blind."

"You're nuts, Jo." Cameron raised himself on an elbow. Joseph could feel him scanning the room, trying to locate the door that led outside, where light had the best chance of seeping through. Cameron hopped to the floor. He shuffled through the *Gehenna* and clicked his tongue. "Light's on, Jo. What do you say now?"

Joseph shot up, banged his head against the underbelly of the top bunk, and scrambled out of the covers. "I can't see!" he screamed. "Jesus, I can't see! Help me, help me!"

"Geez Jo, what are ya—" Joseph made a straight bee line to nowhere and pummeled through the metal door. He didn't think about the geography he was getting into. There was a steep hill right next to the camp cabin, pocked with small cedar trees, prairie grass, and ant hills, and it flattened out at the bottom into a parking lot where the church van was parked. He tread on thick crab grass for a second, filling his feet with stickers as he flailed, but couldn't regain his balance and so somersaulted down the hill. He got mashed up against a tree stump, diverted course, and then dribbled down the twenty remaining feet until he slumped by the gravel, back against the hill. Cameron shouted up above. Other voices joined the chorus. The manhunt was underway. Markie yodeled rumors of apocalypse—just read Revelation 17. Joseph winced, whimpered, felt the rocks when he put his skin torn hands on the ground. For now, he saw nothing.

But he cricked his neck upward and made out the stars. There were so many of them. No moon. Just stars and the tops of the trees making contiguous lines against the sky. The stars were like imprints of quantum ink, perhaps no longer there, erased by time, and yet shining in their non-existence. "Oh, ouch," he whispered. Then he said, "I can see. I can see, I can see!" He was in so much pain. "Oh gee whizzers, thank you, thank you, thank you." He didn't know it yet but he'd fractured a disc in his spine. "Thank you, thank you. Ha, I can see!" He'd catch hell about this from

Cameron for the remaining tenure of their friendship. "Thank you." The concussion was pretty severe.

He said that over and over until Pastor Todd found him through the beam of a flashlight, and until his father and mother pulled up later that night to take him to a hospital room back home. His father would sit in a chair across the room until he woke up.

Alexandra

I just want to tell you I'm sorry.

The minute the boat left for the sea, I threw a bottle into the water and watched it ebb to the shallow part of the bay only to surf there among the foam spots.

I'm sorry this voyage isn't going to end any time soon. Strange. This tipping and riddling of water with no land in sight. Only God's out here, teasing you with his requiems of silence.

Can you practice your dancing for me despite my absence? Captains need to know their daughters are safe and happy and dancing. Captains can't steer their ships if their children are drooping their heads and crying.

I'm sorry that you broke your ankle when running to go play with the other children. How acutely I remember your cries. Carrying you home through trees and brambles with thick raindrops beginning to fall. Your wailing when the bone was set. Your wishing that Mother was by your side, the delirium of your pain recasting her image before your eyes, setting itself next to me, tricking you with smiles and calm hands.

Out here, it's unclear what we're looking for. The pirates, former citizens gone bad, who have harmed and plundered our people, yes, but where are they? They are ghosts in the mist, shadows of Leviathan that taunt with the tips of their vessels and then vanish. Every sailor looks beyond the confines of his original mission and hopes to find more—to chance upon another world. We cannot even find what we're supposed to be looking for.

Rubies, emeralds, and gold bars, form the curvature of the earth and ridicule my view of what really matters. You!

Every man over the history of the world has sought the mystery beyond the horizon while forgetting to tread his own waters first. Till your soil and unearth the gems therein. Toss your ambitions to the winds! Turn your eyes to the trees in your midst. Stop trying to build wings to observe and control the forest.

If it were only that simple. This new world we're living in is simplicity subverted, dear one—an innocent hand pricked with brambles and left to bleed.

If we don't go, they strike at night. If we don't pursue them, they will pursue you. If we don't sink their ships, they'll sink ours.

You once asked what the hardest part of a voyage is. I say it's the loneliness. We are a month into the quest and the ship has become the sole organism and the sailors are its trembling parts, the limbs sharing in the same desolation. Pretty soon the creaks of her great sides indicate our longings for a harbor. The whining of a mast in the wind is the creaking of my heart. We are alone, alone together, until the ship signifies the whole world, spinning through the waters of the cosmos.

I'm sorry we have not found and killed the pirates yet. They set a strange course. They melt into islands and become waves. They slip past us in the dead of night. They are the shape shifters, darts carving wounds in an ocean designed for happier ventures.

Sometimes it pains me to the point of wakefulness that I've left you with your uncle, who is a good man, but have nevertheless left you for a quest whose object feels so evasive. Days pass without even a hint of these macabre men. The other day we had a bout of doldrums. The ship stayed in one place for a week. The men sunned themselves on the deck. We fixed everything that needed fixing. The top of the foremast. The splintered decks near the cabin. The arm of the Madonna reaching out to the great nothingness. I joined my midshipmen at the helm and explored the crystal horizon through eyeglasses. An albatross wheeled and glided a mile away. It burned white, cross-like, and then vanished.

But enough about me. Enough about this voyage. How are you, daughter?

Have you planted the strawberries on the plot of soil your uncle gave you? He was kind to let you have your own section of the land. What all will you do with the strawberries? Will you mash them to make a jam? Will you juggle them in your hands and then feed them to the deer that move slowly through the forest?

I'm sorry that such questions will never reach you. We are so far from any port city. I'm sorry that the only person I'm writing to at the moment is myself. Madness is aloneness turned in on itself. And it's worrying that the pirates have drawn us out only to skirt us and attack you while our best men are at sea, chasing ghosts and dreamless horizons.

I'm sorry, Alexandra. We're lost, lost, lost. Another bottle into the sea, with no message inside. No message will do except our ship itself announcing itself in your line of vision. I want to see you running on the edges of cliffs with no fear of falling. I want to catch you if you were to fall. That's all I ever wanted.

With a storm ahead, and monsters swimming beneath me, I fear this is a eulogy, self-written, gone to be unread as you plant your strawberries so far away. Just plant them deep, water them when it doesn't rain, and wait for me.

I'm So Tired

Why'd you join the chatroom>

?

I joined because I was bored

Really?

I think so.

You think so

Yeah.

. . .

Sorry, I had to pick my son up from practice. So . . . what do you do for work?

I'm a soccer coach.

Oh yeah?

Yeah . . . pretty exciting, huh?

Sounds like it.

It's not, haha.

Well, if you say so!

So what about you? Why'd you log on? Young Platypus.

I do love a good Platypus. Hence the avatar. But seriously, my name is Sharon, if you were wondering. Ummm . . . .well, i don't know. I'm a single mom and thought maybe it was time to put myself out there, or whatever.

Get back in the game, so to speak?

Spoken like a true soccer coach.

Can't help myself . . . .here's the real kicker . . . oops! Did it again . . . let me uhh . . . *field* more of your questions. Here's one: how old are your kids?

I have one son. His name's Shawn and he is four.

Oh, okay. Cool. So how old are you, then?

Ah, you asked sooner than I expected, haha.

Should I not have asked? I was just curious.

No, no, you probably should ask. I just turned twenty-three.

Oh, wow.

Yeah . . . now I'm scared.

Scared to what?

Ask you the same question.

Well. I am older than you, that's for sure.

Oh Jesus.

Ha. But nothing crazy. I'll be thirty-two in October.

Oh . . . okay. Yeah, not a terrible age gap.

Although I guess there's no real way to prove it just by texting via chatroom.

. . . .

Hello? You out of here?

I'm sorry

Don't be sorry!

Thanks for bearing with me. It's just . . .

It's just what? Nothing kills a dude more painfully than ellipses

I'm so tired.

Tired of what?

Of staring into a screen and feeling alone in the world.

Oh.

Sorry . . . didn't mean to be dark.

I don't think that's dark

I mean, I could be lying to you. How would you know whether or not I'm 23? There's no way you could know that.

Are you 23?

Yes.

Well, then, I know you're 23.

But it's the principle of it . . . ugh, idk what I'm saying.

No, no, keep going.

Just like . . . okay . . . i guess what I'm trying to say is that we could be anybody on here. You know? And, idk, it's just sort of weird having that . . . sort of power? That sort of control? Like, how can we actually trust each other on here?

That's pretty deep.

I don't mean to be so existential. I'm just desperate.

For what?

Connection. Aren't you?

Connection might be overrated.

So why are you on here?

. . .

Oh, right. I remember. You were bored.

Steps

We won't necessarily blame you if you go Penn State with your girlfriend, but . . . Cornell. It's where your mother went. It's where I went. Not to mention your grandfather. Don't you want to be part of the legacy?

Legacy. What a weird word. It was one of those words that the more you repeated it in your mind the odder it sounded. Legacy. Legacy. The legs are getting gassy. Lettuce-sheeves. Lettuce eat peas. Leggo of me.

Step number one for fighting those mantras when he woke up with the cold gray band of light seeping through the window was to sit up and try hard not to look at the cell phone on the sill. *Dalton, this is your conscience here, and yes I can be a real bully—just sit there in this funk and remember that you're alone in here, it's okay, Kip has not stayed a night in this dorm room since he met Michelle.* Once Michelle came by the dorm looking for Kip when Dalton was at his desk responding to a discussion board about the French Revolution. Was it just? Is justice a relative concept? She was smacking gum and wearing eight-inch-thick FILS shoes. She had Dua Lipa's number. Her father knew Joe Biden. She shut the door after blinking at him through artificial lashes. Kip? He was the son of a Goldman Sachs man. And he probably wasn't coming back to the dorms anytime soon.

He told himself that he was alone, that he could afford to steep in his morning depression, swaying forward with his arms crossed and fingers gripping his shoulders. He got runner-up in tennis a year before and now he had to crack his wrists and elbow and knee every morning. It was like he aged fifteen years in three months. Is that the "freshman fifteen" everyone was talking about?

Second step was to *not* to think about her, no matter how much the breakup still hurt and the memories of Miranda in arms on the couch back in Philly tempted. Twenty seconds of this silence and the mind became aware of itself, remembered the despair it wore twelve hours before. *So, get up. Step three.* He got up and trembled. A Keurig machine, thank God—the best gift his mother ever sent him. Caffeine dribbled into a Penn State mug and Dalton was now shirtless and waiting to have the boldness to check the time and decide if he wanted to go to Spanish class. *Mi corazon, Miranda* . . .

Maybe you should go see a counselor. There's nothing wrong with that. That's what they're there for.

Below the footbridge on the way to campus, there were mesh nets to keep people from jumping off into the rushing river below. The river was steepled by the gorge walls that, in winter, hosted icicles as long as windmill blades. Dalton remembered hearing about a kid who tried to leap the distance last year. He almost made it but ended up just getting tangled up in the mesh until the fire brigade came and fished him out with ladders and not a little existential encouragement.

"How's classes?" his father asked Dalton two days prior. He was sitting in the Green Dragon with a mug of Witch's Brew.

"Fine, fine!"

You're not going to tell him? Who are you going to tell?

Tell him what? That things aren't "fine"?

Bantering with a pugnacious conscience had Dalton teasing the edges of his beanie.

"Well, I'm glad it's going all right. Your uh . . . your mother and I are taking a trip to Santa Cruz next week with your sister . . . and uh . . ." Shuffle, gristle, car door unlocking. "Wish you could come along, too!"

Do not make the walk back from the Green Dragon fast. Amble on the walk and put those mittened hands in your pockets, recall that it's a privilege—yes, a privilege, to walk the corridors of this great Ivy League kingdom. It's an honor to peruse the books in White Library and clutch a cup of steaming coffee as you walk one of the many paths across the arts quad. Why look for Miranda in the crowd? It's your own fault for initiating a dumb high school relationship. Those only really work out if you start the kinship back in the second grade and make unspoken vows at recess, and by the time you're at Penn State together, you're as good as married.

Dalton didn't tell his own dad that he wished he'd followed her instead of him. He was chasing a paternal legacy around campus like a mirage. *Enter this classroom and be considered enough.* He hung up on Dad at the Dragon's door. Wished them well on the cruise. Tell Sammie I said hey. I miss playing pickleball with her. I miss everything! And that's a real nostalgic and pathetic thing to miss. "Everything."

You can hang up on your parents but not on your conscience. *Remember, there's always something more productive and interesting you could be doing. Why not run instead of walk? Why not tea instead of coffee? Why not study instead of shower? Why not apply to this internship instead of study? YouTube scroll on the pot? Glancing at all these girls? Seeing which ones have shoulder length brown hair and blue eyes. You're eighteen. You have NO idea what it means to love another person. You can't even love yourself. Love yourself? Narcissist much?*

He was at maybe step five or six. Putting one step in front of the other across North Campus. That morning saw a cold rain sweeping through and drenching the slow-moving train of students, hooded in parkas, mostly walking alone except for the one or two pairs of siblings and couples. It was the quiet of the morning and the way the tires grated on the pavement at the crosswalks that put the daily dread in the pit of his stomach, verifying this as a place where no one knew him and where no one wanted to know him. In no universe, though, could he blame them, because when push came to shove, he wasn't sure he wanted to know them either. Some of the faculty remembered his father. A few more in the English department remembered his mother. It was hardly social capital to thrive off of.

They say it takes six or seven months to feel acclimated to a new place. It was the first week of November, felt both like a week and a lifetime, and Dalton was on speaking terms with George, who scooped his noodles in the cafeteria.

A girl he had seen only once punting volleyballs to herself off the wall in the gym somehow found him on Snapchat and sent him the top hemisphere of her head every night with captions like: *Avoiding responsibilities at all costs.* Or often there were zero captions—just her wide eyes and admittedly cute bangs hovering over the screen.

So, no, even though he hadn't reached the six-month threshold yet, he couldn't really imagine things getting any better. There were no seeds planted, no connections made that might yield a harvest. *It'll be an adjustment, college. But you'll be okay. You'll make the best friends of your life at Cornell. Just give it time, son.*

But now, as he stepped into Zeus, a student center abuzz with technological fizz, Dalton knew that "adjustment" was not the same thing as displacement, of forced immigration, trying to live in a place so unfamiliar that the only way to make sense of it is to choose certain geographical plots on campus and stick to them, like oases in a desert. The Green Dragon. Class, of course. Never College Town. The arts quad and the student center and on special occasion, the A.D. White Library, where he would rarely read but sometimes sat in the soft chair facing the window just to encounter the quiet and the light.

Step . . . which step are we on? It feels like one million, and only thirty minutes into the day! Only a half hour into consciousness! He wanted to get coffee. *Sorry Mom but the Keurig just doesn't always do it for us.*

The chatter and the laptops punched him with its chorus of nervous energy. All the voices bouncing off each other, all the open laptops, the AirPods, the girls with one foot over the other as they waited in line scrolling, the tall guys with scruff and hoodies and perfect haircuts. *You all look better than ever. The most beautiful generation to exist. Wow. Are you up to par, buddy? Did ya forget to check yourself out in the mirror this morning?*

Dalton, it should be noted, wasn't non-athletic, was far from hideous, and even attracted some glances from the finest females in the room when he entered. He played squash ball below the law school—played alone, whacking and whopping the rubber sphere against the scuffed wall. Played until he yelled at the ball and the way it kept bouncing back like a comet all the astronomers think might destroy the world.

He saw the billboard and the ad for the squirrel watchers' club. Next to it was a hand drawn invitation to join the squirrel watchers' *watchers'* club, and about twenty people had scrawled their names and emails on the margins to join. "We watch the squirrel watchers watch the squirrels, and watch you as you watch the squirrel watcher watchers!"

Next step. Try to look into the barista's eyes when she takes your order. Don't look at the register or the menu above her head. Know what you want in advance and ask her for the coffee, don't order her for the coffee. She probably doesn't care but she might.

So sentimental! Doesn't fly in the real world. Just get the stupid coffee and go, dude. Don't have to make a Sermon on the Mount of every detail of your day. Hustle and hurry, kids are stamping their phone-bonded thumbs behind you! There's only so long a TikTok scroll can satiate one's patience. Only so long . . .

"Thanks," he said when she handed him the paper cup, which he had to fill himself over by the coffee canisters by the door.

"You're welcome!" She was cheerful. She flipped his card, swiped, and tapped it like a cartridge of mentos tablets on the counter, waiting for the funds to compute. *Supposing we incorporate a step in which we . . . I don't know . . . ask such a one for her name?*

You're kidding. Off limits. Guys who ask girls those kind of nutty questions (like, "hey, what's your name?") are considered utter creeps. No redemption for those who intrude on the sacred, on the untouchable.

He was late for Spanish class by waiting those ten minutes in line and ambled on the trail in the general direction of the Olin Library, that mid-campus monstrosity of pale walls and darkly glinting windows. The wind had softened but the morning drizzle still fell, straight and hazy, with the day's first batch of students now tucked into classrooms, taking off coats, sitting down, checking phones.

Well, what now? Another first hour missed. You have three hours until your 11:15. Congrats. Yet again we've trespassed into unoccupied territory! All for a stupid cup of coffee. Cup number three. When do you get off? We didn't pay your way to Cornell so you could skip classes for a caffeine boost. Following the legacy is supposed to mean *something. You don't get to . . . whoa, hold up, where are you going?*

A walk past Olin will put a man in spitting distance of the red-bricked Sage Chapel, where today, the voices of singing children floated out of the open doors. Dalton paused in the rain, adjusting a strap of his backpack with his free hand. He sipped the coffee. He had a burnt tongue and a curious wet ear. He was late to Spanish. He wasn't going to the library to study. Intro to Latin could wait until the afternoon—the loneliness of studying the dead language in the foyer of Olin Library could wait forever. No, now it was time for something different. A step out of the traditional trajectory. Maybe he'd risk a little diversion into unsanctioned territory—the holiest place on a decidedly secular campus, where Dalton, irreligious but not immune from beauty, veered left through the grass and slipped inside the doors of the chapel.

He blinked, trying to get his eyes to adjust. He had been here before when he came to campus with his parents for homecoming weekends and class reunions. They always wanted to stop by Sage. His parents were married there twenty-four years ago. But now there was the choir of boys and girls no older than twelve in the loft off to the side with the organist going away at "The First Noel." *A choir concert this coming Christmas . . .* read the A-frame sign next to him. *All are welcome.*

Well this is cute. What? You're gonna sit down and listen? Oh, watch out for that little stand there with the handout flyers on it. What does it say? Cornell Center for Meaning Making? Huh. Maybe you need to check them out. Could probably use some meaning in your life, right?

Dalton sat down behind the midway partition in the sanctuary and rested his forearms on the top of the pew in front of him. He was the only non-musical substance in the room. The organist, though, was too caught up in Noel-ing that he didn't notice him, jerking his head up and down so his gray mane flew, tawny fingers dancing along the happy keys. A few of the children tilted their devoted eyes in his direction. Surely they had their share of amblers walk through, hands in pockets, observing the painted intricacies on the ceiling and the flower-shaped mosaic at the back of the sanctuary. The secular and religious mingling in the stained-glass figures of the apostles and Enlightenment philosophers. Philosophy crowned king behind the altar. Christ the other king flying in above, heralding what? Human knowledge? Meaning-making? But it must have been rare for a college student to plop himself down on a back bench and park his arms in front of him.

None but the truly desperate are willing to postpone their distractions to actually *look* at *listen* to something. That's what Dalton realized. *Wow, how long as it been . . . hmm, trying to wrap my head around this. How long has it been since I've . . .*

Trying to figure it out? How long's it been since you've stopped and listened to a choir singing Christmas carols? Well, lemme perform some advanced mathematics for ya bud. Beep beep boop boop . . . CALCULATING, CALCULATING . . . according to these calculations it's been eighteen years, three months, and fourteen days . . .

The First Noel ended, pages were turned, and a young, pale man in a suit, who Dalton hadn't noticed during the singing, readjusted his position at the helm of the choir and reminded the tenors to keep steady during "Silent Night." This was a slow rendition of the tune, so a consistent pitch over time is crucial. Step one: breathe. Step two: remember to breath throughout the song. Step three: Listen to the group, and not yourself. Listening to yourself makes you self-conscious.

*Ding dong! Sing song! Lebron James . . . Jim Halpert! Jimothy, James . . .
ah, that doesn't sound right. Is it all right if I call you Jim? Peter Jackson's in-
terpretation of King Kong is pretty insanely good CGI-wise, even after almost
twenty years. That New York skyline? So well done!!!*

Dalton sipped his coffee and tried to imagine it turning into a salve
and do away with Dr. Jekyll upstairs.

*What's it take for peace of mind? Would I have it at Penn State? Would
I have it with Miranda? Would I have it if I chucked my stupid phone in
Cayuga Lake?*

"Silent night, holy night,
All is calm, all is quiet . . . "

*Here's a hypothetical: when was the last time you experienced silence?
Real, unadulterated silence? Can you think of a moment?*

Dalton's hands trembled. He felt lightheaded and his stomach roiled
from the coffee and lack of breakfast. He bent over, still wearing the backpack. The words coming at him were beautiful, but not meant for him.
What was meant for him?

They finished singing "Silent Night." The conductor dropped his hands
to his sides and the organist sat still in his holy office, white hair calmed,
gripping the edge of the piano seat. The conductor put his fist beneath his
chin and worked his jaw as if in deep thought, while the children all looked
at him, music books open.

They were a good choir but not spectacular. They weren't the Norwich
Choir or from the Mormon Tabernacle. Dalton knew that. But the way the
conductor had paused in the aftermath of the choir's performance, an amber beam of light shining on his bald-spotted head made it seem like those
kids were angels, the cream of the crop, and the best thing to ever happen
to God's green earth.

"All right, kids," he said, clapping his hands. "Wonderful. That'll be it
for today. Tomorrow at the same time!"

The children stuffed their music books into their bags, chattering
while Dalton walked out the doors opposite the ones he'd entered and was
greeted by an unexpected sunshine.

Campus was quiet. He listened to his own brain, breathed, and looked
at the empty little academic city in front of him. *Nothing? How can that be?
No comment, o interminable conscience?*

Which step are we on? Seems like a hundred. The center for meaning
making stood a hundred yards away. Maybe he'd drop by. The counselling

center was even closer. It would be a good idea to get some sessions in. He wasn't at Penn State, and he wasn't with Miranda, and he wasn't back home. There was a lot to walk through. But, what now?

Let me start over. Step one: go to Spanish class, even though I'm late to it.

Endings

On Thanksgiving afternoon, time took a break in the treehouse in the birch trees out back.

American's favorite dinner was over at two and the dishes were already clean by three, with Uncle Darren smoking his annual pipe in the sunroom at the back of the house with Emily's Dad and the crop of cousins, seven total, ambling out to the back pasture with a new football.

Emily took off her apron and hung it on the peg by the refrigerator and clapped her hands free of labor.

The last Thanksgiving meal in this house was already over and she had to work later in the evening at the hospital in town. And the next day. Not to mention the Christmas shift in four weeks. She didn't hate her job, but she didn't know how to opportune the holidays when they came around. And three p.m. hit her hard with the doldrums and that feeling that the day was already over and that she might as well drive back to reality.

"Thanks for the help, sweetie," said Aunt Lisa. "I guess it'll look a little different next year. Think you'll fly down to Prescott to see us?"

She said that sure, she'd love to if she could, but there was no predicting her life a year out anymore.

Lisa and Darren were off to their sunny southwest in January after hanging their aprons on a life of well-ordered work and child-rearing and would sell the century-old ranch to a young couple from Enid who wanted to try their hand at the trade. But for now, the house was the same. That old Osage blanket lay draped on the sofa in the living room, tattered edges touching the shag carpet, flattened by years of foot traffic. The bust of the eight-point buck still stared stoically out the window across the plain, alongside the rainbow trout in glorious mid flop above the mantle. Uncle Darren's fly-fishing manuals lay on the coffee table. The old woodstove crackled and popped, and Emily recalled herself belly down in front of its warmth just a few years prior, listening and giggling and delighting in her little orb of eternity.

"I might go for a walk," Emily said. "It's been a while since I've seen the treehouse out back." Her mother walked into the kitchen, talking about how Cameron, Emily's cousin who followed her, ought to show young Jeffrey how to throw a football. Jeffrey was crazy about his Uncle Cameron. He wanted to be *just like* Cameron when he grew up, if he could manage it. "It's always 'Cameron this, Cameron that!'" she said. Cameron watched Emily put on her coat by the front door as he held a fist up to his mouth to obstruct a yawn.

"I gotta food coma, Aunt Helen. I think I'm 'bout to vomit."

"Well go walking with Emily then. Y'all don't get to spend time together much anymore." Emily peered upward as she pulled on her boots and motioned towards the door with her head. "Was going to see the old treehouse," she said.

Cameron, who had spoken little at the banquet and was earlier in the morning seen shooting aimless baskets in the gravel driveway, cracked his knuckles and gave her a wistful smile that told her he'd be going along, too. The aunts had returned to the sunroom and Emily straightened up and slapped her hands on her sides.

"The treehouse, huh? Feeling nostalgic?"

"Eh. Might be our last chance. Or MY last chance anyway."

Cameron lost the smile and nodded. He blinked his tired blue eyes and went into his old bedroom to retrieve a coat, and soon they were traipsing through the field towards the young band of birches a couple hundred yards away from the house.

"Last one, Em," he said.

"Yeah. How're you feeling?"

"I mean, I don't know, you know? Grew up here. Haven't lived here in seven years, but yeah, it was always . . . here, you know?"

"Yeah. No, I get that."

"You have work tonight?"

"Ugh, yes. Couldn't get out of it."

He shook his head.

"What?"

"I don't get why that kid likes me so much."

"Yeah, he was all over you before dinner."

"I'm not the cool uncle."

"I guess you are to him."

He shrugged. "I feel like every kid in the world hates me. That's what teaching feels like."

At 27 years old, they were still fresh enough out of college to recall the thrill of having a newfound sense of vocation but far enough down the road of their lives to have encountered the ordinariness and downfalls of the daily grind. Emily was a nurse, certified midwife, and would soon become a surgical assistant. Cameron taught fourth grade at the elementary school both he and Emily had grown up in. He didn't have that in his playing cards originally, believe it or not.

"At least you have those long winter and summer breaks!" said Emily, only a little tinged with envy.

"These kids are wild. It's more discipline than teaching. And I can't be their parent. I want to shoulder all that weight they're carrying from their broken home lives but how are you supposed to do that when there's like three hundred of them?"

They hopped over the creek that trickled from the cow pond and hiked up the little grassy rise, which the wind now whipped handily in the midafternoon temperature drop, and beyond, there they were: just a few yards shy of the birch trees and its post oak stationed like a beachhead in the middle. Emily tried to calculate the last time she was there. Could it have been ten years? When they were both seniors in high school? Before then the Thanksgiving trek was something of a tradition. And who had built that old treehouse, its triangular base and tee-pee shaped construction of two-by-fours, remained a mystery. She checked her phone. 3:06. Cameron let loose and ran up to the trunk of the oak tree once it weaved into view. He planted his foot on one of the nubs at the base and hoisted himself up so he was hugging the tree as if it was a long lost friend. "Oh I missed you! Mmmwua!" He slung his arm above the next rung. Two more moves and he crawled into the dank cavity of the tree house. "How is it up there?"

"A little dingy, not gonna lie." He rotated inside the treehouse and stuck his head out, hair mixed with twigs. Emily took off her parka and dropped her phone on it and started to follow suit. The tree bark was cold, dry, sweet smelling on her hands. She thought, as she hoisted herself up on that final branch, that she wasn't sure why they decided to do this today.

Then it returned to her. The last Thanksgiving at the ranch. There wouldn't be a next year. There would barely even be a next *month*. Her mind and her body were used to taking the ranch for granted. Her family lived in town but this had always been the little focal point of escape and enchantment telling her that a broad world of straight prairie and countryside still stretched without apology. And now this was it. She had to enjoy it before the aunt and uncle zoomed off to Arizona for the aridity of retirement. *I mean, it's not like Cam and I won't see each other anymore. We live two miles apart for Pete's sake. And he's probably going to propose to . . . oh nuts. What's his girlfriend's name again?*

She squeezed herself in next to him. At first it was all dark in the musk. But gray light came in through the cracks of the boards and the four-foot-long opening.

They caught their breath, hunched with hands interlocked at the knees. Cameron had his head bowed. Even as teenagers, they hadn't felt this sequestered. At ten years old, this must have felt like a mansion.

Cameron laid down so the upper half of his body was sticking out of the treehouse and he was looking at the branches above him. Emily asked him when he planned to propose, but he just smiled and laughed, and said "ohhh man" and then plopped his hands on his vested stomach. "Laura's a great girl," he said. "She's awesome."

"Do you're gonna propose?"

"Just looking for the right time, I guess."

"Have you got a ring picked out?"

"Sure. Settin' on my dresser back home."

"Really? Can I see?"

"I don't have my phone on me."

"All right. Well, you better hurry up or she's gonna fly the coop."

"Seems to be a trend these days. People flying the coop." He raised himself on an elbow to look at the woods. Emily noticed, for the first time, how still the trees were. They were frozen in their skeletal white branches, like cold flames. There was a bed of mostly untilled green and yellow leaves on the forest floor, welted with the occasional fallen log. She craned her head to get a look at the overcast skies, which also seemed to have paused in their cross-country parade across the prairie.

"What time is it?"

Cameron checked his watch. "3:06."

"Huh."

She leaned back into the dimness and picked at one of the unkempt boards above her, trying not to wonder whether roaches hibernated within. Once a man came into the hospital with a very green arm. It was a miracle they didn't have to amputate. And she'd have to shadow for the surgery if it came to that, sitting with a clipboard in the corner of the room while the anesthesia and tourniquet were applied, the shining instruments evoked. She didn't know why she thought of that.

"So teaching is hard?"

"Teaching is easy!" Cameron sighed, sitting up. "When I get to actually do it, it's a dream. Problem is they won't let me do it. I swear. These kids. There are projectiles, Emily. Projectiles of unspeakably gooey objects on the daily. Some of the kids are shy and quiet. But about a quarter of 'em, like, I don't know. It's like they can't take no for an answer. No is the end of the world."

"Could you move up to junior high?" Cameron laughed and brought his hood up over his head.

"Junior high is worse apparently."

"Gosh. Well, I'm sorry."

He shook his head. "I hate talking about it because at the end I feel so ungrateful. These kids are rough and wild but I can't help thinking that it's not their fault." He shook his head again and wiped his nose. "But what are you supposed to do?"

He flopped on his stomach and laid his head down. "I don't want to go back."

"Are you sad about your parents moving to Arizona?"

He said that originally he was indifferent about it. They'd lived here for decades but always told him and Cassie, his sister, that they wanted a change of scenery for their "rich in years" season. "Plus," added Cam, "they can't keep up the ranch anymore. Not at their age. They asked me to do it, but..."

"You felt called to be a teacher."

"Something like that." He laughed. He asked what her respective woes amounted to, and that he needed to have her over to hang out with him and Laura more often. They lived so close. But, living close can mean that you feel like you never need to see each other, or that it will happen organically. And then you go to work, you come back, you go to work, you come back, and then suddenly you're up in the treehouse together realizing you're long-lost cousins and not the old confidantes and companions you used to be.

"The job's fine. It's just tiring," Emily said. "I've been working a lot of the night shifts and traveling to the city sometimes to work shifts up there. It's just a lot."

"Yeah. You told me last time we talked that it was crazy busy. I can't imagine."

"I knew what it would be like. All throughout nursing school I knew and was excited about it. And I love it. I do. It's just . . ."

"A lot."

"Yup. A lot. I don't feel like I really have a life."

"Well. Maybe you should cut back."

"I don't know how to do that." She settled her chin on her knees and for some reason had this hankering for a cigarette. Had she ever smoked one before? Maybe once. On a lunch break or two.

"Must be nice to have the break," she repeated.

"Oh sure. But it'll fly by. It'll fly."

Cameron groaned and rolled on his side. There was no way he could have taught young Jeffrey how to throw a football that day.

Emily's back burned from crouching, so she plopped on her stomach too and peered over the edge of the planks down at the ground. "Wasn't it windy when we came out here?" she said.

"Mm, yeah I think so." She remembered once when she woke up at home as a girl one Saturday morning and she knew upon the dime that she was alone in the house. The chimes gently hummed outside on the front porch. Early morning shadows from the trees lashed the windowsill, like rippling water. And it was quiet. Quiet like it was now. An unendurable kind of loneliness hung in the air, making the world mute and tied up. She raised herself on an elbow and asked Cameron what the time was.

"When is your shift?"

"Six."

He checked his wristwatch. "Huh. Weird . . ."

"What's the matter?"

"Still 3:06. Watch must've stopped."

"Seriously?"

"That's what it says, champ." She craned her neck to have a look for herself, but her eye landed instead on a doe frozen in mid-step about thirty feet away from the tree. Its front leg was raised close to its downy white chest, head lowered as it sniffed the human invaders with its marble black eyes pointed at the ground. It didn't move. It didn't breathe.

"What the hell." Cameron got on his knees and shouted, "Hey!" The deer stayed like it was, twitching not a hair in fright. "Hey!!"

"Is it . . . a fake?"

"A fake deer? I don't think so, Em."

"Well. Is it dead then?"

"It's standing up."

"I know it's standing up."

"This is weird."

Cameron found a chunk of bark and hurtled it so it landed inches from the deer's hoof.

"Uncle Darren must've put something in the stuffing."

"Dad wouldn›t do that. If he'd do anything it would have to do with moonshine. Maybe bad hemp. But no, he's soundly opposed to legalized marijuana."

They stood up on the narrow platform, using the tree trunk for support, and scanned the birches for any other signs of natural taxidermy. Emily found a cardinal stuck in a jump from a branch, its wings spread. "Oh wow," said Cameron, pointing. "See the creek?"

The creek was a black line in the leaves, un-flowing. They paused, not breathing. "I can't hear anything."

"Nope. Nothing for me either."

And the time? 3:06 p.m. Emily had a two hours and fifty-four minutes before she was due at St. Francis's Hospital taking care of patients on the brink, of men with green arms and children with bursting appendixes. Cameron had three days and ten or so hours before he was due at the helm of a classroom teeming with thrown boogers, hurt feelings, and a phone call from his girlfriend that this wasn't working, that it would never work, and she didn't know what she was even thinking trying to make it work.

Two years ago, a guy Emily was dating, Mark the barista who had two loves, Christopher Nolan and Coldplay, drove her to the top of a hill outside town by the bowling alley where there was a good view of the sunset. He stopped the car and let it stay in silence for a few seconds, and then after they'd kissed a couple times, he said he wished such moments might last forever. He said there had been a few times in his life when he was confronted with overwhelming beauty, like the *Interstellar* soundtrack or "A Sky Full of Stars" in concert in Dallas, that time is suspended, loses its damnable way of speeding up the moments you want the most to endure. "We want eternity in the moment," he murmured. He was a hopeless romantic.

He never learned who Emily really was, but maybe she didn't want to tell him, or didn't know how. She didn't remember him asking her many questions at all on that hill. But maybe he was right.

"Emily. I'm kind of freaking out."

"Me too. Uh, okay. Well, maybe let's get back down the tree and head back to the house?"

"I'm for that."

He climbed down first and helped her to the ground, and the minute her foot touched the bed of leaves, the deer snorted and started, the cardinal flitted to higher terrain, the wind rushed through the woods, and the creek resumed its quiet gurgle. They both ducked and covered their heads as if a plane was flying overhead, and by the time they'd straightened up, the deer was gone, and the day had made it all the way to 3:07.

They looked at each other, almost suspiciously, like they could have each been druggists or magicians who had lured the other out here for some experiment. Emily hoisted herself back up into the treehouse and made room for Cameron as he came up next to her, and again the forest stilled, the creek quit, and they were pretty much all the way convinced that time itself had stopped.

"Okay. God? Hello? Are you out here?"

"What is *happening* right now?"

They went up and down the tree again three more rounds just to make sure they weren't crazy, but they stopped at 3:20 p.m. up in the tree house, out of breath and sure of the miracle.

"Magic woods?" Cameron said.

"Or we're dreaming. Can we be dreaming?"

"I'd have woken up already if was a dream." He clapped the back of his hand against the tree trunk and winced. "Real."

Cameron climbed all the way to the top of the tree and stuck his head above the woods. "I can see the house!" he shouted. "I can see the smoke stuck in place, the kids playing football, not moving." He hesitated. "Can't see Jeffrey, don't think."

Emily saw the deer farther down the creek. Its nose was an inch above the water since it had stooped to get a drink, a marble faun. Cameron came back down. "What do you know about that?" he whispered. "Whole world's stopped."

They knew they weren't seeing things and they knew they weren't dreaming. But she started laughing to herself. She bowed her head back and laughed so Cameron laughed too. "This would happen to us. Of all people."

"This is where we used to hang out. Remember? Every summer."

"You know how we can know if this is really for real?" Cameron said. "We go get someone else. My dad. Maybe your mom."

"Are you kidding?"

"They'll think it's stupid. But that way we'll really know. We'll know that we aren't just accidentally high or something."

"We're not high. We don't get high. This is real."

"What if we got everyone else up here, though? We could drag it out. You know I wasn't being honest earlier. I don't want them to move to Arizona. Are you kidding me? This place is part of who I am. You can't just rip that away from someone. Let's all come here, together, and we can spend who knows how long out here."

"Cameron, hold on."

He started to climb down again when Emily spotted, totally by chance, a bow-shaped figure through the haze of branches. The figure itself wasn't a branch although it might have been mistaken for some large bird, like an owl or maybe even a vulture. When she peered closer, however, she saw that it was a boy falling from the high branch of a birch tree. She gripped Cameron's hand and whispered, "It's Jeffrey."

"What?"

Cameron clambered back up to elevation and matched his line of vision with hers.

"Jesus!" he hissed. The boy, who had abandoned his football pastimes with the other nieces and nephews and struck out on his own to imitate the big kids, was probably about twenty feet from the ground. His body was leaning backward, head well below the elevation of his feet. He could easily break his neck or his back if he fell all the way down.

"I didn't see him come up. When did he come up?"

"I don't know. I guess when we were experimenting."

"If we go down again, he falls and breaks everything."

"If we stay up here . . ."

"Good Lord."

"That stupid kid. Stupid stupid kid! I should've stayed to help him throw the football. Not as if I can even throw it all that great. Your mom thinks I can."

"What can we do?"

Cameron ran his hand through his hair and worked his jaw.

"Well, all we've got is time, I guess."

He blew warmth into his hands and offered Emily his gloves, which she took with gratitude.

"Hold up," she said. "What if just one of us goes down? And one stays up here? Do you think that you could catch him?"

He furrowed his brow and looked back at the falling child. "I'm still trying to wrap my head around the fact that this is happening, but that makes just as good of sense as anything right now. All right. Let's try it."

Cameron started down again, gripping the branch and leaning back with his feet on the trunk, but he hesitated, swaying in space with his chin nestled against his shoulder.

"Emily," he whispered.

"What's wrong?"

"I'm not getting engaged."

"What?"

"I'm not getting married to Laura." He looked up at her, red-eyed. "And I want to quit my job. I want to quit everything. I can't lose this place. Haven't you thought about it? We could take turns. One stays here while the other goes and travels, or something. We could have the whole place to ourselves."

"Cameron, c'mon . . . " Although, at the mention of this, she wondered where she would go. Maybe New York City? There she could walk through seas of unmoving people. She could sit in on a talk show or run around Central Park and sit for a long time on one of its cold sunny knolls. Then she could drive all the way to California and sit by the beach near San Fransisco watching the waves tumble on the black sand and see the children playing in the shallows. But there would be no crashing of the waves and there would be no movement of the children. There would only be her own body, frail in the silence. She'd be needling through a tomb.

Even now, she could roam back to the ranch house and lay next to the crackling fire of the woodstove, but it wouldn't be crackling, and the kids in the backyard would be little statues with their joyous football swaddled in the air. One more eternal day at the ranch house would turn into the lonely sound of her own breathing.

Emily's gut lurched when Cameron started to cry, and unabashedly at that, with the figure of his nephew still in mid-plummet behind him, frozen in time and blessed with the chance of being caught. "It's all inevitable!" he said.

"What's inevitable?"

"I screw everything up!"

"Oh, stop that! Idiot boy."

"Yes! Idiot boy. Idiot boy! What the hell happened to me, Em? God!"

"Just come back up here a second. We'll figure it out."

"I'm nothing," he wheezed. "Hurt her so bad. Can't do my job. Wouldn't even throw a football with my nephew. Nothing. Nothing in high school, nothing in college, nothing now. Jesus, Em. Help me, help me."

"You're scaring me. Come back up. Come back up and talk to me. We always used to talk here, buddy."

It wasn't a long distance to the ground. He'd maybe sprain an ankle on a rogue root or fall weird on his hip and get his breath knocked out. He bowed his head, so his chin now nestled against his chest, reddening, and then went, "Ahh, I'm so stupid," and climbed back on the platform. The didn't say anything now. They just looked at Jeffrey falling, not falling, twenty feet from never playing football again. "I'm sorry," he said.

"Don't be. I didn't know. You want to talk about it?"

"Ah, well. Probably at some point."

"We've got time."

"This doesn't feel like time. It just feels like postponement."

Emily sighed and stood up and leaned against the gable of the teepee. She didn't like that there was no wind or noise. It made her ears ring and her brain hum. Here they could stew in their own problems until kingdom come and nobody would complain about their absence. Jeffrey could remain as he was. He could stay unhurt, in everlasting safety, though cupped in nonbeing. Cameron caught his breath and even laughed a little bit to himself. "How long have we been up here?"

"No way to tell, is there?"

"Haha."

"Oh Jeffrey."

"But seriously, we'll have to report this. To somebody . . . I mean, who would want to hear about it? Who'd believe such a thing? Some zany physicist? We could win the Nobel Prize for science."

"No, we couldn't."

"Well."

"Let's talk back in the living room. After you catch Jeffrey."

"I may not catch him right. He could still get hurt."

"What else are we going to do?"

He cracked his knuckles.

"You're right. As always, you're right."

"It doesn't feel real." Cameron stood up and faced her. He rubbed his eyes, as if this might get things moving again.

"I actually had the thought coming up here. I think even prayed. 'God, just let it feel like it lasts a really long time. Let me hold onto this moment, because right now, it feels like everything's ending.' Call me, I don't know, a doomsdayer! Call me a hopeless romantic. Maybe God has a sense of humor."

"Yeah. It feels weird. Hard to explain."

"All right. All right. Let's do this, then."

"We'll talk," Emily said. "We'll start talking more again. I promise."

So, the plan was devised. Cameron would station himself beneath the tree and Emily would count down before touching the ground. Cameron climbed down and trotted through the trees until he stood underneath the lad, judging the angle, positioning his feet so he could bear the multiplication of weight created by that kind of fall. He heaved a nervous sigh and then spread out his arms. "All right, Em!" he shouted. "Whenever you're ready!"

She scooted to the edge of the treehouse and planted her foot on the branch below. She used the edge of the planks to lower herself and then dangled from the branch from both hands, so her feet hung about five feet off the ground. For a moment as she swung, she saw the bed of green and golden leaves below her as people. They were children bawling in arithmetic class. They were patients lying on cots and they were moments of time piled and assorted and creating some magnanimous design that the home tree had in mind but that she couldn't yet understand.

"Em! Ready?"

"Ready! 1, 2, 3 . . ."

When she hit the ground, the world started up again, and ahead of her stood the man holding the child, knees bent but not broken.

Mr. Poet

"See the sun riddle a band over the new day, honey! Pond lighting up like a lamp now. Hey, gloom be gone, light rife with it—yeah, the stuff of life!"

The old man who Bradley knew as Mr. Poet hiked up the hill and stashed the end of his fishing rod into the earth and hauled up the little fellow behind him to set him on the horizon.

"Pacific Ocean in our backyard," he said. "How about that, honey?"

It was early. Blue morning. Mixed with apricot-colored smudges of dawn. "Check out the snow clouds coming from the North. How about that?"

"It's cold!"

"Cold nothin'! C'mon closer to the water. We're up before the whole world. Did you know that? Everyone else is asleep."

They got close to the muck and balanced on its edge and Bradley stuck the end of his boot out, so it touched the crust of ice. The mud crackled under their weight and the hoarfrost gleamed on the grass. He blinked and balanced on one foot and clutched at Mr. Poet's Carhartt jacket.

"Hey now, you know why I took you out here?"

"To see the Pacific Ocean?"

"Well, hey, this here is the Pacific Ocean, don't you know it, but see it's more than that."

It wasn't the Pacific Ocean, if you were wondering, but Mr. Poet had this way of making little ponds become seas, trees become mansions, and even grass blades turn into flutes. Say, he'd chortle, it's all in how hard you *look* at things, you know? Now when you get all big, and the world gets all small, *that's* when you're in a meager bind.

"Say here I go, tossing the line into the shallows, see?" Swip, flop, zzzz! Mr. Poet reeled in the line out of the cold reeds and brought back nothing to show for it except the silver minnow blinking at the end of the line.

"Well, see that ain't half so bad. Toss your line out and most times you bring back nothin' at all to show for it. But then ever oncet awhile you'll haul in a marlin. Try it!"

The boy stuck the worm on the hook and swung it round his head and launched it, glistening, into the puddle of possibility. "Bull's eye!" He shuffled his feet and gripped the rod. Mr. Poet threw his own cast a few feet down the bank, so it settled in the hole, too. "Sharks, marlins, eels, dolphins . . . "

"All that in this pond?"

"All that and more. Don't you believe me?"

"I dunno. Haven't got a bite yet."

"What I tell you? Won't always get the gold medal on your first try. Reel her in and cast again!"

He did. His aim wasn't always so good. Once the hook snagged on a wart of ice and wouldn't come loose no matter how hard he tugged. Mr. Poet jigged on the ice and pushed the line up with his pole so the boy's was freed. It was probably on the twentieth or so cast that the boy got a nibble at the end of the line, and then a tart jerk, and finally a thrash. A monster ate the end of the line.

"Oooohh it's a whopper!"

"Yeah! It's something HUGE!" He got on his knees and got out on the ice, trying to keep the line from pressing against the edges of the waterhole and snapping.

"Yep, closer! Reel her in, reel her in!'

"I think it's a marlin! I think it might be . . . a narwhal?"

"Here I'll help ya! I'll help ya!"

But Mr. Poet didn't come. The boy slid toward the hole like a dart to a target. My land! The fish must've been a deep diver, a resident of the Titanic. The boy flopped on his stomach, ate some ice, felt Mr. Poet grab his ankle but then lose his grip, and then toppled into the cold water headfirst.

"Sonny! Oh honey, sonny!"

Bradley opened his eyes. Good. Here was bed. A pond of covers. He was sweating and his sheets were wet. Naturally. He'd just fallen into the water. Of course he'd be wet. Momma moved on the other side of the door, speaking with Daddy. Daddy was tying his boots, like every morning. And like every morning, things were gray and fuzzy, and *quiet*. They had to be quiet this early in the morning or the baby would wake up. For two months now, everything revolved around the baby. When she slept, ate, needed attention.

Momma stopped talking. Daddy's shadow passed beneath his door. Or at least Bradley thought it was Daddy's shadow. Through the window, a bit of young man Mr. Sun peeked over the horizon. It was six a.m. He had a few more minutes to sleep but rolled over and planted his feet on the floorboards and tried to wrap his mind around another red-letter day in the life of Bradley Summers: sixth grade. P.E. today, not music class. Since it was Friday, they would scrimmage each other in basketball. Right on. But he remembered the math test two periods prior—unprepared? Just slightly understudied. Who could expect him to master long division by his lonesome? And with Daddy tramping into the house all plastered in oil and his mother dandling a bawling baby on her hip, and since Mr. Poet was just an occasional visitor in his dreams and in the corners of his eyesight, he had to figure it out by himself. Would that old Mr. Poet had a math degree and came out like a genie in a bottle!

So there's good news and bad news, as with every waking day. Christmas break was over. February was almost here, but who cares about Valentine's Day? The sixth-grade basketball season ended the last week of January, but the seventh graders played a full 17-game schedule and went into March. So *next year*. When sixth grade was over and his baby sister got old and could walk and he perfected the jump shot and the crossover, then he'd stop having those odd dreams about sunshine and marlins and the beaming love of Mr. Poet. Then his life *would* be a marlin haul. Yes sir, absolutely.

He crawled into his overalls and pulled the ratty hoodie Momma hated over his shoulders and gripped the pigskin on his desk. Just had to feel the pigskin before anything else. It put a pack of manliness in his inner gut. Like shave cream would do if he had the scruff to shave. He pulled on socks and his Converse high tops.

"Brad? Time to get up. Won't call ya again," Momma said on the other side of the door. Daddy gasped after finishing the rest of his coffee and then put the mug into the sink. Bradley slipped out of his room and padded over to the growling coffee pot. He didn't like coffee yet, but he was trying to convert and show Daddy before he left that he needed the black magic to get him through the day, too. Mr. Poet drank coffee. At least, Bradley remembered him snorting something dark from a green thermos every so often. And Mr. Poet would tell him to "drink up" because every big man has to face giants.

Daddy walked through the living room tightening his hat and swiping his wallet and keys from on top of the mantlepiece in the living room. Bradley had just poured himself some elixir and burned his tongue trying to force down the first sip.

"Mornin', son. Mr. Sunshine."

"Mornin' Daddy."

"Do you like it?"

"Um . . . yeah."

"You'll like it someday."

Daddy took off his camo hat and ran a hand through his hair in front of the mirror. Momma walked in holding baby sister on her shoulder.

"All right."

"Headed out already?"

"Well, I got called out to a site farther away so I gotta head out."

"Oh. Okay. Wait, can you hold her for just a sec?"

She put the baby in his arms and went into the bathroom down the hall. Baby sister cried harder, wriggling for freedom. Bradley tried the coffee again and winced.

"You don't have to drink it, bud."

"Okay."

"You'll like it someday, promise."

Daddy laid the baby girl against his chest and patted her back. Momma was still in the bathroom three minutes later.

"Hon? You almost done?"

"Yeah!"

"I really gotta go!"

"I'm *coming!*"

They heard rustling in the bathroom, but the door stayed shut and baby sister bellowed. Daddy's phone started to ring. He had a duck quack for a ringtone. The phone quacked away on the arm of the sofa.

"Crap." He backed up, trying to reach down. He nudged the phone so it fell between the sofa and the stand beside it. "Crap! Hey buddy, can you grab my phone? Or no here. Can you take her? Careful now. Yeah, you got her. I gotta get this."

Bradley took baby sister. He'd held her once a day after she was born, just a couple of months ago.

"Yes sir, understood. I'm on my way out the door. Just gimme twenty."

He hung up and looked at Bradley beneath his camo cap. His jacket was scarred with oil stains and his whiskers were rusty red. "Can you hold on to her until Momma gets out? You got her?"

"Yeah."

"Thanks champ. I'll see you after school."

"Hey Daddy?"

"Yup?"

"We goin' fishing later today?"

"Ah, it'll be tough, chief, but I'll try and get home before four so we can get a couple casts in. Sound all right?"

"Okay."

"All right." And he hurried out the door into the permafrost, jumped into the mud-sullied Ram truck in the driveway, and barreled down the gravel drive until hooking up with the highway.

"Shh, shh." He wished Mr. Poet would give him a hand. The old man could always get a baby to go to sleep. Once when they fished by the pond, his baby sister crawled through the field to get to them, as if she was jealous of being left out. Mr. Poet saw her from a distance. He scooped her out of the grass and brushed her off as she cried, and then brought her next to the pond where she slept in his arms as Bradley cast and reeled, cast and reeled, all afternoon long.

"Momma?"

"What?"

"Are you comin' out soon?"

"Just a *minute!*"

"Daddy left!"

"*WHAT?*"

"Daddy *LEFT!*"

The toilet flushed, and the door swung open. His mother walked into the living room brushing her hair out of her eyes. She was turning twenty-nine the next week. She and Dad were sending Brad and baby sister to the grandparents' house in Asher while they stayed in a hotel for a couple nights in Tulsa. She gathered the baby in her arms and told Brad to finish getting ready. The school bus would be there soon.

He went back into his room and sat down on his bed. He had brought his steaming cup of coffee with him and took another sip, but then set it on his nightstand and watched it steam. Baby sister kept up her crying, and Momma kept up her shushing and rocking. The sunlight had matured and now painted the slight hills with a wondrous amber. Harvest was already over, with the grain and corn stalks chopped to the nape. "Brad—come out and eat your breakfast!"

When he did come out again, trying to flatten the hair that stuck straight up on the top of his head, his breakfast was on the counter. Eggo waffles, orange juice, and cereal. It was all still unopened.

"You finished your homework?" Momma came back out with baby sister strapped to her chest.

"Yeah."

"You lyin' to me?"

"No."

"All right, well hurry up, bus'll be here soon." She went to the window and peeked through the curtains.

"What time will we have dinner, tonight, you think?"

"Uh, I don't know, haven't thought that far ahead yet. Why?"

"Daddy and I are gonna go fishing but he said he wasn't sure when he's gettin' home."

"You won't be able to fish today. It gets dark too early and your daddy won't be home in time."

"But he said he'd try."

"Yeah, buddy, he *says* that because he's nice. But you know how late he's been getting in lately."

"Yeah . . . "

Morning was the time for shooting straight. In the morning you get all the facts presented, like a stats list in the newspaper, or a weather forecast on page six. Given x, y, and z, it will almost certainly snow today at 4 p.m. This might be one of the coldest days of the year, with a high of 23 degrees Fahrenheit.

He finished breakfast in plenty of time and rinsed off his plate and put it in a dish washer that was so stuffed with dirty dishes that he had to perform Tetris in the cup section. Baby sister was sleeping again and laying in her crib in the living room. Momma turned on the TV. It landed on a real estate channel. A young couple walked around a southern estate outside of Savannah, Georgia, arm in arm, admiring rooms with hardwood floors. The dining room included a chandelier from a ceiling arched like a cathedral dome, and the outdoor patio had white pillars. Bradley watched from the kitchen table, scratching his arm. He read in the subtitles that this house was starting at one million dollars. And the couple nodded along with ease, stealing satisfied glances at each other, looking self-assured when they were interviewed. Momma watched while biting into a breakfast burrito and didn't look away while she chewed. The real estate agent took them to the backyard. Here the wife bent down and petted a softly tilled garden patch, letting the soil run through her fingers. She could plant strawberries there, said the subtitles. Or even vegetables, like potatoes, onions, or perhaps even corn. The only real problem was that the house stood twenty feet from its neighboring estate, leaving little to no room for cross-country hikes to the pond. Where were the *ponds* in a place like that?

When the commercials came on, Momma took the last bite of the burrito and checked her phone. Bradley could see her scrolling through Pinterest, Instagram, and TikTok—a flurry of people far happier than they. Meanwhile he took out a book from his backpack about pirates in the Indian Sea and opened up to page three where he'd been marooned for the past week and a half.

But the bus saved him from all these things, slowing to a stop on the shoulder of the access road fifty yards down the driveway. "You're late!" Momma cried.

He didn't know why waking up a little earlier than usual made time go by all the faster. But it did, and after scrambling his stuff, he jogged down the road in his parka and tried to keep his loosely tied shoes from falling off. Luckily Mr. Poet showed up to egg him on. "That's it, sonny, that's it! Hehe, run like the wind and feel that happy cold sun on your cheeks! Run wild and don't drop a book. Run free but don't forget to check the ditches! Run, run, run!"

He hopped onto the bus in a sweat, almost throwing himself over the driver's seat. Coach Soren swung the door shut right after he got on and said, "Next time I'm leaving ya."

He checked to see if Mr. Poet was still there after he sat down, but the road was just an empty ribbon of gravel, a straight line to the little one-story house with a pond waiting somewhere behind it like a frozen mirror.

Mr. Poet didn't show up halfway through Pre-Algebra as usual. He oftentimes joined Mrs. Clacker by the whiteboard with his hands behind his back, surveying the squiggles on the board with a contemplative frown, stealing winks at Bradley.

"Did ya do the homework?" asked Clay, leaning forward.

"Yeah!"

"Did ya get 'em right?"

"No!"

Bradley realized with terror that he forgot his shorts while the other boys jigged into their sporty get-ups for P.E. No, no—he couldn't be the fellow shooting layups in denim jeans. James told him that he thought he had an extra pair and rooted through his gym bag past sedimentary layers of Axe cologne bottles, Funyuns, and an ankle brace, but came up empty. "Shoot."

He found a pair hiding in the corner of the locker room beneath the bench; sure, they were dusty and smelled like death, but far lighter than the burden of humiliation.

He did okay during practice. He made his layups and touched the bottom of the net when Joel jeered and said he couldn't do it. So that was good. Oftentimes the layups and the short jumpers were the shots he missed the most. The shorts made him feel like he was staying at a friend's house for a sleepover and had to borrow old clothes that no one wore anymore. Mr. Poet, though he often showed up beneath the basket and commended his shooting, picked him up off the floor when he fell, and clapped him on the shoulder at the end, only shimmered briefly in the doorway of the gymnasium next to the concession stand and then vanished. Why was he so shy today? Hard to tell. Some days he was as real as the ball in his hand. On other days he was like the trapped swallow in the corner of the gym, fluttering for escape.

He almost fell asleep with his head leaned back against the wall in Social Studies and doodled on the margins of his worksheet in Spanish class, and had a whole bus seat to himself on the ride home. It was around three p.m. and the warmth of the sun seeped through his jeans despite the cold pressing through the grubby windows. He messed with a Rubik's cube and wondered if Dad would be home to take him fishing, as promised. But Dad didn't promise.

When Coach Soren dropped him off he just stood there by the cattle guard with his thumbs hooked in his backpack and figured that he didn't even need to go into the house. He had his fishing rod stowed away by the bodark trees on the rim of the pond and could just wait for Daddy. So he trotted off through the field, crunching the ice-crusted grass and dodging cow patties, wary that Momma might be watching from the kitchen window. He hopped over the creek and caught himself after rolling his ankle in the soft ground where a mole had tunneled. He got his tackle and pole and overcame the little ridge to overlook the pond to discover the obvious—a sheet of ice stretched over Mr. Poet's big ocean.

He grinned at the sight. Friday at last. Daddy on the way. Hot dog.

He slid down the hill until he got to the bank and tested the ice with his big toe. No Mr. Poet yet. A vulture circled overhead. Stratus clouds decorated the west, suggesting a snowstorm.

"You can do it, sonny!"

"Where've you been, Mr. Poet?"

"Oh here and there. Doin' this and that. Sometimes I'm a busy man." He couldn't see Mr. Poet but he heard him slide down the hill and start whistling, then say, "Well, you gonna walk on ice? Like Peter walking on water toward the Lord Jesus?"

"That's the plan." He planted a foot on the ice and tempted its strength by forsaking the weight from his other. Nothing cracked. He relaxed and settled both feet on the ice.

"Now move slow, and don't forget that you gotta drill a hole once you get to the deep part."

"Yup. You gonna fish, Mr. Poet?"

"Aw no, honey, not today. Today's just for watchin.' Besides, you know how to fish. You got what it takes."

He got on his hands and knees and crawled to the middle of the pond. It was cold enough that the sun didn't melt the surface of the ice. There were fish under there, though; marlins, trout, and whales, no doubt. He brandished the butt of the fishing pole and tapped it against the ice. It didn't give.

"Might have to hit a little harder, sonny, but careful! Don't fall through!"

He hit the ice again with the pole like it was a pickaxe. The brittle crackle that echoed the length of the pond signified that he had jabbed a nerve. He pricked the pressure point of the ocean with just one small hit, and after watching the ice turn into a spiderweb, plunged right on through.

He remembered his dream the night before as he slipped under the water, trying to grab the edge of the ice around him for a grip. His pole started to sink as he thrashed. There was no getting *that* back. He didn't know whether to try and launch himself back on top of the ice and try to crawl on the fractured plain, or swim beneath it and break through when he could touch the ground.

"Easy, sonny! Easy! Breathe! Just breathe!" Mr. Poet shimmered on the edge of the pond, darting back and forth along the bank. Bradley's legs didn't seem to obey him when he tried to kick. He dipped under, trying to shed his waterlogged sneakers, and came back up shocked and trying to settle his arms on the ice. He was able to remain stationary like that, head and shoulders above the ice, but his legs were too numb to move. "Help me," he gasped. "Mr. Poet, you real? Please, please, help me."

"I'm helpin' you, lad, just keep your eyes right here. See me?"

"Who are you?" Bradley never thought to ask before. He knew the image was fake, that he was seeing things. But still, that didn't answer his question. He never knew where Mr. Poet or his songs came from. He couldn't remember reading him in a book or seeing him in a movie. There was no one in his life who looked like Mr. Poet. And he didn't tell anyone about Mr. Poet, fearing ridicule. None of his friends had mentioned imaginary friends for years. They were too old for imaginary friends, and nearly too old now for real ones too.

"Hang on, buddy . . . oh my dear. Sonny, don't let go."

"Help me."

He lost the feeling in his lower body and his arms kept slipping. It was only a matter of time before he would duck under the ice and follow the fishing rod. Mr. Poet could not help him. He could only run up and down the bank, waving his arms, shouting about there was a world of awe and wonder beyond the ridge, right in front of his nose. Bradley's breath quickened. He watched Mr. Poet dance, wave at him to pull himself out, to follow him into the world. And then the old man up and vanished, away into nothing, as if he'd never been there in the first place.

He made one last go at getting on top of the ice, but ended up losing his grip and sliding back into the water where he first fell in. He started to sink, feet first, the solitary vulture roaming the heavens. He didn't know what it would be like to die, but he figured that, if anything, a figure like Mr. Poet might be meeting him behind the curtain. Maybe all those dreams were supposed to prepare him for this. Maybe that was why the old chortler kept showing up. To make this hurt less. After all, he had woken up that morning after falling into a hole in the ice and getting dragged into cold by some unknown monster at the end of the line. He reached his hand above the water, thinking of his family—his mother's impatience with him, her very real burden that she carried. His father's justifiable busyness. His baby sister's needs, more important and pressing than his own.

"Brad!"

Someone, not Mr. Poet, snatched his body and crashed back through the ice all the way back to the shore. He recognized the face of the man who laid him on the bank, dripping wet in his camo hat and red beard. Who was it? "Jesus Christ." Daddy wrapped him in his Carhartt coat. He laid his ear to Bradley's chest and then hoisted him up in his arms with a bellow. "Emily! Call an ambulance!"

He still felt like he was in the water when Daddy carried him back home. He still saw the same sky and its vulture, now drifted to new terrain. He still figured he'd be joining the dead at some point that day. But that was later, way off in dreams. "I knew *you* were real," he whispered.

A Certain Ghost's Long and Final Fall Back to Earth

I 'll just skip the pleasantries and let you know the basics, which are that I died on Christmas morning and woke up to find myself suspended against my ceiling with the full cooperation of this here incorporeal form, and that for the past five years, my belongings have been stripped from my quaint little flat but yours truly has remained nested in its empty halls.

Nobody wants to live in the flat where the previous tenant vaulted to his untimely demise. You know, I hardly remember what happened myself. I woke up ready to continue my tirade against consumeristic X-mas-shopping maniacs and how the holidays are occasions for eggnog and nostalgia and kitsch Christmas gnomes and religious myths, went to the window balcony to shout it like I did every morning of the holiday season, and somehow that early morning lack of balance and a failure of depth perception had me flailing twenty stories to the snowy walks below. The railing broke. That much I remember. My balcony railing, a paltry assemblage of welded iron, gave way and sent this twenty-six-year-old philosophy grad student kicking against cold Christmas air until splatting into the Village. And when I opened my eyes, I was bunched up in the corner of the room, my flat, stilled stymied with junk food and magazines and pizza boxes, now fuzzed over with the gray light of semi-nonbeing.

Five years. The movers came and went. Some morticians in white suits carted the body away and the bellboy had to shovel the bloody snow into the sewage grate. Some other guys came up with my aunt and uncle, showed them the hellhole of a flat, sorted through what they wanted to keep I guess, amid the sniffles and head shakings of my courteous aunt, and then for five years, nothing.

No one can see me. I've tried it a million times. Let people walk through me. Stood with the groomsmen in I don't know how many weddings. The bellboy can't see me, nor the secretary, nor those who flurry down the streets of New York. And I regret to report that Joey can't see me either. That one tends to kind of hurt, but whatever—it is what it is. She's moved on anyway. Furthermore, apparently the community of local ghosts is a scrawny one, because I haven't found any ghoulish compadres along the way either.

But that's enough for now. I'm a postmortem prospector in a city filled with souls of those who are still scrambling for the golden egg at the end of the tunnel. Only, I've got news for them—they're scrambling for residence in an empty flat where they'll watch their nuggets of success get carted away by forgetful minds.

It was December 24th and on the eve of the fifth anniversary of my glorious plummet to ghost-dom when the door to the flat opened as I was hovering over the countertop in the kitchen replacing a chandelier bulb, and a middle-aged man and a boy of maybe ten tramped into the living room. They were carrying boxes. The boy sneezed and the middle-aged fella, who wore a Patriots beanie, thick ski gloves, and large round glasses, said, "God BLESS you, Stevie James!" And then they put the boxes down.

"So your first deposit includes this month and next month, and comes to $3100," cooed the landlord from the hallway. "Drop it off when you can, and WELCOME home!"

"Thanks, Marta!"

Marta. Oh yes, good old Marta. I hadn't checked in on her in a while. But my first reaction here was to still the chandelier and duck behind the counter. I can't be seen, except maybe in the brightest modes of sunlight (haven't verified this but have gotten some doubletakes whilst walking through a sun-banked Central Park last summer) but I can still touch the broken chandelier, and my hand isn't so disembodied that it can't rustle someone's bedsheets or turn over a vase on the coffee table.

They were tenants, obviously—the first tenants the flat had seen in five years, and by the look of them, seemed pretty much over the moon to be here. "Wow," the dad (presumably) kept saying. "Just wowza. I mean gosh. Isn't this place so much better than our last place, Stevie?"

Stevie rooted around the hallway, went in and out of the two bed-rooms, and reported back on the "nook" he'd found with a few books and magazines stowed away. I didn't want him touching those. That was my nook, and this was *my* apartment. I hadn't really thought of it that way until they came marching in there like that, but you get used to the silence and solitude after a while, and despite being ethereal, can't help but feel like you've still got some property rights. At least he won't find the stash of literature I've got stowed beneath the floorboards. That's all crap from childhood. *Huckleberry Finn* and *David Copperfield* and all that stuff you feel embarrassed to like as a grownup.

Stevie lugged back a stack of the *New Yorker* magazines and splayed them on the floor as if they were cowhides. "Whoa! Hey we'll read 'em soon. We gotta help those guys with the other stuff."

Over the course of thirty minutes, the father and son joined ranks with a couple of moving guys and brought in a measly grand total of a sofa, almost caved in at the center, two twin mattresses (which they put in the same room), a coffee table with so many gashes and scratches it could've been plucked from the rubble of some revolution, and a rug of many colors—not to mention the final addition, which was a spindly arti-ficial Christmas tree, pre-decorated with wretched flossy twine and glass icicles and stars.

They stuck the tree in the most coveted corner of the room, stepped back to observe their work, and then Dad paid the movers and then shut the apartment door. I whooshed back to the kitchen with folded arms.

I was no millionaire in life—please understand. But I wasn't . . . like *this.* They unpacked their boxes, filled with old pictures, dishes, a candle, and some other garbage. Most of the photos were of a young woman with dark eyes and a light, pensive smile. These they enthroned in various high spots in the apartment. Gosh. They were the real impoverished. Whether they'd signed a vow of poverty and disavowed the poisons of capitalism and had a portrait of our lord Karl Marx hiding somewhere in the box I didn't know, but I started to get curious. These might be *my* kind of people.

They didn't have much to set up, as you might have figured, but the kid Stevie felt the need to explore the nook again, reemerging with another bundle of literature I'd snatched from the nearby Barnes and Noble. Why the accusatory looks? It's not as if I could buy anything anymore. Besides, none of these corporate hogs deserve my cash—not that I have any to spare of course. Being invisible except in intense beams of light affords you the kind of liberties you should have had as a flesh and blood guy. Remember Gollum and the Ring of Power? He could do whatever he wanted, and for five hundred years. Sure, no one could see him or love or know him in such a condition, but he probably got what he felt entitled to, and without the repercussions. Obviously I'm not going out robbing banks, but a ghost has got to read his Nietzsche. I'm trying to be a refined person, okay?

They set up some more dingy Christmas decorations, including all these awful crayon depictions of reindeer and wise men—were the wise men *riding* the deer? And they even pulled out some "Advent" devotional book with illustrations of the nativity and angelic hosts and whatnonsense. I'm anti-consumeristic and anti-religion, so you can imagine that double whammy that accosts me amid the annual yule. So, they were poor, I guess, but shoot—they were the *devout* poor, and that puts this agnostic ghost in a tough spot empathy-wise.

After they were done adjusting the sofa, they stocked the cupboards with their paltry collection of mugs and plates, and I decided to flutter out for some fresh air. I fell the twenty stories as gentle as the dusty snowflakes cascading on the avenue, and swished my way to the sub where I sat between a man thumbing through a sudoku booklet and a middle-aged lady who kept dabbing her nose with a tissue although she didn't seem to have a cold or anything. I got off at the square and "walked" into the Central Park amid the happy hordes of tourists, the ear-muffed runners in leggings and purple vests, the literary couples from 5th avenue who knew they were above the sentiments of the season, and the few cohesive families who threw frisbees to dogs and let their kids roam on the stony knolls. One time I saw Paul McCartney here put in eye droplets on a bench. I followed him for three or four blocks and then stopped when a group of college kids assailed him for signatures.

Today, though, couples were hobbling in skates around the rink and men held their coffees to their professional chests, and I sort of got to missing it all. It's a weird thing being able to see everything but not being able to participate in any of it. It's like watching the world from a magic window. The window lets you get as close as you want to anything in the world, to any person, city, or treasure, but refuses to let you be a part of it. I whisked myself up above the trees to get an atmospheric view of the place, then zoomed back to limit my territory to a portion of bench by the pond. And just as I got to feeling more that sort of way, who should sit down next to me but the woman herself, the embodiment of tender perfection, the

Venus standing in Botticelli's clam shell—Joey Lander, dressed in a brown knee-length coat and a red beanie, brown curls bobbing from beneath. She crossed her legs and extracted a cigarette from her purse and struggled to light it in the wind—I put my blank flipper up to block the airstream and miraculously it worked. She piped away and breathed the smoke out into the cold air, and rested her arm on the bench backrest. Almost so it was around my shoulder.

When we were dating in grad school, I asked her to move in with me—yes, the paltry flat that's now being invaded by Stevie and his pa. I asked her that a couple weeks before my death, and when she was packing a suitcase in her apartment in the Village getting ready to go to Vermont for a ski trip with her parents. She raised her eyebrows as I pleaded and snagged a cigarette—that's still her prime vice, I guess, and then she said she'd think about it while criss-crossing down the powdery slopes. It doesn't take much guessing to know that she didn't move in with me. Something was holding her back. "The stuff you talk about . . . " she said the next morning over coffee, kneading her forehead. "I don't know. It worries me. I'm no religious nut but what you've got is some real anger. Some genuine bitterness at some cosmic daddy in the sky, and that . . . God, that really freaks me out."

You might say that her silence on the ski slopes impelled me to become a slob that Christmas season, defame the flat into something of a pigsty, and conclude that if I was going to be an angry nihilist I might as well live like one. One too many drinks on Christmas Eve. One too many self-pitying rambles down the street and back. And then over the railing I flew, wishing my descent was like Joey's on the mountain of snow—soft, elegant, and beautiful.

Today she looked almost the exact same as I remembered her. She had that spray of freckles under her green eyes, now webbed a bit with creases, courtesy of turning thirty-two. She pursed her lips a lot, because she thought a lot, and had those dimples in her cheeks as she drew in a deep breath and brushed her button nose with the knuckle of her thumb.

"Joey," I said, loud and clear. Was it sunny enough? Not even close. I stood up in front of her, reached out my limp gray arm towards her, watched as she smoked and frowned at the scenery and checked her watch. Was she meeting someone? Why wasn't she in Vermont skiing with her Neo-Con parents? Why wasn't she at work sketching bridges and skyscrapers and all the infrastructure for all these bozos to enjoy? "Can we talk, Joey?" I said. "We never really got to do that, you know. I know you were sad about me dying, but that's a minor hangup. Let's talk about you moving in. Will you? No one will bother you there. There's not a soul in the flat . . . "

She stood up and took off her beanie and ran a hand through her mousy brown hair and started off towards 5th avenue.

"Hold up, I can explain everything."

Clip clop went the duck boots.

"Can't you see me? Won't you talk to me?" Somehow I stumbled on the sidewalk and went haywire, like tumbleweed, and ended up in some thistles by the water. Gravity's no friend to a ghost. You need real momentum to get going. Wind helps, and sometimes earnest desperation. "Baby!" I swam through the thorns, but she was walking fast and momentarily got lost among a horde of garish bikers.

It occurred to me that it was Saturday, and that it wasn't out of the ordinary for her to go on weekend jaunts with no particular destination in mind. She usually abjured the subway and walked the length of upper Manhattan. Only occasionally would she invite me to go with her. She said once, in jest, I hope, that I'd just chatter about nothing the whole time, and she wanted to hear the engine of the city alongside the mechanics of her own brain. She said all that stuff was calming, and that sometimes she'd even speak out loud.

"To yourself?" I asked.

"No, not to myself."

"To . . . like . . . the people around you?"

"No . . . I don't know who I'm talking to on those walks. Call me sentimental. Sometimes it feels something like prayer. A really free and uninhibited type of prayer. Walking and talking."

No wonder she didn't want me with her on her pilgrimages. To talk out loud in New York City without caring if anyone thought you were crazy? To speak words not necessarily caring for reciprocation? As I squeezed through the pack of bikers, flowed through a potbellied man smoking a pipe beneath a 1920s-looking ballcap, I caught up with Joey and joined her in stride with my airy fingers tucked in my pockets. Her lips were still pursed, and she still smoked, finally discarding the yellow nub of cigarette into a nearby bin. Was she going to do it? Talk to the great nothingness? We walked beneath a bridge, passed the Balto memorial, and by the time we were a ways removed from the populous rim of the park, she actually did it—she started talking. Her voice was quiet, exasperated. She was ranting about someone at work who wasn't submitting designs on time, and now they had to stall a series of housing projects until at least March. Then she closed her eyes, considered another cigarette, declined, and kept going, "I don't know what to do," she said. She opened her eyes wide and shook her head. "It's been what . . . five years? Was it my fault? God, was it my fault? I probably never should've been with him, but there was something about him . . . ah, I do this every stupid December. Get all weepy about it and wish . . . what am I wishing for? That he'd come back so we could wrap a bow on the relationship? Finally get some 'closure' as they say? I don't know." She huffed and brushed a tear from her eye, took a deep breath, and said, "Here's the thing. You were a thoughtful guy. You were SO smart, and really going places with your education and career, but you were wounded. Angry and wounded. I could see it every single day. You didn't tell me much about your relationship with your dad but I figured . . . well, I don't know what exactly. Just that he wasn't around that much when you were a kid."

Was she talking to me? Christ, was this actually happening?

"You never told me what happened. But I'm sorry about whatever it was that happened. You were mad. I get it."

"Do you? Do you get it? What're *you* so angry about if you can so easily relate?" I shouted.

I was barely getting over the fact that she was talking to *me,* nonexistent *me,* and that I had the insanely good luck (or misfortune) to witness it. Is this what she did when I was still alive and was this why she didn't want me along with her on the walks?

"Five years," she whispered on. "Five years ago, and I'm still living in the same city with the same job, while everyone else comes in and out, in and out. I guess I'll be out of here too, one way or the other. Either by death or rent, it's probably gonna happen."

We were grazing 5th Avenue, where the women wore mink scarves and the men wore furrowed brows and walked in arrow-straight gaits down the street.

"I want to say goodbye," she said. "I know I want to say that much."

I didn't follow her across the street. I was starting to feel exposed, and the sun was out. It was a cruelly bright and cold sun that still permitted the crystal flakes of December to mingle with the trees and the building and the woman with the red beanie who had finally said goodbye to me, or to the ghost of me, rather. Maybe she said those same words every week on her escapades. Maybe those were the words she didn't know how to articulate to any other human being so the best she could do was recite her woes to a ghost. Well. I can't cry anymore but I wanted to.

I wandered the park some more, drifting out over the ice and gliding a few feet behind a young couple who kept having to hold each other up so they wouldn't fall, and then, blue to the bone, I went "home."

The father and son weren't there. They probably went out to get some food or Christmas caroling or some such sentimental tripe. Here was another Christmas Eve and now the place had a ratty couch and an empty bag of Doritos on the coffee table. Man, how I miss the taste of coffee. I tried to drink it once out of a cup some lady abandoned in a café down in the Village, but it burned holes in my incorporeal vestments and I had to spend the next three days mending myself in the sunshine.

Oh well.

I went out to the balcony. The place where the railing broke five years earlier had been stitched back together with zip ties. Not exactly the most prodigious form of bonding, but it seemed to have held pretty well. Cars beeped and plodded down the street twenty stories down, with those crosses etched into the buildings for Christmas, and hurried professionals scampering down the walks to make it home in time for granny's home-made minced pies and peas. Back to their fathers and mothers and wives and children. I bowed my invisible head as the wind picked up and snow once again started to swirl.

About the books in the floorboards. They were presents from my old man. That's the reason I hid them and the reason I kept them. But something in what Joey said earlier made me want to uncork the locks and take another looksee at the original literature that got me started on this long academic track in the first place.

I reached beneath the floorboard in the master bedroom and used the heft of the spine of *Huckleberry Finn* to pop it loose, uncovering a modest array of goodies: *Moby Dick, Don Quixote, David Copperfield, The Brothers Karamazov,* and even the Bible, if you can believe it. Some of the best stuff ever written—or at least some of the most widely and highly regarded. I sat against the wall beneath the gray window, teasing through the dogeared pages. He didn't write a note or anything. My father told me that if I read these books, and reread them, my life would probably be deeper and truer and better. He said that as a major financier, a Wall Street bro. He said that as a millionaire if you can believe it.

I read them when I was twelve. At the time they were perspiring with the old man's very presence. These books were like the word of God. But over the years, when the guy didn't call all that much because of his "anxiety" following the divorce, when he forgot my following birthday and neglected the next consecutive ten Christmas gatherings, those volumes, I'll admit, garnered a stench of suspicion. In college I discovered a lot of things. Liberal women, postmodernism, and intramural soccer, but I also found that, do a little digging, and your average student can make a career being markedly dissatisfied with the way things are. I was so pissed off and didn't want to know what at exactly. Intellectualize your sense of abandonment and you'll end up like me.

So, what now? It was Christmas Eve and I'd had enough of my continuation without participation. But a proper goodbye was in order. Joey said it, and now I had to say it, too. I took the old sappy library and salvaged some wrapping paper from the living room, where a roll of it lay half-used already, and set it underneath the Christmas tree, which, shabby though it was, glimmered with gold and blue lights. I stood there watching it for a while, floating midway between floor and ceiling. By eight p.m., Stevie and his father were back in the living room, and I was hovering above the tree, stashed in my old corner.

I didn't sleep, but I managed to "close my eyes" that night curled up beneath the Christmas tree next to the gift. They might think it was weird to find a nicely wrapped package under their tree, which is why I changed course around midnight, wrote a note from Marta the landlord, and set the gift outside their door. When Christmas morning came, I summoned up every ounce of energy in these quickly dissipating bones and blew against the door, so it rattled. Then I slid underneath the door as the father came over to open up and stood by the glass door leading to the balcony.

"What is it, pop?"

"It's for you! From Marta!"

"For me?"

"Well, geez, open it, open it! It's Christmas, isn't it?"

It took a double take to confirm that there were a measly total of three gifts beneath the tree, each no bigger than a chicken egg. And as the boy tore into the wrapping paper, heart pounding so loud it liquified my already disembodied state, the father knitted his brow, rubbed his chin, and turned around so he was facing me. Facing that Christmas morning sun. Who's to know whether or not he really saw me, or whether he suspected that his son had a ghostly benefactor? I don't know, but he got as close as a man has ever gotten to looking me into the eyes. That look was enough to conclude that I'd been made a little bit solid again by the sun. It was enough for me to tumble off the balcony after the dad smiled in my general direction and make

Margo's World

They were at the caboose when the whole space station popped like a balloon a clean billion miles away from the gently spinning core of the earth. Luckily for Paul and Margo, they were in their spacesuits. They had been floating around in the antigravity room, bumping against each other and playing Hole in the Wall. Great game. One of the millions of little pastimes to pass the time on the ship called Salvation. Their new home was how many years away now? The station how impenetrable? Their boredom how acute?

Paul couldn't stop spinning for about ten minutes, ears whining at a high pitch—maybe he was on the way to going deaf. Maybe he was dead and this was heaven. Or he was asleep and this was the dream. But no. There was a lineage of events. Boom, scream, spin. And his heart was sobbing too loud to be fake.

And now he had to wonder: Who else? The neighboring cosmos was a big pool of stars above and below. When he finally quit the spinning, rotating slowly like a pudgy windmill, what should he see but a flaming mass of humanity's last hope, and the embers of the World Hall blinking sadly in the ruins?

"Oh cripes."

He slapped his wrist and pushed back the vomit in his throat. This slap on the wrist was to initiate contact with survivors. The vomit was due to his being horrified. "Uh, hey hey hey! Help? Help!" He got static and the whizzing sound of what could've been an alien, then nothing.

Project Salvation was a no-go then. All those courageous world leaders, once enthroned on ivory chairs endowed with the ideals that were supposed to propel them through the heavens and onto the next evolution-ary step—reduced to stardust. Sure, there were some poor folks who opted to stay on that little blue dot, but as far as the Saviors were concerned, if the voyage to Planet 45X failed, humanity had failed.

Margo, incidentally, told him that she was going to give him a surprise that night. She just had to choose the end of the "world" to tell him. They lived on the same hall like college freshmen in a unisex dormitory, and as of three weeks ago, read in some archaic book that when two people have the "fuzzies" for each other in their intestinal regions, this most likely indicates you should bump wine glasses and later bump something else. He wasn't exactly sure of the order of things.

Have you ever missed someone you've never met? You look for them in the hallways of your workplace and imagine them sitting across from you in the cafeteria amid the flurry of passersby and noise. And this person isn't asking anything of you. She is sitting there playing with something on the table, maybe a pack of sugar, maybe with a toothpick in her mouth, but she is saying nothing. All she's doing is looking deeply into your eyes to as-sure you that she understands who you are and what you're going through, that no, you're not alone, and no, you're not a space alien orbiting a planet of non-belonging. That's how he felt about Margo. She had big brown eyes behind a pair of thick-lensed glasses and was the daughter of one of the billionaire honchoes who had originally funded the expedition. She spent hours at the Big Window staring at the little blue speck tucked in the folds of Andromeda, sipping her coffee with a book tucked beneath her arm. She was short—only five feet tall, with a bob of brown hair and a round face and a chin that went double only when she laughed. She never capitalized on her beauty—she was pretty much perfect in the eyes of the passengers, many who were conditioned to want to bang her type, including Paul. But she belonged in a world of her own, apart from the Salvation ship, floating out there in the cosmos in search of an old planet. An old memory. He was running laps around the Space Auditorium and kept seeing her in one of the chairs by the Big Window, spinning slowly in circles with her feet tucked beneath her thighs.

"Margo!" As if anything in the universe could hear him. "Margo!"

Can you swim in space? Paul did breaststrokes, but there was no way to tell if he moved forward, backyard, up, or down. He kicked the atmo-sphere and reached up like there might be some sort of bar to hold onto that would lift him to safety. He wanted to see her more than he wanted to get back to safety. There was no getting safe and saved now, of course. But he saw the fiery rings of debris, the electrical tailspin of cutting-edge pieces of machinery, and knew that finding her was almost definitely out of the question.

"Margo!"

His spacesuit could furnish him with the nutrients he needed to survive for up to six months. When the time came, nodes would attach to his forearms, like an IV, and keep him alive and kicking. The humans on Project Salvation were really good at keeping people alive. They weren't so good on letting people know *why* they should want to be alive in the first place, but they were first rate at survival and bio longevity. Probably the best in the business.

"Margo!"

"You know, friend, we are not as safe as we appear." They were munching popcorn in the basketball courts just yesterday when she said that, looking off into the bleachers. The gym was a model based on an old similar kind of facility from Earth, a small, dusty junior high dungeon with gum under the seats and scuffs on the court. There were lots of artifacts on the ship like that. There was a little country post office, a gas station that sold bad coffee and corndogs, and even a country church. There were no cemeteries.

"What do you mean we're not safe?"

She swallowed her popcorn, pensively knitting her brows. "I mean we're not really safe. We're hurling through the outer reaches of the cosmos in a tin balloon. Doesn't that . . . " She cocked her round head. "*Perturb* you at all?"

"I'll tell you what perturbs me. If I can be honest. Knowing that nothing I do really matters." She cocked her head, frowning. "I mean," he continued, "I was made in a laboratory. In ice. Almost everybody here was. I look a lot like hundreds of the other guys. If I die, they'll just cook me up again and it will be like I never existed at all. Isn't that what they were going for all along? Do you know what it's like to feel like you could do *anything*, either something really good or something really terrible, and have it not matter at all because you're not related to anyone and no one seems all that affected by what you do anyway?"

They had left the gym and walked down the garish hall of the mockup junior high. Homecoming was next week according to the posters of glitter. They walked outside and stood by the flagpoles under the light of the artificial sun. She was dipping low now, easing into the bottom of the cylindrical space station while the real stars burned effulgently through the windows.

Margo gripped the flagpole and swung around it a couple times. She watched him while she swung.

"So nothing you do matters, huh?"

"Sure feels that way."

"What if you pinched me?"

"What do you mean?"

"I said 'what if you pinched me?' It would probably hurt pretty bad. That would matter." She stopped swinging. She held out her hand, almost like she was wanting him to kiss it. "Go ahead. Do it. Pinch me. Pinch me real hard. See if I care!"

"No, I don't want to do that."

"Ha!" she snapped. "Why not? Why don't you want to pinch me?"

"Well, because it would hurt you."

Margo smiled and spun on her heels. She spun in more circles by the flagpoles and tossed her scarf around her neck, so she looked like a caterpillar. The artificial sun went out so Margo became a shadow against the distant windowpanes. Only a moment later, a digital moon sprung at the apex of the space station, and a hologram of President Nielson appeared against the ceiling. "Good evening, fellow pilgrims," he softly boomed. "As we make our historic journey into the far reaches of the cosmos, remember that every stage of the process is of eternal significance. You are the carriers of the future. The intermediary generation. Humanity forever after will thank you for your sacrifice. You are the heroes of the cosmos." Nielson, a spindly man with a hooked nose and unconvincing smile, gave a little salute, and then disappeared into the pixels. Margo mouthed the words as he spoke, cocking her head at him again, looking regal.

"See?" said Margo. She was a silver twig in the moonlight, arms spread. "Old man Niel says you matter, Pauly!"

He wasn't convinced. This ship would not land in their lifetimes. He lived here so someone else could live there. Carry the flame, soldier. They came to an empty cobbled street that led to what was supposed to be a Bavarian village. A film of snow even fell under the lamppost by a German bakery: *Deutcher*! "Are they open?"

"Nah. It's Saturday."

"Saturday. Everyone's at the Ball of Brilliance—remember?"

"Dad wanted me to come. And I told him I'd come. Gosh. Guess I'm a traitor to the cause." Margo opened her hand. A couple of the snowflakes landed and melted on her palm. She cupped her hands against the window, peering inside to study the cakes and rolls on the platters just inches away.

"What cause are you talking about?"

"You know. The 'cause.'" She shrugged and kicked her heel against one of the cobbled stones. "No one tells you what the cause really is—only that it's the most important thing—" She stopped. "I was going to say 'the most important thing in the world,' but you know, I guess that wouldn't be right. Because we don't live in a *world*. We live in a floating tube, filled with little fake worlds that are supposed to make us feel at home. The cause is causing me to be quite caustic." She turned to him, evading the light of the lamppost by pressing her blue ballcap tight on her head, and he felt it again: that near irresistible draw to bring her in, put his hands on her hips and . . . sway? Move side to side? In the old movie *Casablanca* they danced in the bar to piano music. He took a step closer, face reddening in the dark.

"What if we all had spacesuits on?" she said. "What would be different about that?" She slapped her arm and clicked her boot against the post. "Because really, that's what we are anyway. Suits blocking everything out." That drove him up the wall. To touch her like they touched in the movie! He could see Messieurs Rick drawing close in the shade of his study, Ilsa's eyes brimming with inconsolable longing—complicated, impossible desire! But their desire wasn't about bodies touching. It was about that and something more. What?

"People wear armor here. Do you?"

"Do I wear armor?"

"Yeah. Do you wear a spacesuit? Keeping out all the bad air? The air that will kill you if you get exposed to it?"

He checked himself with a shrug. "Not that I know of."

She stepped closer. "Whenever I go into the antigravity chambers and try on that stupid suit I feel like I am becoming just like everyone else. I am putting on a covering so nothing will ever hurt me. Spinning through space in a machine that keeps me alive but . . . "

"Keeps you alive for no particular reason," he said.

That's when he sprung forward, charmless as an old bear, and touched her hand. Just the tips of her fingers were available beneath her sleeves.

She flinched her shoulders but didn't pull her hand away. He sputtered and thought to himself, *Conditioned. Conditioned to like her type. That's what they said in orientation . . . don't worry when you feel drawn towards them. That's all natural. It was in the programming—our top minds know which matches will prove to further the ideal development of humankind. Don't be disturbed! It's natural! It's all natural!*

"I'm . . . sorry."

"For pinching my index finger? It didn't hurt."

"I don't know what I'm sorry for."

They left the Bavarian village and walked into a grove of pine trees, heavy with artificial fragrance. They found a stream so clear and deep they could see trout rummaging their silver fins ten feet down. Margo stooped and dipped her hand in the water. Paul just listened to its current. He vaguely felt like he had stood here before. He remembered being alone in a forest and feeling the wind on his face, and mountains off in the distance. But he had never *felt* the wind. He had never *seen* mountains. Memories, his mentors said, were images of the primordial past programmed to drive a man towards survival. It was all in service to the continuation of the race. All these relics—the gym, the flagpoles, the forest, Margo's face—were supposed to make him want to pass on the fire.

Margo stood up and held her wet hand above his head. A couple of the drops fell on his cheeks, rolled down to the edge of his jaw. She took her hand away and dried her hand on her sleeve, and they kept going.

They left Corridor Ten, wove down the passage and into the Central Hall, where they heard the shouts of celebration coming from the Ball of Brilliance in the auditorium, all the way to her pod in Hallway 45. They talked about other places in this maze of a ship they might explore. There was always the beach, a simulation of the Blue Grotto. They could go to the cliffs of Dover, even though they were only about a quarter the size of the real thing. Of course, there was always the Grand Mall. It was always chock full, but the movie theater sometimes showed old stuff, taking a break from the predictable cycle of AI-generated flicks and rom-coms. So maybe a movie?

No, they had seen all of this. They had done all of this. He didn't want to "see" or "do" anything else. She held her wrist against the reader by the doorknob of her pod. The chip beneath her skin gleamed green and the door slid open, and she stood in its open space facing him as if wondering what she was supposed to ask him—as if there was some secret script they both needed to read to sustain their relationship.

"So . . . " He sighed. "Antigravity room tomorrow? After you finish your book, of course." He could see her stack of literature on the desk next to her little flatscreen TV.

Her eyes fell to the floor.

"Antigravity room," she said, nodding. "We can play Hole in the Wall, or whatever it's called."

Ironic, he was thinking now as he chewed his lip behind a wall of plastic, alone in the void. *She thought the space suits would make it harder to talk to each other. Now they're the only things keeping us alive.*

Why not hold on to blatant optimism? What on "earth" did he have to lose? He floated past a chunk of a cafeteria. He thought he recognized the bar where he slid his tray behind the other clones. In that old world, once so predictable and secure, were the blonde variants piling up on donuts as if they were made for them, and the tall brooders with a love of art and prophecy in a far corner needling their fingers and looking grim. And the Supremes, fit as fiddles in their uniforms, strident and holier-than-thou at the round table near the Big Window, looked over the cosmos they were designed to colonize. Paul shook the images out of his head. The noodles made cursive lines by a big pot and half of an oven. He grabbed one like it was a lasso meant to wrangle planets and let it trail behind him.

"Margo!"

"I have a surprise for you."

That was the last thing she said to him in the antigravity room when they bumped around the walls and tossed their balls through the holes in the wall. He had twenty scores; she managed three.

"I have a surprise for you," and then there was the BOOM followed by the soundlessness of space.

He thought he saw her waving her hands during the explosion, trying to grab his arm, but she hurtled in the opposite direction. He wondered what had happened. The space station was self-sustaining, he was told, and no comet or enemy would ever bring it down. He read something about an ancient ship called the Titanic. People thought it was the future, how it would never sink. All those centuries ago people still thought they had made a ship that would never sink.

He let go of the noodle, going head over heels for a couple of rotations, and then found, almost like transmitting into another dimension, himself floating among dozens of books. He hadn't seen this coming. It was like they were dropped there by an invisible hand, offering some leisure in his free time. Many of them were charred and bleeding with embers, but others were still intact and asking to be looked through. He reached out and snagged a copy of *Anna Karenina*.

He looked inside the cover. "Property of . . . Margo."

He almost swallowed his tongue and swam after another volume. *Pride & Prejudice*, *The Hunger Games*, *Harry Potter*, *Catcher in the Rye*, *The Westing Game*, *The Adventures of Huckleberry Finn*. They all belonged to her—every dogeared one of them.

He tried to hold them all to his chest but had to let a few of them go so he could reach for others. He would not be able to carry them all. He didn't have a house to keep them. There was a portion of her little desk, the flatscreen TV, her smartphone, cleft in two, and all four pairs of shoes she owned. "Margo!"

What was the surprise? Had she solved the meaning of life? The meaning of the Salvation ship? Paul reached out and grabbed a small purple leather-bound journal. It didn't take long for him to know that this was not just another book. It was *her* journal, scribbled all the way through the final page in sleek cursive. He didn't know where she learned to write cursive. He never knew she kept a journal at all. He would not have looked through any of it if she had never mentioned the surprise, or if he wasn't careening towards his imminent doom in space. But he cracked it open to the last page, squinting through the fog of his helmet to read:

Day 7,234

A surprise for you today.

I float in space every day. That was the story at the end of the last journal and that is the story at the end of this one. I walk through the line at the cafeteria and avoid the calls from my father, who still cannot fathom why I would choose to live near the caboose. I get my food and read my books and stare into space. Only I do not think that is a very kind word to describe the universe. An author I read recently said a much better word for it is "heavens." The last thing this big universe amounts to is "space." I see stars, the tails of galaxies, distant black holes. But I don't see our future home. And it's become frighteningly clear to me. This IS our home.

We're not sailing toward any future planet.

And I figured it out last night while walking in the Bavarian village with P. When President Nielson hailed us as the intermediary generation, instrumental to the thriving of the future clones, I realized that he and his successors could all say that and convince everyone on board that they're still going somewhere. Even when they're not. Every dinner with Dad and it's the same answer when I ask him about the planet: "It's beautiful. I've seen pictures." Then when I ask him if I can see pictures: "Sorry hon. It's classified right now. The experts are still putting together schematics and drawing up the data for where we'll be landing. It'll come."

I don't remember much about the world. I do remember, though, once walking hand in hand with Mom by a stream. It was clear and deep. You could see fish swimming at the bottom of it. I let go of Mom's hand and bent down to touch the water, but lost my balance and fell all the way in. I remember opening my eyes underwater after hitting the bottom and sitting upright. It felt like falling into another world. The current against my face, the cold water, and the green reeds weaving through the stones; although I couldn't breathe there, I never wanted to leave. I could have been happy there forever. But of course, Mom pulled me out, and two weeks later we were aboard the Salvation. I am not convinced that there was ever anything all that wrong with that world.

I have a surprise for P. I want to surprise him with my scary theory that there is no Planet Salvation. And then I want to make that okay by telling him I love him. And that there are real mountains out there. There is real water. There is a world that maybe someday he'll get to see when he is older and he has learned how to love me back.

Reached the end of the journal. More to come in the next one.

Paul turned toward a new horizon where a distant sun shined openly on his face. Wreathes of nebulae shimmered like pillars of gems. Blinking, he thought he saw a figure dressed in a spacesuit facing it all, as usual, with her arms stretched open wide collecting the light. He could get to her if the currents directed. He could get to her maybe if he prayed for a miracle.

"The world," he said, inching closer to her side. "I can see your world, Margo."

The Observer

We went to Tommy's party on a brisk evening in October when it was starting to feel a little ghostly and haunted around the neighborhood. There was an orange tinge in the air. It smelled like hay and pumpkin spice as we passed by the local Starbucks. An androgyny draped in a sheet passed us and saluted me with a swish of an index finger, like they knew me. I'm sure I didn't know *them*.

Tommy and his wife Anna live three blocks away, so it was an easy walk, but we almost didn't go because of our highly anticipated trip to Colorado the next morning. Sarah had a lot to pack, and she's very particular and organized when it comes to trips. If we don't have everything figured out to the dime, we have to turn back, even if it means sacrificing hours of the vacay. But somehow we had the suitcases jammed and zipped by 5 p.m., free from other obligations because it was Friday, and she said, "Let's go to the party. I'm tired of worrying about tomorrow." She always wants to go on our vacations, but the night before the journey, usually recounts aloud in our bed the thousand different things that might go wrong. Flat tire. Speeding tickets. Inclement weather. Head-on collision with a rogue semi-truck. Abduction at the hands of weed-smoking vagabonds usually makes it on the list, too. I always tried to resist her fears by suggesting we go for a walk around the park, or watch a TV show on the couch, etcetera, but tonight she beat me to it. To Tommy's we'd go.

I hadn't told her about my own recent bouts of anxiety. The problem was it had nothing to do with the trip. It had nothing to do with anything, so far as I could tell. It's hard to explain. It's maybe something they'd call a "spiritual crisis" back in the day, but that might be a bit too dramatic. Today people call it low self-esteem, bad vibes, or mental dysfunction. Maybe what I'm going through has elements of all that. I haven't been able to really put my finger on it, and every time Sarah has noticed me brooding over the dishes in the kitchen with the water still running, I told her I had just gone blank. Zoned out. Nothing going on upstairs. If I could articulate it point blank, though, it would be this: college was over, marriage was underway. *Voila.* Good job secured, plus benefits. Middle-aged parents within comfortable driving distance. And yet, I don't know—it was like a specter in the sky was looking down to suggest that this was it. There wasn't much beyond this nice little package, except repetitions of the same old patterns. You better get used to it. And then one day, you'll die.

Tommy was my roommate in college who, like me, never fled the metro after graduation. Like me, he was a business major at OU. Like me, he married the girl he met at OU—Anna, Sarah's longtime sorority sister—and like me, tended to sometimes wonder if we'd already topped the apex of our lives. We don't talk about stuff like that, but every little party he throws, you can sort of feel it in the air. Tommy would be drinking beer and laughing across the room at some comment, but then turn slightly away with a subtle flash in his eyes that said: "Let me out of here."

We walked the three blocks to the house arm in arm. I carried the wine. Sarah carried a card game in her jacket pocket next to her phone.

"How long is the drive tomorrow again?"

"Ten hours. Not too bad. Why?"

"I just need to get a Spotify playlist ready. Do you have any road trip music?"

"Are you kidding? Babe, do you even *know* me? I am the king of the road trip jams."

"The fact that you said 'jams' strongly suggests otherwise."

"Bob Dylan. I'm in a Bob Dylan kind of mood."

"Who?"

"Don't even . . . "

The sunset shone down the street, painting everything orange. College kids walked down the sidewalks and older couples came in and out of different shops, peering through glass windows at rings and dressed-up manakins. I saw a window with a Christmas tree in it.

Tommy and Anna were both night owls in college, so they'd prod us to stay until at least midnight. But no, Colorado called. We'd chosen the cutest Airbnb outside of a little mountain town called Basalt, an A-frame with a deck and a loft above the kitchen. A river flowed right next to it so close you could hear it flow at night. We felt like we needed this week in the mountains all to ourselves. Our honeymoon got cut short when Sarah's dad had a stroke two days in and we had to fly back from Costa Rica. He ended up being okay, thank God, but we just didn't know for a while whether he was going to make it. That was in January. Since then, I've worked at the office, she's taught special needs kids, and the ten months have swept by without giving us a warning.

We reached their little green one-story house a block removed from the street and rapped on the door.

Frankenstein's monster answered. Sarah yelped and I flinched, but immediately remembered with a pang of remorse that we'd been summoned to a Halloween party. With all the packing for Colorado, we forgot.

"Hey, what's the deal, buddy?" said Tommy. He had the bone thing fake-sticking through his throat, the black eye shadow, and a wig on. I would have mistaken him for another person if not for his wide grin of perfect, white teeth.

"Where's your costume?"

"Oh God." Sarah was laughing now, doubled over. "You scared me."

"Sorry man, totally forgot that little detail. Plus, you know, not really a costume guy. Haha."

"Forgot? Bro it's October 29th! You didn't think it would be spooky-themed?"

We followed him into the foyer. I had to clear away some artificial cobwebs as we kicked off our shoes by the door. Anna met us at the helm of the living room dressed as . . . a vampire? I wasn't quite sure with the blood streaks at the corners of her mouth, but the cape and collar made me think she was a vampire. Our crop of frat and sorority friends sat on the L-shaped couch in the living room while others poured drinks in the kitchen, all dressed as cats or pirates or barbies or Taylor Swifts, all replicates of their college selves. I recognized everybody after a round of hellos and handshakes and side hugs, all except for one. Someone wrapped in a sheet with holes cut for the eyes, a ghost, perched on the corner of the couch. He wore a pair of worn-out Hey Dudes and jeans underneath the sheet but didn't move a muscle.

Tommy clapped me on the shoulder.

"Gonna get the game on! We'll watch *Hereditary* later." I took a couple steps forward holding my Coors light and bent my head to get a better look at the eye-holes of the ghost. There were eyes behind them, all right—little brown beads that stared right at me, unblinking but still believably human. I straightened up. Maybe it was some kind of joke. The ghost would disclaim his identity by and by and we would all get a big laugh out of it. But I'll be honest. It was a little creepy because no one else seemed to notice he was there at all.

Tommy put on the football game and sat on the couch next to Anna, leaving Sarah and me the little loveseat against the far wall, which faced our friendly Mr. Ghost.

"Who's playing?"

"It's Bedlam, babe. OU and Oklahoma State."

OU was up by ten and driving again OSU's thirty-yard line. I sipped the beer and put my arm around Sarah's shoulder and tried to pay attention to the game as everyone else settled into their spots. I couldn't help glancing back over at the ghost-dressed fellow on the arm of L-shaped couch, though. He, or she, or "it" still stared. The eyes were dark brown and opened wide. He seemed to have settled his hands on his lap. The feet were uncrossed and hanging just a couple inches above the floor. I couldn't even tell if he was breathing or not. I turned back to the game. Interception. A pick six and OSU was right back in it.

"Stupid!!"

"What just happened?"

"The quarterback threw it away."

"Oh." Sarah doesn't care about football. I usually do. I got up to get chips, bean dip, and some orange-frosted sugar cookies, and sat back down. The sheet hadn't moved during my exodus. Through my periphery vision, I could tell he was still looking right at me.

"Babe," I whispered.

"Yeah."

"That guy on the couch keeps . . . staring. Getting kind of weirded out."

"Huh?"

"The guy on the couch, damn it!"

"You don't have to cuss at me."

"I'm sorry. But you see him. He's sitting right there."

"Hon, what are you—are you talking about George? He's dressed as a strawberry shortcake."

The buffest dude in the room was indeed donned as a piece of dessert, but that was the least of my concerns.

"No, not George."

"Okay . . . a ghost? Babe, I don't see a ghost."

"What do you mean you don't see the ghost. He's sitting right there, dressed in a sheet." I was still whispering. Sarah leaned past me, scrunching her brows, and then stared quizzically at me as if it was high time I saw a neurologist.

The room erupted in cheers, and I spilled my beer. OU recovered a fumble and ran it for thirty-five yards to make it into the red zone. The guy under the sheet, though, didn't lift a finger of excitement.

At the next commercial break, I set down the beer and slipped into the restroom down the hall. There's a little blurred window in there, and the orange blob of the sun shone through its lower half, indicating dusk. As I sat on the can, tomorrow's trip no longer felt like a mental priority. I pulled out my phone and checked my email for no reason and then scrolled through Twitter and YouTube, finally watching a #fail compilation video for the next three minutes. I probably would have stayed way longer than that if someone hadn't tried to open the bathroom door. "I'll be right out!"

"That you, Jason?"

"Yup." It was George, the buff croissant.

"What're you doin' in there—jerkin' off?"

I washed my hands and looked into the mirror, which was so clean that I wondered if Tommy, a notorious domestic slob, actually ever used it. George rattled the door. My forehead suddenly popped with sweat. I put my hand on my chest. My eyes are brown but looked kind of red around the edges right then. I rubbed them and clapped my cheeks as if trying to wake up from a dream.

"You good, bro?" he asked once I came out.

"Hey man, yeah, doin' all right."

"I gotta take a major dump."

"Go crazy."

I paused for a moment in the hallway and looked at the pictures on the wall as I wiped my hands on my jeans. There were lots of wedding photos from the summer, including a few shots of the groomsmen. There I was, standing next to Tommy in a gray suit with a fresh haircut, a white smile, and every reason in the world to be happy. Sarah was in the bridal party. Her radiance came on me strong there in the hallway. Her smile made me miss her, even though she sat twelve feet away in the other room. We are all so young. The gray suits and the bright blue dresses of the bridesmaids told me that we were all at the beginning of our lives, that there was so much still to look forward to, and to see, and to do, and to be. Maybe, though, all of us in these pictures were pining for something that had already passed, partying in Tommy's living room as if this was just another semester to endure. College came and went in a flash. A portion of the crew made mad dashes to the east coast for big jobs. Others stammered after graduation and landed back with their parents, shamefaced. But a good few of us were there at Tommy's that night, making it just fine, comfortable, rich, and full.

I wiped my forehead again and returned to the living room. The ghost was still there, of course, slumped against the wall and looking like a dead body wrapped in medical clothes. It could have been a sheet-covered scarecrow for all I knew. I snagged Tommy by the Fritos in the kitchen. "Who is that?"

"Who's who?"

"Don't mess with me, bro. The ghost on the couch."

Tommy chomped on some chips and thrust his hand in for more as he surveilled. "You mean Candace? She's dressed as a sexy nurse. Not quite the same thing. She ghosts every guy she dates, though."

"Seriously, dude, don't do that to me. You see him. C'mon now."

He hesitated, blinking at me with those doleful Frankenstein eyes. "Are you okay?" he said.

"Is this a big joke that everybody else is in on? Did y'all start a group chat and orchestrate all this?"

"Bro, what are you *talking* about? I legitimately don't understand what you're saying to me right now."

At a loss, I grabbed another beer from the carton and sat next to Sarah again, pale faced. The ghost sat up now, rejecting any notions of its nonsentience, still without blinking, and leaned forward with its eyes remaining trained on mine.

"God, Sarah," I whispered through my teeth.

"Babe, what is *wrong* with you?"

"I swear on my own grave, if you're lying to me . . . if this is one of Tommy's pranks . . . "

"Lying about *what*?"

I stood up and took a step or two forward so I stood in line with this unwelcome observer, poised to strike. The girls on the couch peered up at me and Tommy just stared from the kitchen, Fritos dangling from his lip. "Who are you?" I said. I got nothing in reply except for those blank, dark eyes, wide and aimless though aimed fixedly at me all the same. "Is that you, John? I thought I saw you in the group chat. You're all playing a joke on me, yeah?"

"Jason, hey, buddy, who're you talkin' to?"

"Shut up, George."

"Damn, okay."

"I'm not kidding."

Without asking again, I shoved the ghost, hard. It was a sudden decision, and never in my life had I ever done anything like that. Sure, I'd been riled up before, and once had wanted to hit someone once. More than hit him—but that's another story.

I shoved him, but the gesture passed straight through the apparition as if he was made of mist, so I fell headfirst into the couch. My feet flew into the air and I caught myself on Claire Sully's lap. Claire screamed and spilled some wine on my head while the others on the couch rolled away in instinctual defense. My shoes were Hey Dudes shoes and my pants were light denim jeans, and when I had toppled to the floor, OU had scored a field goal and there was no ghost on the arm of the couch. George got it all on camera.

Just about everybody started laughing as I toppled to the floor. I was known to do random stuff like that from time to time. Once I face planted on the carpet and did twenty pushups at a frat party in the basement. Another time I climbed into Tommy's Christmas party through the window and threw hot chocolate packets at people. My first impulse now, though, was to stand up and scout out the ghost. I did. I peered over the edge of the couch. There was nothing there. I rushed into the kitchen and ducked underneath the table. Then I went back into the hallway and even opened the bedroom door until Tommy and Sarah grabbed me from behind. "Hey, hey, hey, brother, take it easy."

"Honey, what's wrong?"

"I saw him! You saw him, too! He was *right there in front of you!*" I tried to pull away from Tommy but caught a glance of Sarah's eyes. She looked at me like I was a stranger. A crazy man. A real wacko. I stopped then, catching my breath. "Babe," I whispered. "Can we go home?"

We left a few minutes later after I crawled back into the bathroom to straighten up under the sorry excuse that I wasn't feeling very well and hadn't been for the last week or so.

"Are you still going to Colorado?" Anna asked us on the way out.

Neither one of us answered as we walked back into the orange air, trick or treaters emerging by the dozens from their hovels, including more than a few flailing little ghosts carrying plastic jack o' lanterns.

* * *

"I've been thinking a lot, Sarah," I said the next morning. Sarah took the first leg of the drive and was frowning towards the Kansas border, sipping her coffee and staying quiet. "I've been thinking about how empty all those parties feel."

"That's really interesting, hon." I could feel her eyes on me even though I was laying my forehead against the glove compartment, and she was looking at the road. "But right now, I'm just kind of worried you have schizophrenia."

"That's not it."

"Well then I don't know what to say."

"Can you pull over?"

"What?"

"Pull over?"

"We're on the interstate."

"Please."

She slowed down and veered to a stop on the shoulder of the highway, leaning her head back against the seat and closing her eyes after snapping the Corolla into park. I sat up and took a deep breath, but it was honest to God a legit deep breath, not one of those phony ones we often use to punctuate a meaning. "They feel empty because it does always feel like someone's watching. Waiting to spoil the whole thing."

"What do you mean?"

"Don't you feel it, too?"

She threw her hands up next to her head, fingers clenched. "You're so *cryptic*! No, I don't know what you're talking about."

I almost kept trying to explain what I was feeling, that inarticulable sense that everything was already over even though life had just started, but she was looking at me with her big brown eyes, brimming, now, with tears, with all the early morning cars and trucks speeding by towards a ghost-pale horizon, and I just couldn't say anything else. Maybe I didn't see anything last night. Maybe it was a weird trick of the brain, the sum total of the angst

I'd been feeling taking on a ghostly form. Maybe it was Death, dressed up like one of the boys.

"Just don't look away for a while," I said. "Will you do that for me?"

She started crying, then—the big teardrops kind of crying, splotches of saltwater dabbling on her cardigan. I held her hand. We looked at each other for a long time until I forgot about the ghost on the couch. I forgot about everything that was going to end someday.

"Don't ever leave."

"I won't."

We switched spots. I put the car into gear, turned on Bob Dylan's "Blowin' in the Wind," and we drove to the age-old mountains.

Polaroids from Tomorrow

T he first photo from outer space or that spare dimension undiscovered by mortals arrived on a Monday when Markie was mowing his lawn, achingly slow. It was the morning after his brother's funeral. The grass was drunk with last week's flash flood, thick and mined with fresh ant hills, and Markie man was tired.

The photo wouldn't have been so weird if his mail lady hadn't already come that day and left him a pie with his trunk of condolences. The UPS delivered it, with the guy in his brown safari shorts flipping the envelope in his hand as if asking himself why *he* was the messenger of so small a memento. But he stuck it in the slate gray box, slapped down the flag after extracting the care package Markie was sending to Grandma, and toiled down the driveway with Markie peering after him beneath the ball cap.

The swooning type of sorrow made mowing tough when it hit. But it was better than the armchair by the window. Better than a fifth cup of coffee and a smidgen of whiskey. God, Jeremy. Why'd you have to die, in this lifetime out of all the ones you could have chosen? And from a simple wrong turn. One wrong turn, Jeremy once said, will put you in a maze that only God can save you from. Just one.

But now, there was the envelope—maybe a late bloomer of a distant cousin sharing his grievance. Or asking for money. Randy. That was the cousin always peddling for cash. *Dear cousin Marcus, I need help, please, get me funds! I won't ever ask again . . .*

The envelope, though, when he got it from the box and looked down the street, finding it chippering with locusts and totally empty, didn't have a return address. And it was white as whipped cream. He was almost sorry to sully the cover. He opened it up, noting how it was marked for him, and pulled out a polaroid of a girl. Not a girl he recognized. She was auburn-haired and smiling with a cup of coffee in front of her on a coffee shop table, arms folded in front of her with one hand cupping an elbow, dressed in a black turtleneck. The edges were faded into white, and her face was faded into white, too, but not in a way that faded the details, the ridges of the sweater at the forearms, the ivory teeth barely biting the bottom lip. Secret admirer? That was a first. He was thirty years old in December and hadn't had the pleasure since college.

It was enough to make him abandon the mower in the middle of the jungle of his front yard and retreat to the living room, where he went ahead and brewed that fifth cup and sat down in his armchair by the window with the picture still snug between thumb and index.

Not every day does this happens to a dude. Not every *decade* does this happen to a dude. Of all the lifetimes he could've occupied, in this one he'd been nudged with beauty in polaroid form. The stuff of college dorms, forgotten desk drawers.

Who is she? And is the UPS driver an angel? God with a grin behind the truck?

Coffee now ready, dripping on the stove, made him plant the photo gingerly on the sill and get his mug from the counter.

Tomorrow? Tuesday. Working from home through Wednesday. Nephew with a baseball game on Thursday night. Jeremy's kid played summer league. *Please,* he though. *Let's not get all sappy right now.*

He was the saddest he'd ever been in his life, but there was some good in that. For one, he wasn't really worried about anything. Seven days earlier, he worried that he'd left the door unlocked and that the IRS might find a miffed comma in his returns. He worried that a sidelong glance he'd given to the barista handing him his coffee saw him as a creep. (She didn't.) When Jeremy took his wrong turn, Markie froze in the kitchen as he scrubbed a plate, and by nightfall, still standing there with the phone buzzing in its hung-up static on the counter, wondered if he would move even if a truck busted through the wall. He wondered if he'd do anything ever again, or just stand like this in the silence with the moonlight coming in like it always did. Pure, mercurial sadness. A confidential brush with the Real.

Well. He wished a near death experience would have sufficed to get him feeling again.

Twenty years ago, they'd been sitting at the dinner table about to finish their bowls of chili, Friday night special. Markie, ten, Jeremy, seventeen. Mom. Dad. Mom asked Jeremy how his day was as he picked the final tomato from the bowl. He used a spare hand to brush his bangs from his head and glanced sidelong at her. "Fine."

"That's it?"

Dad put the spoon down, twiddled his calloused fingers, quivering down to the mustache. "Boy I don't know what's gotten into you, but you'd better quit hunching over the table like that and start *talking* to us."

"Honey. What's going on?"

"Let's go look at the universe, Markie man. Take a walk maybe." He nodded to Markie as Markie swallowed and went cold, not sure what side to take. "I'm going to take Markie up on the roof."

"No, you're going to sit here and *talk* to us. Your mother asked how your day was."

"What's in a day? You know?" He shrugged, slipping Markie a sad wink. "There's nothing in a day."

"What does that mean?"

"You don't want to know."

"Maybe we *would*, if you *talked* to us."

"The days are long. They are slow. They are rapid. They race. I wonder, Mom, about enlisting. Would it add some purpose to my bones?"

"Enlisting in what?"

"The army."

"You want to join in the army now?"

"If I quit drugs, maybe."

"WHAT?"

Later that night they looked at the universe from the roof, or the fragment they could detect.

"Don't be like me," was all the big brother said, who lay on his side, teasing a shingle. "Markie man. Don't be like me. Okay?"

Markie decided to leave the mowing for another day, and without putting the machine under his porch, drove to the café on Brunson and Fifth for a late-day reprieve. He'd stuck the mystery polaroid in his pocket, and his drive over there was a mixture of memory. He remembered his brother, who studded his past like railway spikes one uses to build a semblance of a life, the kind that, once expired, have you looking for another foreman who can tell you how to keep laying track. Who isn't there. And he remembered this auburn-haired girl who he had never met but now flooded through his mind as if she was next up in taking the helm of his life. Always hiding in the bright shadows, beaming at him.

So, his surprise, then, when he walked into the café and noted how familiar it was with its scratched up wooden floor, crusty brick walls decorated with paintings of trees each in their seasons, to see the spitting image of the girl sitting by the window and looking out on the sidewalk.

He ordered his coffee first and waited for it by the countertop, feeling the polaroid in his pocket after he took out his wallet to pay. Time for the subtle double take. Yep. It was her. Down to the black sweater and final freckle, it was her.

"Here you go."

More black coffee? At this hour of the day?

"Thanks."

And now what? He sat down on the usual brown couch by the window on the other side of the door so he was facing her. She glanced up from a book, one not pictured in his polaroid, and flipped a page, leaning her cheek on the heel of her palm. Well. Was he supposed to talk to her? Had he been sent a polaroid from the future? He piddled with the coffee lid and looked out the street, the tart flumes rising to meet him, bringing his senses front and center, denying him the notion that he might be dreaming. He thought about work the next day, the baseball game on Thursday, the strange way life just sort of moves on after the wrong turns, after death. The girl proffered another glance at him; he wouldn't stare, though—he didn't want to be that guy.

He'd seen people sitting like this at the café a million times over the past five years. Living here, he became one of them, hiding behind a screen—that polite film of distance. It's common law these days to speak only with the barista and then hunker in your corner.

He stood up. She looked up. He turned sideways and peeked down the empty corridor of the shop for no reason. And he stepped forward in a way that could've either been toward her or the door. Outside, when he was a ways down the walk and had clambered back into the car, he rooted in his pocket for the picture. Odd. It wasn't there.

Randy, his neighbor, was setting his garbage out on the curb when he got out of the car and back into the balmy evening, reeling with confusion. Randy, a hulking Vietnam vet who donned the black hat and spat tobacco into the sewage grate, said, "Looks like you gave your lawn a mohawk, champ!" He didn't know about Jeremy.

"Oh." Markie tried to laugh and scratched his arm, and added, "Got some coffee. Gonna finish up now." Randy nodded, resituating his cap and rummaging at his feet to retrieve his hose. He tested the trigger, so water spurted and nodded at his clean-cut yard. "One thing I told Jan. Can't let the yard get crazy. She said that if you can't keep you're yard clean then chances are you can't keep your life clean, either." Randy, who was not an asshole, rubbed his jaw and qualified, "Not that your yard looks bad, buddy. Heh heh. Just something she used to say. Anyway. Anyway."

Jeremy didn't even go inside before hauling the mower out, and managed to finish weed-eating by dusk, when the chirpers were yowling in the branches and the summer night was a little bit cooler. He went inside and poured the rest of his brewed coffee into the sink, blinking at the little folding table he had set up in the space between kitchen and the living room. And then he went to bed.

The second photo came before the mail the next morning. And this time it was a polaroid of an old man in suit with paint flecked all over it in the middle of applying a coat of paint with a roller on the outside of a Mexican restaurant. Bright yellow and green. He didn't recognize him. But he knew the building. It was El Chico's on Eighth and Main, not far from the coffee shop with the auburn-haired mystery. But he had to work. He set the picture on the kitchen counter as he reapplied coffee to his nervous system, ate two eggs, scratched his puzzled head, wondered if this was a trick of the subconscious or if an anonymous pal had actually figured out time travel. Two days after the funeral and his PTO was exhausted. So, he worked for two and a half hours, took an early lunch, and cast his lot with El Chico.

It was another hot beater of a day, but the painter rolled away in the shadowed side of the building, true to the polaroid. Markie walked past him on his way into the restaurant, but like the day before, didn't say hello. Telling a stranger that you carried a picture of them in their pocket didn't feel like the way to start the conversation. So he went inside, got his basket of chips and little cup of salsa, and pulled out the polaroid to give it another scientific examination. Was it time to handle it with gloves and take it to a personal investigator? He bet he'd stump the detectives with this one. But it didn't matter, because as soon as he'd eaten his churro and empanada, a modest meal for the sedentary man, the picture up and vanished again, and the painter was packing up his Ranger in the parking lot, job now finished.

The next week included photos of a Latvian woman who ended up checking him out at Target, a barista who whipped out the best latte he had ever tasted, a construction worker who the cosmic photographer had caught on a smoke break, helmet off and bald head gleaming in the sun. And on Sunday night, one week after the funeral, one week of these polaroid premonitions that never produced a single conversation, Markie got a photograph of the last person in the world he expected. Someone he knew. Someone who knew him. Someone dead. Jeremy. And not just Jeremy, but Jeremy sitting at that rugged table of his that stood between the kitchen and the living room. His brother had a finger looped through the handle of the mug and was looking head on at the photographer with that half smile that could always be interpreted as a lament, a surrender to sadness.

"Jeremy?"

The last conversation they shared had been at that table just two weeks ago. Jeremy was visiting from Knoxville, where he worked at a pawn store, among other secret professions, and although Mom told him to fly out for the Fourth, he decided to make the drive. His job was terrible, he said in a call to Markie the day before he drove up. "I'd take McDonalds over this place. Who knows? Maybe I won't leave the hometown after the holiday. I'm sort of in trouble, Markie."

But he did leave the hometown after the holiday. He took a few wrong turns that Markie and anyone who knew him knew were going to take him to Little Rock, where he had a girlfriend and some no-good buddies who always seemed to suck him into their orbit. His ex-wife, Cassie, showed up at the funeral and stood in the middle of the aisle in the church for four minutes before the service started, turning left, turning right, and finally sitting by herself almost at the very back of the sanctuary. Markie tried not to look back at this woman in black, still beautiful, alone and without her new husband.

"I think we could make things work," Jeremy said in that last conversation, talking about Cassie in a moment of surprising reflection. "If she'd just . . . see things from my perspective." He shook his head, rubbing his jawline, now stubbled. "Don't be like me, Markie man."

They had always been very different people. So why the admonition not to follow suit? Markie adored his brother. Jeremy could have hijacked the Pentagon and Markie still would have seen him as a patriot. So, it was always so weird that Jeremy always felt like he had to temper his brother's love with the "truth." He could remember the litany of crimes that undercut him. *Struggling with the drugs, little bro. Don't do drugs, Reagan's woman said. Well. Made me want to do 'em all the more. Don't you understand who I really am? You know I've taken every single kind—please don't be like me. I found some magazines under Dad's workbench. Listen to me, and don't forget it. Don't ever look at them. And I know what you're thinking: Well, NOW I'm gonna go look. But listen. Please don't give any of that shit the light of day. It'll screw you over for life. Do you understand?*

Markie sat down at the table and leaned into the silence. His eyes brimmed and his neck hotly trembled, like it was being fracked.

"Jeremy?" he whispered. "Are you here, man?"

No, I'm not here. But you're here. Took a wrong turn, didn't I. Couldn't see what's been coming after me my whole life. Took a wrong turn into the opposite lane. I wasn't the only one killed. Did you know that? Of course, you know that. And still you spoke words at the funeral. You're a better man than me. You're holy. So holy. I don't mean that as a joke. So don't be like me, Markie man. It just takes one too many drinks, one too many pills, one too many glances until your wife notices you looking under Dad's workbench, until you slam right into what's been coming at your face your whole life. Don't be like me.

"Then what am I supposed to do?"

Remember the pictures?

"Yes."

Talk to any of them?

"No. I didn't know how."

Hmm.

"Teach me."

How to talk to people?

"Everything."

I can't teach you anything. You know it already. You just don't know you know. I just want to see you happy. You know? I want to see you with a girl who gets you. She's out there. What if you've already seen her around? Who knows. Maybe you've already seen everyone, you just haven't realized it.

"I want to see *you*."

I know. And I'm sorry. For everything. But I made some choices. Some wrong turns. You haven't made many turns at all. That's how we're different. And because I told you not to follow me, you decided not to go anywhere. That's what kills me. You didn't travel far for college, and landed an easy re-mote gig in marketing and live just a mile from the parents. Nothing wrong with that, by the way. But I know how this goes. You'll keep wondering about the road. About what could've been. Just because you shouldn't be like me doesn't mean you can't start choosing. Take wrong turns . . . better than not turning at all. But you're better. Better than me, Markie . . .

"No, I'm not."

See ya, buddy. You got this, bud. I'm just a snapshot away . . .

He slept with his head on the table and woke up confused about where he was, with his laptop leaning against the wall. The polaroid was gone, and he was already tempted to think he dreamed up the whole thing in some post-funeral hallucination, if such a thing existed. One thing was sure, though. He needed coffee again, and soon.

The street was almost empty on Fifth and Brunson, but a red Mazda was parked in front of the glass windows, and when he walked in, the espresso smells billowing at him, he noticed the auburn-haired woman sitting at her usual spot by the window, reading again, brows knitted. She couldn't be bothered.

He walked home with her number in his pocket after a long internal debate about whether he should even go up to her at all. But he did. He studied the number for a long time before picking up his phone and making the call.

He got no mail that day.

The Fisher's Man

At first it was just the fisherman on the river, up to his waist in the water. He sent long casts out into the current with his fishing pole and slowly reeled back his catch. I was standing on a little knoll farther upstream but could see him well. I could see his green waders, his broad-brimmed straw hat, and the cigarette in his mouth producing a thin trail of smoke. The water was dark. You could see nothing beneath its surface. All you could see were the ripples caused by the little worm at the end of the fisherman's line, and the evening sun laying golden fingers on the far bank.

I did not know where I was. I stooped to touch the water at the base of my feet. It was not as cold as I might have expected. And it mercurially clung to my hand when I drew it out, like it was asking me to stay. The air was silent. All silent, except for the fisherman's bait making soft plops in that slow, deep, broad current of the river.

Something told me I knew this man who so passionately fished. Had I seen him somewhere before? Was he an old visitor in my dreams come to haunt me one more time? I didn't know. There was no telling. All I knew was that I saw him raising his big arms overhead to cast, time and time again.

He brought in a fish. It was a trout, violent red. He tucked it in a basket by his side. At the next cast, he brought in a golden bass. Next, a small marlin. And finally some grubby catfish, a wriggling green eel, a cantankerous gar.

He caught each one without upset. He tucked them all in the basket like they were books being put on a long shelf.

162

How many fish he caught I will never know. It must have amounted to more than fifty. For a long time, he caught nothing. But he never altered the rhythm of casting and reeling. Not once did he take a break. Not once did he raise his shadowed face to look at me standing there overhead, trying to articulate the frontier before me.

Beyond the river there was a wall of pine and spruce. The front trees were ignited by the twilight. The spaces between the trees made columns of golden light but exposed no living thing in their ranks. The rest of the forest was dark. A mystery. I wanted to throw a stone into the river to see what kind of sound it might make. I wanted to swim in the river, but felt like this was not a river for throwing stones into or for swimming in. One needed green waders and a broad-brimmed straw hat to get into the river.

As I was looking across the water, a figure appeared on the opposite bank, right across from the fisherman. I could not see his face, but he wore a gray trench coat with a gray hood over his head. I had no idea where he had come from. The only explanation is that he just stepped out of the trees. There was no other place he could have been hiding. But he took out his own fishing pole, and after tying a silver hook to the end of the translucent line, made casts into the river. He made long casts, so long that the hook fell right next to the fisherman. I mean right next to him. The man on the other side of the river would raise his pole over one shoulder and loft his missile with perfect precision. But the fisherman did not seem to notice the hook. Maybe he did not want to notice. He kept up his own fishing. He drew in trout, salmon, cod, and narwhal, even a small whale, and kept tucking them in his wondrous little basket at his hip. But still the man on the other side of the river made his generous casts, pulling in no catch himself. They must have been at this for hours. Neither one showed fatigue. At least, not for a very long time.

It was only when the fisherman had caught absolutely nothing for about three hundred casts in a row that he began taking longer to reel the line in and hesitated before making the next throw. But the man on the other side of the river did not stop making his perfectly precise casts. Soon, the fisherman tucked his pole into his belt and let the line sidle in the shallows. He put his hands in his pockets and watched the man on the bank cast out to him. The hook twinkled like an ornament in the heavy sun.

It wasn't long after the fisherman seemed to really notice the forest beyond the river and the sweep of wind that seemed to come from its general direction that he reached down and caught the line of the other man's fishing pole and curled his finger around the large silver hook. He paused like this as if asking, silently, if this was what he was supposed to be doing. The man in the gray hood gave a single nod and tugged.

The fisherman knelt by the water, but the other did not reel. Then the fisherman took off his waders, but the other did not reel. The fisherman took off his broad-brimmed straw hat. It floated downstream. Still the stranger did not reel. Finally, the fisherman stood up and held his basket holding all his many fish before him in the water. He looked at it for a very long time with the silver hook still on his finger. The other waited. The sun was so bright on his face. Maybe he was part of the sun; he was so bright.

Finally, the fisherman pushed the basket away from himself and watched it float after his hat and waders in the dark current. And, facing the man on the other side of the bank, he fell forward into the water.

The gray man reeled him in as easy as though there was nothing on the line at all. When the fisherman crawled on the opposite shore, he looked different. Bigger, maybe. Fuller. Like he had adopted a new kind of strength in the undertow.

When he disappeared into the trees, I thought the gray man would follow him, since they exchanged words like old friends. Then I would wake up or learn a big truth and realize where I was, and things would go back to normal. But the man on the other side of the river walked farther down the shore with his pole until he was right across from me. He reached back with his bright gray arms and cast out, so the silver hook landed in the very spot I'd dipped my hand.

Send a Surfboard

T he healing coach or whatever to write about what's going on, to do an exercise that would make things good for the soul, or something. I don't know what to write, but all can think to do is write to you, Jimmy. Don't u remember me? We had a talk that once when I lived in La Mirada. We had a talk about the weather, and then you said something like you can do or be anything you want to be. And that meant something.

I don't got your address. I don't know how I'd ever be able to get that. But maybe they have ways to get this stuff to you. Well, things aren't so bad. All things considered, I guess. This place, my mother put me here. And well, there's this open sitting area where you can look out windows and see some other guys playing basketball, meditating, or whatever. They can't smoke, duh. But that's all right—sort of why we are all here.

A bit about me, and not just the nice stuff. There is a point in the morning when I start to itch all over, and sweat, and then pace the room, and I'm wondering if you have got any tips on that. If it gets bad enough they will put me in room smaller than a cell you would find in a jail. And there is nothing in this room. It is just white, and empty, with a lightbulb sticking out of the ceiling. That make it sound like this a bad place. I was trying to tell you about the trees outside, and even the beach—yeah, man, they let us go to the beach at times to have a lil looksee, and that's pretty cool.

You tol me I cud be somebody, and to perk up, Jimmy, and I've been thinking of those words a lot recently. I don't got a cell phone in here, and some ladies from a church bring by a bunch of books sometimes, but you know, I don't read them. Not many of the people here read them. I saw some try, but they always seemed to end up holding their head in their hand and bouncing the book off their knee. I hope someday I can like reading again. We didn't talk about when we had our little talk in La Mirada, but I used to really like to read. I couldn't tell you what books I read. *Harry Potter* and stuff like that.

But I was saying that you told me I had the potential needed to be someone good. And nobody ever told me that, you know? Maybe my mother did, but can't remember. No, here's what it is. She told me I was good, I just didn't know it. But you, Jimmy, all suited up, looking at the sun as you straightened your tie, you saw me and nodded and said it was a real nice day. And you popped me a twenty. Thank you for that. And said your name was Jimmy. And I said yessir it's nice. If I could surf I would be surfing. And you said why aren't you then? And I said I don't know how. And you said learn then, but I said I didn't have no board to learn on, and no stupid money to buy one with.

Then you kicked out the big guns, Jimmy. Shoot, now I know why I'm writing to you. It's a lot of sweat coming down this pencil now sir, but I just have to say it—you give me five hundred dollars to go buy a surfboard, or put down some rent, or get a haircut—and you put that hand on my shoulder and said I could do it, I could be somebody . . . first twenty bucks, then something lots more, but you know sir I didn't spend that five hundred dollars on nothing good, just more of the strong stuff, stronger than I ever had in my life, and it almost kilt me! That's what made them put me in here, and I for real don't want to go back out there like that again.

So I'm sorry. But sorry don't cut it, Jimmy. I've said the word so many times I'm sick of it. I want to take sorry by the neck and strangle it in the weeds. A thousand sorrys later and I'm still pacing the floor and sweating and wanting the stuff I shouldn't want.

Do you know what it's like to have a sad gut feeling and to hate feeling this way but knowing that it was you who put it there in the first place, like swallowing a bowling ball? It goes in, but it never comes out. And so I go out into the little grove of trees they have by the compound and stick my fingers into the dirt and try to get that deep sadness out of me and into the ground, and sometimes it works a little bit, but not a lot. I still sweat through the fingers, still wish I was back home in Orange County, still wish I'd bought a surfboard with all that cash.

So tonight, you know what I'm going to do? I'm going to go down to the beach and sit there with some of the lads and try to bury myself into the horizon. Have one of those transcendent experiences, you know. I'll ask Marty if it's cool to get in the shallows. I won't have no surfboard, Jimmy, but I'll pretend, since that's why I'm best at, and try to get some practice in anyway. You're a good man, a real decent man, and hope this can get out to you—but honestly don't send money. Come out yourself and have a talk with me again. Or if you can't do that, maybe send a surfboard.

The Blues

A red cherry almost too bright to be real glistened like a Christmas ornament on the railing of the lodge of the Big Wolf ski resort. It was like
a speck of blood in the blue shadow of snow, with its question mark stem
budding from its upper dimple.

And it was the cherry that caught Tony's eye when he waddled over to
the ramp for a break, Britney swishing through snow powder on her board
behind him, feeling that early brunt of adrenaline that he hoped would get
him through the whole day. Britney had wanted to *ski* at first, but when
they got there, she decided snowboarding was more of her vibe. She hadn't
graduated from the bunny slopes and didn't seem to want to.

"Tony, we gotta get a picture! Before it snows. It's gonna snow right?
God, I hate this."

He half fell on a wet bench, still pumped from the steep blues he'd been
courting out there on the mountain; no black diamonds yet, but who knew?
This was real powder, the best drenching the mountain range had seen in
a decade. The resort, including the platform of the ski lodge, bustled with
international color and creed despite the pain it was to drive all the way up
the mountain. A Korean family went up on the lift behind a lone business-
man nursing his wounds over a bad deal. The college dropout danced on
the moguls, blonde locks flowing as he got air and ducking low when he
lucked on a stretch of fresh pow.

But what *was* it about the cherry? It wasn't an abandoned tangerine
or discarded from somebody's limeade. It was an artifact put there but that
no one else seemed to see. It was nothing. It was nothing and he noticed it.

Britney sat next to him, leaning her board against the rail so the cherry wobbled, and punched him in the arm. "Photo time!"

She tripped out of the snowboard and sat down on the rail after sweeping the cherry off right off the ledge and into the snow ten feet down below.

He snapped the pictures of her holding the snowboard with her tinted goggles still on, silently beaming. Her lips cherry red.

"Are you ready to go?" she asked.

"We've only been here an hour, babe."

"I mean . . . "

"I'm going to go up a couple more times at least, if that's cool with you."

Britney nodded with a huff and a shrug and carried the snowboard inside the lodge. "Let's leave before the storm!"

Christmas Day was four weeks away to the day; Tony, who worked and did well on Wall Street, never missed the countdown. Halfway up to the slope, just a mediocre blue, he saw the storm clouds Britney had talked about make black globules against the peak; the skiers and snowboarders were mice running down the mountain's scarred curtains of white, trying to get away from quickening doom.

He remembered his own phone in his pocket and figured that he should probably snap a shot of the glory, but his hands were comfortable in the gloves and he didn't want to incline his body on the lift to risk slipping out of the seat.

The pine trees were Christmas nettle on the incline, giving glimpses of untrodden trails through their mixed branches; he didn't think anyone would ski through those perilous columns, swishing back and forth with grace, but towards the top of the lift, a woman in a blue snowsuit proved him wrong.

He had to look hard to keep track of her bouncing, calibrated form, but it was an unmistakable dance of skill. She ducked and flew. Then she aborted and veered, left leg strained and locked so she could avoid a small family of baby spruces. When he had to turn around, she was making a tapestry of the tree trunks. The invisible thread on her tail made zig zags, wrapping up the forests in twin ski paintbrushes. He could almost *see* the design of her path. And then she was home running out in the open with the ski poles tucked behind her, easily and swiftly redefining the hashed-up slope already cut to ribbons by traditional skiers like *him*.

He wouldn't try to copy her trail—it was already forged. This was the final run of the day, but he had an odd peace about things on the way down. There was a peace in knowing mountains like these existed way deeper beyond the touch of other people. He did venture into the outer seam of the forests, even cut dangerously close to a gully jammed with drifts, but he leaned on his thirty-year-old thighs and, by the grace of the mountain's magnetism, broke out into the newly started snowstorm.

The wind stirred tufts and columns of crystal all up and down the mountain, and along with the fanfare of snowfall, blinded Tony and put him at the mercy of the natural order. And it got colder too. It got so cold that his beard froze in a glaze of sweat. But he'd seen the woman in blue before the storm, the weaver who had redeemed the day, and he was imitating the art in his own turns and glides, and would be okay, now, if he didn't get a chance to go up on the mountain again. And he *wouldn't* have another chance.

He came to a stop at the foot of the slope as a loudspeaker roosted under the corner eave of the lodge called for all skiers to come in from the mountain—that the lift would close until the storm had safely passed. Tony snapped the skis off and looked down at his feet to find the cherry he'd seen on the railing when it was still sunny, spinning like a mad top from the storm.

He picked it up. But it wasn't a cherry at all. It was a *Christmas* ornament—a sleek clump of gaudy tin. It turned out that people were throwing them on the trees from the lift, and with the storm, all the fetters and tinsel and aluminum blobs made a commercial foam at the foot of the mountain. It probably wasn't even the original cherry. In fact, dozens of artificial fruits and trinkets rolled past his feet, even hitting him on the head and shoulders like a bad parody of the snowfall.

"Tony!"

He'd gripped the ornament a little too tightly, though, and it cracked in his bare hand.

The God's-Eye Perspective
of Young Bear

B ear got the drone in the yearly family Dirty Santa gift exchange and given that he was sixteen and delighted by all things military adjacent, he tucked the gift behind his considerable girth and miraculously evaded theft.

It was a straightforward gadget, as straightforward as such gadgets can be, with wispy little blades and shiny obsidian legs for landing, and a camera that could hook up to your phone to document the world below.

It being Christmas and all, and the fact that they were at Grandpa's sprawling ranch house with its million crannies of expensive mini statues on coffee tables and window stands, he just *had* to go out to the pasture to give the thing a proper whirl after the last gift was unwrapped.

Christmas at the ranch was always a good old time, for sure, flooded with the usual cousins and that aura of celebration and cheer that virtuous aunts and mothers are particularly expert at inducing, but the crop of cousins was now at that precarious age where they were too cool to have the typical forms of fun. And apparently that included flying a dope new drone, courtesy of a mysterious benefactor.

While the fam congratulated Bear on his new gift, they didn't trail him when he slipped outside to test the Orwellian device. The other teenagers had since slithered into the game room to worship the Wii.

And Bear's dad didn't see him leave the house or he might have accompanied him out to the back pasture, or maybe the unknown gift giver should have come forward to teach the young buck how to figure out how to set it up. But no one came out along with him, and it was that point in the afternoon where the long dwindle of energy really started to take its hold on anybody over the age of forty-three, which happened to be about three-fourths of the household population.

So Bear took his drone out to the pasture, opening the rusty cattle guard gate, which he danced across like an acrobat, and jogged through the crusty Johnson grass until he reached the clearing that was so neatly hedged by a forest of oaks, elms, pecan, invasive cedar trees, and wreaths of green briar.

He had the remote control with him, along with his smartphone, which he could put at the top of the controls so he could see the perspective of the drone. When he got to the middle of the clearing, he stamped his feet on the ground because it was getting pretty chilly, despite it being sunny and mid-afternoon, and set the mechanical creature daintily on the rigid blades of grass.

Part of him did feel a little sheepish for being so eager to try out the new toy, but he'd been watching YouTube videos of drone footage recently, avid as a sportsman, and up to that point had seen radical vistas of Niagara Falls, the Redwoods, the Saharan Desert, Calcutta, NYC, and the Rocky Mountains. The drone represented man's final dominion over nature, so far as he was concerned. Who wouldn't want a miniature satellite at one's command, or to rise above the earth with the eye of an eagle and fly like Icarus, only to have one's feet still safely plugged into the clay of the earth?

He mainly thought a drone made rad videos, and the buzz of the drone made him feel like he could be conducting some secret operation in eastern Europe, infiltrating the Soviets or something like that.

It took a while to get the drone up and running. First it popped up like a jack-in-the-box and fell on its side. He was more gingerly with the controls after that and got it to whir and hover about five feet off the ground. The camera was connected to his phone, now, too, so he could see its limited view of the patch of hoar-frosted grass beneath it.

He eased the right knob upward and got the drone up above the level of the trees, then let it hesitate in mid-air to determine its trajectory. North it was, toward unoccupied territory.

A cluster of cows dawdled on the edge of the clearing while Bear made his calculations, curious no doubt about the faint buzzing contraption in the air, flicking their tails on their haunches and blinking at their invader. Bear didn't see them, though. He had no time to see them! For the drone was zooming like a robotic bird across the world of trees and hay bales and cow patties, fast as the speed of sound, and now it was zooming back, obedient as a hound dog with a duck in its jowls and was finally set again to rest above the ranch house and its assembly of tiring family members within.

Bear paused at this juncture, wondering if he shouldn't zoom in a bit closer on the familiar view, which now looked totally alien through the new angle, and see if he couldn't locate Misty the cat by the barn.

Misty did come out, but then sped under the house when she detected the ominous presence above her, so Bear zoomed himself up and tottered over the ring of cars parked chain-link style along the roundabout.

The cows ventured a bit closer in the meadow, but he still didn't look their way, give them due. He discovered that he could zoom all the way to the ground on the phone and was pleased by the clarity of the picture. There were the front steps of the porch, newly stained and gleaming, with the knots of brown tangled weed curling along the base of the brick wall.

This was a cool gift. Who could deny it? He figured he could drone his way all the way to town and see what was up, or zoom like a metaphorical fly on the wall, witnessing the hidden crannies of the universe. Then he could record everything and announce his findings on YouTube. That's what you were typically supposed to do, anyway.

After about five minutes of exploring the ranch house, Bear started to retrieve the drone but soon noticed two figures at the back of the house, right by the whirring heating and air conditioner units. It was his Uncle Freddie and . . . was that his mom?

The red dress and Freddy's bright heavy green coat seemed to affirm that yes, his mother and his father's brother were smooching heavily by the heater, apparently oblivious to surveillance, whilst the rest of the family, Bear's unwitting pop among them, still lounged in the house.

They made quick work of it and didn't do anything gross. They just made out passionately like a pair of teens and then sort of fell into each other's arms, probably saying something like, "Welp, we did it again . . . we've been doing this dance for so long . . . every Christmas we find a way to get a little bit of alone time, find this secret spot at the ranch house no one else can see, and get our ten minutes of love in."

Freddie was a landscaper from Tulsa and Bear's family lived a comfortable two hours south of him. His mom, come to think of it, had far too many doctor appointments in Tulsa.

When they went back inside, on opposite ends of the house, suggesting strategy, Bear brought the drone back to the meadow and grabbed it out of midair. It was only until he shut it off and wrangled his phone from the controls that he realized he had indeed filmed the debacle. The video was stored in his phone, all 89 seconds of it.

He watched it again to make sure he'd seen right, and yes, he had, and then stood there in the meadow with the cows suspiciously close to him wondering what in the sam hill to do next.

He started back in a numb trot but then hesitated at the first cow patty he encountered, and investigated the drone in his hand as if he was holding a key to the universe, an eyeglass that could detect the good, bad, and the ugly crevasses of the world without discrimination.

He walked back to the ranch house after pausing by the barn door to look at the cat rub its haunches against the tin gate and mew at him through a pair of green Christmas eyes, then trod up the back steps and slipped into the kitchen, virtually unnoticed by the two dozen family members who had somewhat rejoined in the living room to peruse the last year's trove of gossip.

"Well, I wouldn't put it past the kid, and you know I invited him here, but I figured with everything goin' on with Joan he wouldn't wanna bother . . . kid never seemed to want to be bothered, you know."

"You talkin' about Ricky? How's he doin'?"

"Not great. Checked him back into rehab for the fortieth time, but we're hopin' it does him good this time around, since, you know, he said he was serious about changing and whatnot."

"Shame he couldn't be with the family for Christmas."

"A damn shame!"

This exchange happened mostly between Bear's mother and uncle, the very ones who the drone had detected committing what seemed like straightforward infidelity, but they chatted now like they were mere acquaintances who had a yearly duty to somewhat catch each other up on the basics of their lives.

Grandpa came through in his starchy blue Wrangler shirt, slightly bow legged with a handlebar mustache curving against a cherry-red smile, and patted Mom on the shoulder as he reached for his red solo cup of wassail. The younger batch of cousins moused through the grownups with their helicopters and nerf guns, overturning just a couple of chairs, and vanished into the game room.

Bear, of course, didn't really know where to go at this point. He was too sick to his stomach to eat anything, couldn't manage looking at any one person, almost as if the knowledge would spill out of his eyes, or was obviously inscribed on his cherubic cheeks of marred innocence. And yet, before he could go anywhere or deposit the drone in a safe corner away from the corruptible reach of man, Dad popped out of the restroom, clapping his hands dry, and noticed him standing by the door with the drone in hand.

"Hey!" Dad punched him playfully on the arm. "I've been looking for you. We should go try that out. I'm pretty shocked your uncle didn't steal it from you."

Bear tried to gently protest and go, "Ah, well, I's thinkin' about maybe shooting some hoops," but he and Dad were out the door in the outdoor quiet before he could. "Let me see that." Dad, peering beneath his camo hat, snapped out his Oakleys and weighted the small drone in his palm, flicking the wings and making interested expressions with his lips and eyebrows.

"Wonder who got this one," he muttered. "Again, probably your uncle. When we were kids we'd make paper airplanes and model helicopters and would take the engines out of the mowers and put 'em on our bikes and ride 'em around the pastures out here."

"Really?"

"Yup. So how's it work?"

They ventured a little ways into the backyard as Bear showed him how the phone could hook up to the drone and how you controlled it, up, down, lateral, speed, angle.

"Dang, that's somethin' else."

Bear handed over the controls to Dad and watched him levitate the drone so it hovered five feet above the ground.

"How far up can it go? Oh, says here. Three hundred feet?"

"Yep. Hey Dad?"

"Ope, there it goes! Shoot, that's awesome, dude." Dad was looking at the screen of the phone now, shifting the drone well above the ranch house, suddenly absorbed in the image. "I think we gotta get a license to handle this thing, though . . ."

Bear leaned over to check out the perspective. There was the ranch house, same as he'd seen it out in the pasture with the mooing cows, only now there wasn't anybody hiding out by the heat and air units. There were just the figures of a man and his tongue-tied son, standing side by side in the wide open, and that rusty tin roof of the old house where generations had gathered and would gather many times again.

God only knew what they were doing inside, and what was really going on in their heads. Drones can't pick up such things, unfortunately.

Stop, Light

The stoplight on Gray and Lone gives me enough time to glance over and see the drip-dripping water falling off the side of a green dumpster by the Kwik Trip gas station. It's just enough time to see the morning sun catch the murky drops and almost hold them there.

It's just enough time for me to roll down the window and breathe in the morning before getting to the office, and see the woman in baggy cargo pants, tight tank top, and pink crocs with a shade of hair of similar hue take a drag on her cigarette with a spare arm crossed over her stomach; it's enough time for her to cross one leg over the other in front of the dumpster and hide her face whilst scratching her pink head with the index holding the cigarette. It's even enough time to see her cry, like she thinks she's invisible to the traffic. And yet gleaming, along with the falling drops of trash water—she is gleaming, and smoking, and then puts her smoke out and hops into this ancient Corolla with a license plate from a state I never think about.

It's enough time, if you can believe it, for a couple of construction workers to walk up to the dump and toss their McDonalds bags in, swishing their hands clean and tipping their hats against the sun, discussing the job of the day. And they're gone, now, too, in trucks almost too big for the road, bumbling east to a project.

It's also barely enough time for the gas station clerk to sneak out the backdoor, handling a heavy black trash bag by the blue loops and hauling it hence with a grunt. *Man*, I have to think as the kid swings twice his weight into the dump—*he must do this many, many times a day.* And still that water drips from the dumpster's handle.

It's not enough time to stay there all day—just enough for the cruel honk of a horn behind me as the light on Gray and Lone turns green, and we all speed forward without much space to give, like little drops falling, gleaming, smoking, to end up in a puddle most of us might wish to miss.

But on the way home at the end of the day, I see the water's been all dried up, and this time, the light beckons me on without stopping. Quick trip home.

You know, for some reason that maybe I'll figure out when I'm about to fall asleep, I wish the light would stop more, and longer, and finally, forever.

Blind Man

Y ou wouldn't have seen Johnny Case even if you looked keenly from the rim of the pond. He hid behind the burlap duck blind that he'd draped over the branch of a bodark tree about fifty feet from the water. The blind had a flap at the front that he peered through every few minutes, holding a four-gauge shotgun over his knees.

You wouldn't have seen him behind that old duck blind.

You also wouldn't know that he was only halfway there to hunt the ducks in the first place, even though it was November in Oklahoma, and this was the ritual of the year.

Johnny Case had left his truck door open that morning on the side of the county gravel road. He left his wallet, cell phone, and keys, along with an unfinished note (since the Bic pen wouldn't scrawl all the way to the end) all in a heap on the driver's seat. All he had now was the gun, a thermos of coffee, and a blood-red sunrise indicating a heavy round of snowfall later that afternoon. A round he didn't plan on getting caught in.

Johnny Case leaned against the trunk of the bodark and listened. At first, there was just the sound of his own breath and the crinkle of his weight on the grass. He leaned his shotgun forward to the butt set by his hip and looked at the pond through the aperture. The pond was a black coin, throwing back a fractal image of the birches on the rim. Totally duck-less, by the way. And where were those quacking companions? Drifted to other waters to make him hike? He didn't really care about bagging a mallard or a wood duck that morning. If a group of mergansers cursed the waters, he wouldn't even *try* to shoot. He brought only one shell, and it wasn't meant for the usual prey.

A doe, though, walked by and stooped to drink. She was careful not to get her little hooves wet. She passed by him without even notching her ears back or giving him a snort of recognition.

A spatter of swallows flew over the lake and turned into a film way down by the sunrise. Johnny Case could see it all as through a TV screen.

His brother Gage worked as a welder in Amarillo and his hands were too big, calloused, and busy to text back any time soon. His Aunt Sarah still thought he was in Kansas City for college. His parents thought he was content and even thriving as a middle-class manager at an electrical company. His wife Jara saw signs and would be calling him about now, over and over again.

It was nothing in particular. Maybe that was what bothered him. That he couldn't put his finger on the curse. Even if he'd talked to somebody about it, no difference. This was the end of a very long road. Most people didn't know he was on the road or misunderstood the road's curvatures that might lead a guy here. But it was only last week that he stood out on the front porch in sweatpants while his daughter slept in her princess-themed room that he couldn't see an off ramp. No bridge over the waters. No pond shallow enough to hold his trembling knees that were about to fall.

And now, here he was. The end of the hunt arrived, and no one was around to watch the final gunshot.

Sort of peaceful, though, no? A pleasant morning, all things considered. Now the ray of sunshine made gold pellets in the openings of the burlap. Now there were little clues of beauty. Shoot.

A line of deer danced in a line by the water and bolted for coverage in the birch trees. They had a sixth sense for invisible duck hunters like him, maybe. Maybe they were just deer, and this was the way of the world. Maybe they were just being themselves and didn't have to think about what they were for or what they were even doing. A benefit of the beastly?

He always felt like he was part of the world out here. Not so much in the office. Not so much in the living room. God, he hated that. How he never felt like he could a part of his own house—how could *that* be? How could a man become an alien in the mansions he's built for himself, for his family, for a future?

"I'm worried about you, Johnny Case." Jara called him by his full name when he was endearingly in trouble. "I'm worried we got what we wanted but you don't know what it's for."

She could be really on the nose with her diagnostics. But, damn it, she actually knew him, and he bent over and winced with the cold steel on the skin of his throat. She would be calling him about now, over and over again.

Now the sun was up and staring down on the copper grassland and made the pond silver, even more coin-like. Not a coin he could spend.

His wife and daughter. Better off without him? What a crazy thing to think out loud. That was some real pathetic nonsense. That was self-ish talk—that's what that was. He'd been at lunch with Rod a couple days before at Antonio's where they got a booth in the warm depths of the place and while waiting for a twin pair of spaghettis talked about the fishing trip next summer. After that they talked about each other's families not because that's what you do at lunches with your coworker but because both men actually liked their families quite a lot, believe it or not, had no quibbles with their domestic lives except that they wanted to do better, knew they weren't perfect men but knew they probably weren't the scum of the earth either, and after the noodles and Diet Coke, Johnny Case stood in the chip-per November air of the parking lot and decided he would go hunting the upcoming Saturday. Alone.

Today. Saturday.

Wife and daughter were back at home wondering where he was. What he must be doing at this hour. Bringing them back donuts? Coffee and hot chocolate from Starbucks?

They were probably at the kitchen table. Jara heading to the hall to dial again. Voicemails abounding.

It would be so easy to go back to the truck, start her up, toss the half-written note into the Styrofoam cup on the passenger seat, and drive the ten miles home. He could just tell Jara he went duck hunting and that he was sorry he didn't tell her, and that he'd woke up at five in the morning with the itch to gun down some fowl.

It's strange, don't you think, that the things that are technically true can end up being the most uproarious lies?

Enough idle chatter, he decided. The early morning made him feel like he had the edge on the sleeping world. Now the sunshine made the fields garish. Now it felt like he was out in the open and that just about anybody might see him out here.

He slipped out of the duck blind and headed over the hoarfrost to the edge of the water. He loaded a shell in the chamber and sniffed back a runny nose. The wind teased the last leaves off of the mesquite trees on the pond's edge.

He didn't know how to do this.

How could he do this?

He pointed the gun across the water as if he might see a duck spiral like a cross-shaped effigy at the end of the barrel. The point settled against the sun. Should he spend his single shell on the brilliance, watch it vanish into the happy murk of the morning?

No. One bullet, one shot. It wouldn't be manly of him to back down now.

He positioned his forehead at the end of the loaded barrel and stooped to notch his index on the trigger. The butt settled in the mud, confused that it wasn't leveled against its usual shoulder. He stared at his boots for a few seconds and then closed his eyes. The rest was silence.

He thought, then, of all the reasons not to pull the trigger. He had thought about them the whole drive out there, running them over in his head like a windmill churning water. Jana. His daughter, Stacy. Stacy, man. Don't you remember *her*?

And then all the reasons he was out duck hunting for his own hide pranced through his mind. What were the reasons again? Not enough? Enough for who? Enough for himself? Didn't expect to be here in life with nothing else to look forward to except for the drab remainder of a long, American life? A life that asked for a purpose day in and day out, but still a life, you know. Still a gift. Despite what happened to him in sixth grade, despite his other dead brother in the back pasture, despite his father in the living room staring at the TV screen. Still a gift.

He didn't hear the footsteps so much as *feel* them. He was like a deer out here. His sensitivity was seismic. He bolted back to the duck blind and peered through the flap.

Jara marched up the hill wearing her Uggs, heaving for breath, saying, "Please Jesus," over and over in a whisper that sounded louder than a shout. At only fifty feet away he could hear the huffing. She had her hair back in a ponytail and was still in her University of Arkansas sweatpants, the hog now faded on the thigh in a copper spackle. She probably sent Stacy over to Mom's house and started scouting the potential hot spots on her own. Boomerang café. He like their breakfast options. Now she was at his pond, a place he had never shown her before, only mentioned via a broad reference to the general geography. About ten miles north, towards Keller. But she was here all the same, pinpointing him. Looking for signs.

He gripped the loaded gun and backed way up against the bodark, as if this would hide him even further from outsider view. He wondered how hidden the duck blind really was to the "untrained" eye. To him it looked like a ragged brown curtain, but maybe from her perspective it was part of the canvas of grass behind it and would stick out no more than a bramble bush.

She shouted his full name as loud as he could. "Johnny *Case*! Johnny *Case*! Johnny *Case*!"

She walked down to the water and then back up the hill and made her way all the way to the woods, where she disappeared into the fringe of ash and birch trees. He waited one minute. Two. Five. The whole time, he asked his body to get on up and chase after her, but the burden of explanation loomed, held him down like a rock in a hand. Why didn't he give her a shout when she was in plain sight? Well, he'd have to explain himself then. There were many ponds he could have been at. There were many locales in the downy fields he might be hunting in. He could still fire his shot and come home and tell her the lying truth. He still had that option.

But because his soul was now feeling quite paralyzed, he didn't crawl out of the duck blind. He just laid the end of the gun through the blind flap and waited for ducks to fly down and settle on the liquid coin.

Johnny Case? He heard her voice in his head. Combative. Making war with the minions. Being so sentimental and heavy handed. *Don't you know, Johnny Case? Don't you understand that your life means something?*

A group of ducks did fly down about ten minutes later, and he was still alive to see it. Their quacking told of a world apart from the pond and the field where people were waking up, setting their feet on cold floors, making coffee and going through it all one more time.

Just one more time, Johnny Case.

He followed the ducks with his gun barrel as they made a united swoop for the water. The pond, as they settled in a clock-shaped hole, was a golden coin now. Evolving by the minute, shimmering with reflections, collecting everything he loved about these familiar fields.

She looked for me out here. Shouldn't I return the favor?

Heaven

The best thing I saw today was an old man jigging to the beat of a contemporary song most people his age would plug ears at. We had just come in, Jara and me. She dragged me from the edge of a dock where I was seeing how close I could dip my dress shoe into the artificial pond, which was quartered by baby palm trees, slopes of black rocks pocked with jungle plants, and partially shadowed by Georgia forestry. My best friend was married off and although I'm a married man myself, the world had, for a moment, gotten slightly more lonesome.

"You're *dancing* with me. C'mon."

Jara's sleek form pressed and undulated behind her silk green dress, but even so, my cool curmudgeon ways still hadn't quite graduated from high school. Kory and Bryce stood in the dark corner holding their beers with one hand and spare hands stuck in their gray-suited pockets by obligation, barely nodding to the songs they wouldn't join.

Jara had me by the arm though, and if you're a dude in a likewise predicament, you know there is no leverage system more persuading than the female sleeve tug. I looked over the hopping heads for Ricky. Ope, there he was, pulling his bride Julie into the middle of the ring with the invisible twines of love; good. No chance I'd be shoved into the middle of the orb.

I couldn't recognize the song. And I clapped off rhythm, searching the flock of shifting feet in the hope of imitation, but any fool can tell you that you if don't feel the beat, you're dead meat. And man, I wanted out—but Jara! The best thing to ever happen to me swayed and smiled and hugged me where I stood, not caring who saw it.

When Ricky told me he was finally marrying Julie, I sat down at the desk in my childhood room where we were lodging for Christmas and wrote out a letter to him listing his great and serious attributes, but I missed one. No one tells you that having fun, I mean genuine fun, *unselfconscious* fun, is the hidden virtue of the age. The thing that's missing. The groom was getting groovy.

And now, when the newlyweds had waltzed out of the circle, inviting the next kid to get down, this old anonymous man busted through the wall of youth. He was taller than everyone else and wore military honors on his frock, a bald highway lane decking the center of his head, with his academic khakis and evident age misconstruing him as a fellow who wouldn't do such a thing in a million years.

But man, he did. He rattled his knees and kicked out his feet and rolled the shoulders to and fro as the crowd cheered him on. As I cheered him on.

We are so *old*. And not "old" as in we're now twenty-five and pining for the varsity days. No, *old*, like really old, like cantankerous and wizened and infirm as we lay on the cots of our own making. Bryce! Kory! Won't you join us? Won't you do more than watch this truly young man dance, his arms raised up, raised all the way to Heaven? Good thing Jara and the young old man were there. By myself, I'd have already fallen into the pond, like I almost did while hunting ducks last November, and would have looked like a damn fool crawling onto the rocks in front of everyone.